D1631320

Reviewers Acclaim Nash Candelaria's
Memories of the Alhambra, First of the Rafa Novels

"...beautifully handled...Candelaria has probed a question many readers should investigate before dashing off to dig up their 'roots'." —*The Denver Post*

"...the unique and valuable contribution Candelaria's novel will make...is the clarity with which it dramatizes the painful and apparently insoluble dilemma of the New Mexican Hispano." —*Western American Literature*

"...a concise, poetic, intense quest for one man's heritage and life's personal meaning...fascinating to read..." —*Colorado Springs Gazette Telegraph*

"...Candelaria's exploration of the conflicts inherent in New Mexican Hispanic identity is a sensitive, many-faceted one, resulting in a positive contribution to ethnic American literature." —Paula Shirley, *MELUS*

"More than a brown 'Roots'...a story of a people struggling to achieve their ideal of the American Dream." —*Douglas* (Arizona) *Daily Dispatch*

"Candelaria adds a new page to the Chicano novel, testifying to the fact that Chicano fiction is not limited to certain ideological themes or...stock answers to questions of identity and ethnicity...part of the growing richness of Chicano fiction." —*Revista Chicano-Riqueña*

"...perhaps the second novel of the proposed trilogy now in progress...will bring the author the wide reading public his simple, moving story so richly deserves." —*Palo Alto Times*

Bilingual Press/Editorial Bilingüe

General Editor
Gary D. Keller

Managing Editor
Karen S. Van Hooft

Senior Editor
Mary M. Keller

Editorial Board
Juan Goytisolo
Francisco Jiménez
Eduardo Rivera
Severo Sarduy
Mario Vargas Llosa

Address
Bilingual Press
Department of Foreign Languages
and Bilingual Studies
106 Ford Hall
EASTERN MICHIGAN UNIVERSITY
Ypsilanti, Michigan 48197
313-487-0042

NOT
BY THE
SWORD

NASH
CANDELARIA

Bilingual Press/Editorial Bilingüe
YPSILANTI, MICHIGAN

ISBN: 0-916950-30-1
Printed simultaneously in a softcover edition. ISBN: 0-916950-31-X

Library of Congress Catalog Card Number: 81-71731

PRINTED IN THE UNITED STATES OF AMERICA

Cover design by Christopher J. Bidlack

Back cover photo by Pete Nuding

Acknowledgments

Two chapters of this novel originally appeared as short stories in the following publications:

"Only a Yankee" (Chapter 10), in *Hispanics in the United States: An Anthology of Creative Literature*, Gary D. Keller and Francisco Jiménez, eds. (Ypsilanti, MI: Bilingual Press, 1980).
"The Retribution" (Chapter 13), in *Revista Chicano-Riqueña*, Volume IX, No. 3 (Summer 1981).

Then conquer we must, when our cause
        it is just,
And this be our motto, "In God is our
        Trust"

> Francis Scott Key
> "The Star-Spangled Banner"
> September 14, 1814

Your war, sirs, is to be a war of races—the Anglo-Saxon against the Moorish-Mexican American. What will be the causes of such a war? Sirs, the banners of freedom will be the banners of Mexico . . . and your banners, I blush to speak the word, will be the banners of slavery. You are talking about acknowledging the independence of Texas, and yet you are thirsting to annex Texas, Coahuila and Tamaulipas and Santa Fe, from the source to the mouth of the Bravo, to your already extended dominions. Five hundred thousand square miles of the territory of Mexico would not even now quench your burning thirst for aggrandizement.

And again I ask, what will be the cause of such a war? Aggression, conquest and the establishment of slavery where it has been abolished!

> former President John Quincy Adams
> United States Congress
> March 2, 1836

AUTHOR'S NOTE

This is a work of fiction based on history. The Rafas and their friends and neighbors are creatures of the imagination. They inhabit a world replete with real, historical personages: Governor Manuel Armijo, Don Tomás Ortiz, Vicario Juan Felipe Ortiz, Padre José Manuel Gallegos, Padre Antonio José Martínez, Bishop Jean Lamy, Father Joseph Machebeouf, and others who played prominent roles in the history of the state of New Mexico.

The major events around which this story revolves are historical, including the incident of the Irish who deserted the American army to fight alongside the Mexicans. Scenes with historical personages attempt to couple the essence of what the historical record shows with the imaginary roles the Rafas played. The interpretations drawn and any misconceptions or errors are solely the responsibility of the author.

1

"Well, Grandfather. They say that we are to become Yankees now."

The young priest stood in the morning sunlight that streamed through the open door of his grandfather's adobe room, having just come across the patio from his own room. He lifted the skirts of his robe to let the sun warm his saddlesore backside. The old man jerked his fallen head, abruptly cutting off a snore.

"I wasn't asleep," Don José Antonio II said defensively. "I was just resting my eyes. The sun is too strong."

Father José Antonio smiled and moved out of the sunlight. Grandfather's cataracted eyes were covered with a whitish film that screened out the sun even on the brightest days.

"Where are you? Get back in the light where I can see you." Father José Antonio Rafa III, known to his family as Tercero, smiled even more broadly, stifling a laugh. The old fraud. "Now what was that you were mumbling about?"

"They say we are to become Yankees. Americanos. That the Americans and Texans are getting ready to invade New Mexico. Papá and Carlos are riding to Santa Fe to meet with the governor."

"Bah!" Don José raised himself from the earthen floor where he had been leaning against a folded mattress. He groped against the wall for a gnarled walking stick, then moved toward the shadow dimly seen in the sunlight, past Tercero out to the open patio. The old man turned his face toward the sun for a moment, then turned his back toward it and pulled his serape more tightly around his shoulders.

"Do you hear me, Grandfather? Yankees."

Don José waved a hand impatiently. "What does it matter,

3

Yankees? I was born over ninety years ago on this rancho, praise be to God. Born a citizen of the Spanish Empire in this miserable, God-forsaken kingdom of New Mexico. I have never been to Spain. I will never see it. I assume that it is much like this. With people like us—except for the Indians.

"And you. Look at you. Born on this same rancho twenty-five years ago, which makes you a Mexican. My own grandson born a Mexican.

"And now. If a great-grandchild of mine is born on this same rancho next year, you tell me he'll be a little Yankee? Bah! We have always been here, and the world keeps changing. It's lunacy. The Yankees are coming. Who cares? What difference does it make? It doesn't matter."

"It matters," Tercero said solemnly. "But you are right. We have been here always. And the world has been out there." He waved an arm toward the east. "We can no longer keep the world out."

"No importa. What matters is our land and our ways."

From the kitchen came the angry shriek of a woman's voice. Then a servant girl came running outdoors, her hands over her tear-filled eyes, amidst the flurry of hens who were pecking the dirt. Doña Estela Rafa appeared at the door, shouting angrily. Tercero look away, not wanting to see his mother's anger nor the Indian girl's distress.

Don José turned his head toward the commotion and narrowed his eyes, then shook his head. "They never learn, those Indians. You either have to kill them or make Catholics of them. After you convert them, that's when your troubles begin."

Tercero looked away from his grandfather. He had been here barely a day, arriving in Albuquerque last night from the long journey from Durango, Mexico. The joy of being home again after five years had created an aura that masked the memories of the many harsh things he had forgotten about New Mexico. It was not all of a piece, this love for his family and of the land. It was beset with ambushes, traps, dry water holes, wild beasts, scorching heat—like the desert he had crossed coming here.

"Indians. Yankees. I don't know what is becoming of us. Have the groom get me my horse!" Don José commanded.

Tercero hesitated. He was neither servant nor child. Then he looked at the nearly blind old man, his dear old grandfather, and relaxed. Don José was right about one thing. Some never *do* learn,

4

not just the Indians. Old men never learn to temper their imperious manner of commanding lesser beings whom they feel they were born to command: slaves, servants, children. While young men, even those of the clergy, never lose a spark of resentment and lie in wait until they too are old men and take their turn in the hierarchy. It was nothing personal, Tercero realized. He had always been his grandfather's favorite; this he knew. It was just that habit and character somehow transcended blood.

The young priest strode to the corral and ordered his grandfather's horse to be saddled. The groom was new to him. A short, slender, very dark young Indian who looked like he had come from one of the nearby pueblos, one of the genizaros—Indians with Spanish surnames who had lost touch with their own ancestry and could no longer speak their own language.

The horse was old and familiar to Tercero. A tough little mustang who, in his equine way, must have been nearly the same age as Don José.

A slow shuffle of steps was punctuated by the crisp thump of a cane. "Is my horse ready, you lazy good-for-nothing?" The groom bowed toward Don José and hurriedly pushed open the gate, leading the animal out at a trot. "Well, answer me!"

"Sí, Don José." The voice was barely audible.

"Help me on!"

A quick hoist, a tattoo of hoofs, and Don José was ready. Mounted ramrod straight, he seemed to expand on horseback, to lose years of age and almost become once again the young man who fought Indians and killed buffalo.

"Grandfather, where are you going?"

"To the river," came the answer. "I need to be near the water. Don't follow me. I can take care of myself."

As he trotted off, Tercero turned toward the groom who had looked away and waved a signal toward someone in a distant field. When the groom turned back, his manner was less servile.

"So that's how you still do it?" Tercero said.

"Sí, Padre."

"When I was a boy of eleven or twelve they would send me out to follow. He was less blind then, but not much less."

"Sí, Padre."

Father José Antonio watched his grandfather trot west down the trail toward the Río Del Norte. Back of him, to the east, the trail led past the settled valley toward the Sandía Mountains, out

5

where what was here called Rafa Road became Comanche Trail, leading toward the plains with their hostile Indian tribes.

"Tercero!" The call came from outside the kitchen. "Chocolate is ready. Andrea is in the sala."

With a last look at Don José and the boy on horseback who followed at a distance, Tercero turned and waved at his mother who stood by the kitchen door. He hurried toward the house.

It was two-thirds of a league, two miles as the Yankees reckoned, from the rancho to the banks of the Río del Norte. Like many of the old Spanish grants in New Mexico, what was known as Los Rafas was a strip traversing and partaking of the various terrains that began at the river.

From the banks of the Río del Norte, Río Bravo, Río Grande— whichever of its several names one chose to call it—the grant went east along rich bottomland that was alternately claimed, then returned, by the occasional flooding and receding of the river. This fertile land rose in an almost imperceptible slope toward the scratchy high desert that ultimately merged into the Sandía Mountains some miles distant.

Los Rafas contained everything a settler needed. Water for irrigation. Rich soil for the corn, wheat, beans, chili, apples, pears, grapes, apricots, tomatoes, whatever else they wished to grow. Plus pasture for sheep and cattle.

The original grant had been an immense area that crossed the Río Grande and extended west. Now, five generations later, much had been sold, with the remainder devolving to the various descendants of the original grantee, Don José Antonio Rafa I. In the current generation there were brothers, uncles, nephews, cousins until the entire countryside seemed to be named Rafa, with some dozen different Rafa properties of which Don José's was the largest.

As the old gentleman's mustang trotted along the trail, there would be an occasional wave and shout from the neighboring fields.

"Grandfather! How are you today, Grandfather?"

"¡Buenos días, Don José!"

"I hear that Don Francisco has gone to Santa Fe to meet with the governor!"

"They say the Americanos are coming!"

To each shout he would turn and touch his sombrero as greeting, then kick the flanks of his mustang lightly with his heels so as to encourage him along. At the sound of a voice the mustang was prone to slow down and turn eagerly as if anxious for his own exchange of gossip. If one didn't know better, Don José thought, one would think this bag of bones that he rode was an old woman.

"God go with you, Don José!"

"¡Adiós!"

Then the trail grew silent, and he stopped the mustang so that he could listen to something besides the sound of human voices. In the distance came the bleating of a goat. Then the faint grunt of a pig, until a flapping of wings told him that instead of a pig it was a crow in a nearby field. He smiled, wondering how a crow learned to sometimes make a grunting noise. Finally there was the river itself, its flow gentle yet full, coursing its way south.

Don José had always felt an awe and respect for the river. As a boy he had helplessly watched his cousin and closest friend venture out too far into the swollen spring waters and drown. He had seen the drought when the river was a viscous flow of muck that could barely moisten the nearest fields, and their store of food would diminish until they would eat their seed corn to keep from starving. And in floods, the water would rise, leaving ruined fields, uprooted cottonwood trees, and dissolving adobe houses along its rampaging trail.

Don José tapped the mustang on the flanks and they moved on. He could feel the rise of the trail, then the quick drop, like rolling over a hump, and he knew that they had crossed the bridge over the mother ditch that fed all the tributary irrigation ditches in this area.

"Be careful now, pony. I don't want you to land us in the water." But he knew that there was little danger. The horse knew the trails and the river better than most men, turning by the cluster of cottonwoods and heading along the river bank toward the northern boundary of the Rafa land.

They stopped along the bank on a slight rise that gave a view for some distance both north and south. Don José listened quietly. It was not the flow of water that caught his attention, but a land sound that had slowed and finally stopped.

"Well," Don José said to his horse, "they sent the boy out to watch us again. Our nursemaid."

He was neither displeased nor pleased. Years ago, when he

first started to lose his eyesight, it had made him angry to be followed like that. Later, after a few falls in a ditch or a sudden meeting with strangers whose intentions had seemed threatening, he appreciated his watchdog. So now he accepted it—as he did his almost lack of eyesight, the pain of his arthritic legs, and the constant pleasure that this ride to the river gave him.

He stood there for some minutes, almost dozing, until a shout startled him. Don José turned his head, puzzled by the direction of the voice until it boomed at him again from the direction of the river.

"Hallo! What place is this?"

Through his squinting eyes Don José vaguely saw the shape floating on the water. A huge raft. Loaded and drifting slowly.

"Hallo!" the shout came again. "What place is this?" An accented voice. The Spanish words pronounced almost properly, but with a flatness, a harshness that could only have come from a Yankee tongue.

"Albuquerque!" he shouted back. "The plaza is not more than a league down river from here."

"What did you say?"

He repeated the words, more slowly now so that the Yankee might understand. At the same time he prodded his mustang south, following the river's flow to keep abreast of the sound of the man's voice.

"Where do you travel?" Don José asked.

"El Paso." It was a different voice now.

Don José wanted to laugh, but his natural politeness restrained him. Crazy, these Yankees. But what he said was, "That is a long way. A hundred leagues by horse. Maybe more by river."

A laugh answered him. "We've already come much farther than that. A hundred leagues are nothing."

Then the other Yankee voice. "Tell us, grandfather. Are there cantinas in Albuquerque?"

"Sí, señor."

"And fandangos?"

"Ah, yes. Fandangos."

"And more?"

Don José sighed. "Yes. More." Putas, they meant. Whores.

A chorus of loud laughs, one of them shouting like a wild Indian. There were three voices altogether. Trappers, Don José thought. Who else would it be with the coarse, loud laughter and their obvious appetites?

"What business do you do in El Paso?" he asked.

"We sold most of our furs in Santa Fe. We have a few left. And some lumber."

"I see no lumber." In truth Don José could see very little of what was strapped onto the raft. The vague outlines he could discern were obviously not lumber.

Again the coarse laughter. "The raft, old gentleman. We will sell the raft. They say that lumber is worth its weight in gold in El Paso."

Don José turned at the sound of a soft canter of horse's hoofs, hearing it before the others. From the direction and the peculiar gait he knew that it was his neighbor, Juan Griego.

"Hallo!" the men on the raft shouted.

"You must watch out for the Apaches, señores," Don José said. "We hear that they are riding against the settlements again. Three men afloat on the river are no match."

He did not say what else he thought. That the Apaches, like the other warlike tribes, were astir again because they had rifles that they had bought from American traders. More rifles and better rifles than the Spanish settlers had. So the tenuous balance of power, the uneasy peace that had existed with these tribes had been broken by the new technology, Yankee rifles in Apache hands.

"Don't worry!" came the shout from the raft. "We can take care of them." Don José could not quite see what the Yankee held up over his head.

"You wouldn't want to sell that rifle, would you?" It was the deep voice of Juan Griego whose horse had drawn alongside Don José and slowed to keep pace. "Greetings, Don José. May the Lord be with you this fine day."

"Greetings, Señor Griego. May you and yours be blessed by the love of Jesus, Mary, and Joseph."

Then the business-like shout toward the river again. "I have a beautiful horse, fast and strong. He is worth two of those rifles."

Another Yankee laugh. Nothing but laughers these men. "Can you see a horse riding a raft down to El Paso? Thank you, but no señor."

"Well, God go with you!"

"Watch out for the Apaches, señores!"

Don José turned his mustang away from the river toward home. Juan Griego rode alongside him, a man of some sixty years, stick thin in contrast to Don José's protruding stomach.

"I think the soldiers may detain them when they land at Albuquerque," Griego said in an undertone, "if they don't run aground in the shallows first. I'm surprised they were not held in Santa Fe. But then you know how these Yankee traders are. In this poor country not even an honest man refuses a foreigner's bribe."

"Fandangos!" came a shout from the raft drifting south on the river.

"And more!" came the raucous answer that ended in a laugh.

"There are rumors of war," Señor Griego continued in an undertone, as if the raft floated over the land within earshot. "The Yankees are moving west and here we are. If we had guns, we could fight."

"For what? For this miserable land?"

"For our honor," Griego answered crustily.

"You must excuse my coarseness, Señor Griego. Like me you are a man of distinction and ancestry. But what honor? The government in Mexico cares nothing about us. And before that the government in Spain cared even less. Could it be any worse under the Americanos?"

"This is our land," Juan Griego said angrily. "We took it from the Indians, made good Christians of them. It is ours. We fought and died for it. Made of it what it is. The Yankees have no claim."

Don José did not answer. Sometimes if one could not say something in agreement, it was better not to speak. A few ill-chosen words could be a spark that ignited a powderkeg of emotion.

They rode in silence to where a trail branched south. Here Señor Griego slowed and turned his horse. "I must take my leave of you, Don José. I have business in Albuquerque."

"Yes, my shrewd friend. If the soldiers detain the traders, and if they have more than one rifle to trade, let me know."

Juan Griego laughed. "Always these little suspicions, Don José."

"I hear the American rifles can hit a buffalo's eye at two hundred yards."

"Ah, Don José. You know the law about weapons. They must

be locked up with the commandant of the district. It would be nice to own such a rifle, but—"

"Well, God go with you, Señor Griego."

"And with you, Don José."

The little mustang trotted on alone, past the fields toward home. Closer now came the sounds of the boy and pony that followed. Don José cleared his throat and spat viciously at the ground.

Andrea Rafa waited expectantly in the sala for her brother, Tercero. She had been but twelve years old the last time she had seen him. There had been the letters from the seminary in Durango. Few, and therefore each one precious. Full of what was to her news of the greater world. Rumors of what of momentous importance had happened in the capital, Mexico City. What the fashionable women of Durango wore to mass. What ships came and went from Mazatlán and other west coast ports, and what imported treasures might eventually find their way overland to the Río Grande Valley. All one needed was money—lots of money—and one could have dining chairs from Spain or England. Gilded mirrors from France. Little clocks that made music from Germany or Switzerland.

She looked around their sitting room in disappointment. True. Their dining room held an old, treasured dining table, now scarred and nicked, with a matching set of eight straight-back chairs. In its day it must have been beautiful, but now it was only old and ugly.

Here in the sitting room there was only homemade furniture: a few chairs, a bench, a sofa. Tercero had been in Durango, in Mexico City, and now he would see what little style his back-country family had. The unpadded wooden bench felt awkward and rough under her, hand hewn and therefore disdainful. It was a blemish on what was at least elegance in the old scarred furniture in the adjacent dining room. She spread her skirt to cover more of the seat, then noticed her dress: a cotton skirt, a gingham blouse with full, short sleeves and low neck like the peons wore.

The sound of her mother's voice grew louder, accompanied by the soft laugh of her brother. Andrea looked into the closest of the several mirrors hanging on the walls, pinched her cheeks with thumbs and forefingers, and wet her lips with her tongue.

"But he is getting older," Andrea could hear her mother say. "So he becomes like a child again. Pouting. Disobedient. I don't dare tell your father that he rides his horse bareback like an Indian, wearing his old buckskins with a serape around him like a peon. Your father would be disgraced if one of our neighbors would see Grandfather like that, but then what is one to do?"

They stepped from the hall that ran from the front door through to the patio. Tercero was smiling as he came through the door. Only the robes distracted Andrea, reminding her that this was not the same Tercero that she remembered from her childhood.

Tercero's gaze turned from his mother and looked across the room, his face breaking into a broad smile. "Who is this beautiful young lady? This vision. This absolute vision."

A flush inflamed Andrea's face, covering the rosy-cheeked handiwork of her finger pinching. "Tercero!" Unable to maintain her ladylike repose on the bench, she leaped to her feet, rushed across the room, and threw her arms around her brother. "Look at you," she squealed with glee. "Black robes and everything. Just like a real priest."

Tercero laughed. "I *am* a real priest."

"In here. And hurry." Doña Estela Rafa shouted back to the servant girl who followed cautiously down the hall. "Let's go into the dining room," the señora said. "It will be easier." Then to the servant, "Andale! You're so slow."

Andrea took Tercero by the arm and led him across the hall. She dropped onto a chair, resting her elbows on the table and her chin on her hands. "Now," she said. "Tell me everything."

When the answer was only a smile, the questions began. "Are the women really beautiful?" Andrea started. But before he could open his mouth to answer, there was another question. "Are they so rich—with beautiful clothes and jewels and carriages?" Then another. "Are the women more beautiful than those of New Mexico?" Then rushing, because she was afraid to hear the answer to that question, until it became a barrage.

"Andrea," her mother finally said.

"Sí, señora."

"Please serve the chocolate."

The pouring only occupied her hands, so the barrage continued. Tercero sat back and smiled at each new question, knowing that he was not expected to anwer yet, but some other time, perhaps when the two of them were alone.

Doña Estela finally felt that it had gone on long enough. As she spoke, her daughter fell silent. "We prayed every night for your safety on that terrible journey. It used to be bad enough with just the desert, but now they say that the Apaches are at war. Just like the Navajos and the Utes. There have been ranchos raided. More Catholic souls sent to heaven." Here she crossed herself solemnly and slowly as befit the mother of a priest.

"It was a long, tiresome, dusty journey. But safe. No Apaches. We stopped for supplies and a rest first at Chihuahua, then at El Paso del Norte. All together dull and uneventful."

"Thanks be to God." The señora motioned to Andrea who refilled Tercero's cup. "We must have a mass said in thanks. Then we must have a baile so old friends and family can welcome you." But she saw the look of concern cross Tercero's face. "What is it? Don't you want to see old friends?"

"I will need the permission of my pastor. It is not as if I were your son who was not a priest."

Andrea's eyes had opened wide with pleasure when she heard the word "baile." But now a pique of irritation burst from her. "Pooh! If your family wants to celebrate your homecoming with a dance—"

"I no longer belong to my family," Tercero said. "Nor to myself. I belong to God and to the Church."

"I'm certain Father Gallegos would be delighted to join us," the señora said. "He loves to dance as much as the next one. Maybe more."

"You should never have become a priest!" Andrea said, still irritated. "A young man like you mumbling beads and baptizing dirty Indians. Oh, Tercero. What will ever become of you?"

The young priest looked away from his sister's intense gaze and from his mother's shocked expression. If Mamá could read my mind, he thought, she would be twice as shocked. For the words that his little sister had spat out were not new to him. He had thought them himself many times during the years he had been away.

"I report to Father Gallegos tomorrow," he said. "Although I am on leave for awhile before I have to take up my duties, I should see him. I will speak to him about the baile."

Doña Estela smiled as if permission were a foregone conclusion, while Andrea leaned back in her chair and pouted, a dark, glowering petulance spoiling her pretty face.

There will be more than parties and Father Gallegos to contend with, Tercero thought, harking back to his talk with his grandfather. The Yankees are coming. Things will change. What *will* become of us?

2

Rumors! Don Francisco Rafa thought. Always rumors. Like the silly chitter-chatter of women. Never information. Never facts.

At sixty-five his old bones no longer relished the ride to Santa Fe. No longer found the hearty companionship of the campfire desirable. Rather, he would be at home teasing his grandchildren—the children of his two eldest daughters, Josefa and Clara. Instead he was here in this God-forsaken country huddled in a serape around a fire that was too small.

About the Americanos and the Texans—nothing but rumors. But the Indians were not rumors. There was that ranchito across the river and twenty miles south of Los Rafas. The entire family massacred. Women. Children. Babies. The livestock run off. Then back into the desert. Swiftly. Elusive as shadows. And therefore, for this group of twelve on its way to Santa Fe, the fire was small and the sentries more numerous than usual. They could have stopped at the adobe ranchito some miles back, but in their haste to reach Santa Fe early next day, they had ridden on.

His son, Carlos, now on guard on the outskirts of the camp, carried one of the few guns in the group, which was mostly armed with bows and arrows, lances, and knives. It was an old flintlock musket that had seen many a campaign against the Indians. An old musket that Don Francisco's father, Don José, had considered ancient when he had been a young man. But Carlos carried it proudly, looking forward to once again testing his marksmanship, whether against Indians or Yankees. At twenty-five he had already had more than his share of skirmishes with the Indians and had ridden against the Texans who had invaded New Mexico five years ago.

At twenty-five years of age, Carlos should have put behind his exuberant thirst for a fight. It was time to think about crops and cattle and sheep—and a family. Heirs to carry on the family name. There was nothing like a few babies to cool the fighting blood.

Without babies there would be no one to inherit and pass on what the generations of Rafas had worked so hard for. Of the four sons that had been born to them, only two had survived childhood. Carlos' twin brother, José, had renounced his claim to the things of this world and taken a higher calling. Praise be to God. So now there was only Carlos to carry on.

"Don Francisco." The whisper woke him from his reverie. It was the younger Griego boy, a neighbor. A good lad. Perhaps a match for his Andrea. "Don Francisco," came the whisper again. "Do you want me to stand the watch for you? It has been a long ride."

The boy could not see Don Francisco's angry face in the dim firelight. "No. Thank you," he whispered gruffly. "When it is my turn, it is my turn." I can do whatever I have to, you young whelp, he thought. More!

Unrolling himself from his serape, Don Francisco stood and stretched. He patted the old pistol at his side and walked to the outskirts of the camp to relieve one of the sentries. They would be in Santa Fe tomorrow, so this would be the only night of this nonsense.

They approached Santa Fe in mid-afternoon, those on horseback leading the way while those on mule straggled behind.

Although the twelve represented families who owned the large ranchos on the outskirts of Albuquerque, they were an assorted group. Old and young. On stallions with traces of Arabian ancestry and stringy little mustangs or mules. In fine wool suits with short jackets, pants that flared below the knee, silver buttons— and plain buckskin, indistinguishable from that of a raunchy Yankee trapper or an Indian for that matter. Rich serapes imported from Mexico or local homespun blankets were thrown around their shoulders.

Most carried the most primitive of weapons—bow and arrow or lance—while seated on large, rich, ornate silver saddles. In a land where money was scarce, riches were measured by other things: a man's ancestry, his land, sheep, cattle. And these the motley group had in common and in abundance.

Santa Fe lay flat and brown in the distance. The flat-roofed adobe houses seeming to rise from the earth, the houses like a mirage to the distant viewer. As if his eyes were playing tricks on him. Making him see little square habitations where none existed. Little earthen cells that were really shadows teasing the landscape.

Santa Fe! Capital of the province of New Mexico. Largest city of Mexico's most northern province, with perhaps three or four thousand souls and a few Anglo interlopers, and three times the size of Albuquerque. Terminus of the Santa Fe Trail along which wagons from Missouri found their way with American goods that were sought more eagerly by the Spanish-speaking inhabitants than the goods on the Mexican caravans that came north from Chihuahua.

The town was built like all Spanish towns. Square. With a plaza at the center, leading to the inevitable church. With a few narrow trails from various directions ending in the plaza.

Carlos slowed with the rest of the horsemen, his eyes glinting with anticipation at the earthen city. Those damned stragglers and their mules, he thought. We could be there now if it weren't for them. There were things to do in Santa Fe. Places where one could play monte and faro. Where one could win enough to buy the fastest horse and one of those new Yankee rifles, with a little left over for a beautiful silver saddle with all the trappings. Then one could enter the races that were held along the main road from time to time. Horse against horse. With the winner to take all, the loser to walk home on foot.

Carlos smiled and glanced at his father whose horse trotted alongside him. "When do we see the governor, señor?"

"First thing before supper."

"Then we have some time free?" Carlos' eyes gleamed brighter. Perhaps there would be a new señorita promenading around the plaza this afternoon. A beauty he had not seen before, hidden in some magic adobe tower just waiting for her caballero.

"We will be staying with Rudolfo Rivera. We have business to discuss."

"But you will not need me to discuss business, señor."

"We will need you most of all," Don Francisco said. "The business will involve you."

16

Carlos' dark face glowered. He did not dare mutter the curse that flashed through his mind. Business! He did not mind the soldiering and the guns, the hard riding. That *was* business. But this other— Rudolfo Rivera was a distant cousin of his father's. A trader and shopkeeper. What kind of business could he, Carlos, have with Rudolfo?

All twelve were now gathered together, and the senior men nodded to each other in silent accord. Then, in a group, they trotted toward Santa Fe.

The group broke up as they entered town, some toward lodging with friends, others to the cantina for something to cut the dust from their throats, while the more conscientious went to a livery stable to care for their horses. They would meet again at the Palace of the Governors in two hours. The governor would be expecting them.

Don Francisco and Carlos continued up San Francisco Street as the others scattered. Ahead, beyond the plaza, loomed the church of St. Francis, its twin adobe towers standing higher than any building in town.

"I promised your mother I would say a rosary," Don Francisco said. His horse slowed almost to a halt as they entered the plaza. He could see the look on his son's face and part of him was amused, remembering his own young manhood, while another part of him was thinking firmly that a rosary would do Carlos no harm. Remember the commandments. Honor thy father and thy mother.

"I would like your permission, señor, to see after my horse." Don Francisco looked at Carlos noncommitally. "Then perhaps," Carlos continued, "I could stop by one of the trading stores to find something to take back to Los Rafas."

Don Francisco remained silent for a long time. In a land where priests danced and gambled at cards, what was one rosary more or less? Especially for a young man. "Meet me at the Palace when you are through," he said. "If you finish early, I'll be at Cousin Rudolfo's."

With a smile of relief, Carlos hurried across the plaza while Don Francisco rode on to the church, where he hitched his horse and walked into the dark, cool adobe building. He stood for a moment in the dim candlelight, searching for the statue. He walked toward it slowly and reverently. La Conquistadora. Our Lady of Conquest. The patroness of the kingdom of New Mexico. She who had survived the bloody slaughter of the Taos Rebellion. Who had been exiled along with the surviving colonists until once again she had led them back with de Vargas in the reconquest in 1692.

The statue, illumined by candlelight, stood in a small chapel to one side of the church. Don Francisco knelt and drew the crudely carved wooden beads from around his neck. Old and worn smooth by fervent fingers, they were stained dark by the oil from those same fingers. A gift from his son, Tercero, many years ago. One of the early signs that once again there would be a priest in the family. Like Don Francisco's uncle, the twin of his father. And back before that to the twin of the first José Antonio Rafa, José Blas. And even before that, the brother of the first Rafa to come to the New World from Spain: the priest who had preceded them all and had written to his brother of the glories to be gained in the New World by priest and soldier both.

He crossed himself with the small wooden cross carved of cedar and began the prayers. He did not know what mysteries he should pray at this time of the year. A priest had told him once many years ago. But the dancing, card-playing priests of today seemed to have forgotten these and other things of the church. Only through family tradition had some of the basic lessons been passed on from parents to children.

The old, hardened fingers moved along each bead, the lips moving slowly, savoring each prayer almost as if it were the communion wafer itself, the body and blood of Christ, the son of the most holy patroness of the kingdom of New Mexico and its reconquest.

"Hail Mary," he prayed, "full of grace—"

There were others in the church. Women mostly. But Don Francisco did not notice. His prayers were too deeply felt. The statue of the Virgin seemed a living person to him. His prayers a personal invocation to a holy and all-powerful queen. An earthly queen who ruled over heaven too.

For my wife, Estela, he prayed. That she might become a grandmother again soon. For my father, Don José Antonio II, for a peaceful and blessed death that will come only too soon. For Carlos. For Carlos most of all. For heirs and a long life. For calm. Oh, Blessed Lady, for calm most of all to tame the wildness that will surely be his undoing.

The prayers continued. Bead by bead. Full circle. Until the rote seemed to drain his soul of the fears and anxieties he had brought with him. "Holy Mary, mother of God. Pray for us sinners now and at the hour of our death. Amen." Don Francisco crossed himself and made his way thoughtfully from the chapel.

Now that he was afoot, Carlos could not decide where to go next. Since the cantinas thrived in this part of town, he went into one and stood watching the monte game. But he could not get excited about cards. His pockets were almost empty, and there was but little time before he had to meet the others.

He had heard that there were new girls in one of the houses down the street. One of those beautiful Navajos that appeared as if by magic from time to time. Haughty. Proud. With features that shamed all but the most lovely of the local girls. Also two Mexican girls. Rescued from the Comanches after having been kidnaped as children and brought up by the Indians. Versed in the exotic debauchery that Indian captives learned.

Again the almost empty pockets. So Carlos joined the small group that stood around the monte table, watching the shrewd-eyed woman deal to a Yankee trader who had money to throw away. Carlos refused a drink from one of his companions. It would not do for him to attend a meeting with the governor with whiskey on his breath. And then there was his father. A governor one seldom saw was not nearly the problem of a father one saw daily.

After a while, bored, he walked out of the cantina toward the plaza. It was still too early for the promenading to begin. That afternoon custom where the young eligibles would parade around the plaza while the young unmarried beauties would parade in the opposite direction. With a glance at the sun, Carlos mused: Maybe it's later than I think. He shrugged and walked slowly forward. What the hell! It would be a way to waste a little time. Better than going to Cousin Rudolfo's where, no doubt, his father was.

At a strategic vantage point, Carlos settled himself under one of the long portals that lined the plaza. The procession would pass close by. He would be able to watch the girls coming along the north side, turn the corner, and walk along the portal side. The governor's office was just across the plaza within easy view. He tilted his sombrero forward, the brim cutting just above his eyes, rolled a cigarillo of crude, coarse New Mexico tobacco in a cornshuck, and leaned back to watch through narrow slitted eyes that appeared dreamily half asleep. Occasionally a familiar face would pass by and Carlos would nod his head.

Time went slowly. But in a land where time always went slowly, this was to be expected. It must have been his third cigarillo before the promenading became more than a few casual strollers passing by. The talk of the young ladies became more shrill, dark eyes flashed to see who was listening, lips pursed ready to smile at a favored young man.

Disinterested, Carlos searched each feminine face, discarding them all with the same indifference with which he watched them. One or two picqued his appreciation. He rolled his tongue inside his mouth in distaste, but rolled a fourth cigarillo anyway. As he lowered his eyes to light it, a new figure came along the edge of the plaza, rebozo wrapped over her face and flung across one shoulder like a beauty in an Arab harem. The murmur of voices along the portal grew louder, and out on the plaza he could see a cluster of young men suddenly come alert.

Carlos watched the dark eyes approach, saw the animation as the cooing voice murmured to an elderly companion who stood between her and a second young woman with anxious eyes whose rebozo had fallen back off her face.

"Poor thing," Carlos thought. "She could take off her clothes and still we would all be looking at the other one."

His eyes followed as she passed, feasted on the soft sway of hips, and nodded at a man standing next to him who smiled openly. Then Carlos tipped back his sombrero and moved forward to the edge of the portal.

Minutes later she came by again, eyes moving across each male face that walked toward her, then moving slyly to the side knowing that she was being watched. There was more to see this time. A soft shoulder. In the white blouse a hint of breasts quivering like turtle doves. But still the rebozo thrown over her shoulder so that only dark eyes peered out absorbing the appreciation.

Three more times Carlos watched her circle the plaza. Three more times provocative dark eyes peered from the still unmoved rebozo. Across the plaza he could see a congregation of men, his companions from Albuquerque, and he threw his half-smoked cigarillo into the dirt in disgust.

He waited before he crossed the plaza. Waited for that moment when the old dueña, her two young ladies in tow, would turn the corner of the plaza again and walk toward him. Then he stepped off the portal onto the street. He would bump into her, he thought. Gently but firmly pull the rebozo from her face and see— But what would there be to see? Perhaps the face of an old crone. It had happened before. Gorgeous eyes. A stingy, resistant mouth. A smile that exposed crooked, stained teeth. Breath like a manure pile. Oh, imagination! Conjuring beauty where none exists.

They were approaching now as Carlos was halfway across the plaza. With burning eyes he stared at the object of his imagination, ignoring the sharp-eyed questioning look of her older companion. Then, when they were within a few paces of each other, it happened. A voice spoke to him. Soft. Unsure. "Cousin Carlos." It was the other girl. Not the beauty, but her young companion.

In surprise Carlos' glance was deflected. He felt a flicker of recognition. Where had he seen her before? "I'm Celia Rivera," she smiled timidly. He only had time to smile politely and touch a hand to his hat, then they were gone. The eyes beneath the rebozo hardly gave him a glance.

Cousin Celia. Yes. That skinny child who trailed her father in the little store off the plaza. Cousin Rudolfo's homely daughter. A glance, a nod, a smile, and he was across the plaza in the midst of the group gathered on the portal.

"Caballeros," a guard addressed them, "the governor is waiting."

From behind the desk Governor Manuel Armijo loomed large and splendid in his uniform with a brilliant red sash and gold epaulets. Recently named commanding general of New Mexico in addition to his civil office, his natural personality fit more easily into the exuberant pomp of the military. He rose and shook the hands of the contingent from Albuquerque, embracing the senior men who were old friends from his home town.

"Thank you for coming, caballeros. Your governor is always here to help you with your concerns. And now, as your commanding general, there is no need to go all the way to Chihuahua for decisions regarding public safety in New Mexico. Santa Fe is here to help you."

Words, Don Francisco thought. He heard a quiet cough or two. Beside him Carlos tensed and Don Francisco hoped that his son would control himself. Not do something stupid like laugh.

The governor went on affably. An aide read the recent proclamation about the transfer of military authority to Santa Fe, although they had already heard it in the public square in Albuquerque just days ago.

The governor smiled. "Now, caballeros. What is it that I can do for you?"

One of the younger men—one of the hotheads—spoke quickly. "Rumors, Your Excellency. What of the rumors about the Americanos? We hear that war is imminent. That the Americanos plan to invade New Mexico. Either from the east or from Texas, since Texas is now part of the United States. That they've set their greedy eyes on New Mexico. That we will be captives and slaves of the Yankees. We will lose everything. Look at the blacks that they have made slaves. Look at Texas. What about the Americanos?"

"We have more than rumors to talk about, Your Excellency. We have brought a petition from the ranchos near Albuquerque," Don Francisco said. He turned his cold eyes on the young man who had spoken out of turn. Disrespect! his eyes tried to say. Wait until we get you away from here.

But the governor held out his hand as if to intercept the thought. "Of course, Don Francisco. By all means I will receive your petition. I could do no less for old friends and citizens of Mexico. But there is time. First about the Americanos."

There was a general nodding of agreement, especially among the younger men. "We will fight them!" came an impassioned outburst from the group.

Again the governor's extended hand. "I have heard the rumors too. About preparations for war. About invasion. About Texas. But there have always been rumors. How long ago did Lieutenant Pike come through on some pretext to spy out our defenses? Almost forty years? There were rumors then. But what has happened in forty years? Nothing.

"As for the Texans—," the governor smiled at pleasant memories. "How many of you were in the party five years ago that captured the invaders from Texas? Your son, Don Francisco. And you. And you," nodding to others in the group. "They had come to claim the Río Grande as the western boundary of the Republic of Texas. That meant much of New Mexico. But you know what happened. We strung up their ears like strings of chili. Like Indian scalps. Not many Texans came out of that alive."

"A great victory, Excellency," one of the men said. What he didn't say and what they all knew was that it had been the governor himself who had led their military forces to that victory.

"I don't worry about the Texans," the governor said.

"But what about the Americanos from the east?"

"I don't know," the governor answered. "I hear the same rumors you hear. We have agents, citizens of Mexico, in St. Louis. In New Orleans. They see. They listen. But even so, it is a long way to Santa Fe so what news we get is old. There is an outcry in the United States to move west. To engulf the entire continent. 'Manifest destiny' their politicians call it. There is an equal outcry to be friendly with their neighbor, Mexico. And there are many Yankee Catholics who consider themselves our brothers in God more than our national enemies.

"So far the only invasion has been the wagon trains of goods from Missouri. Every day we see Americanos here in Santa Fe. They are our friends. Our business associates. They marry our daughters. Some have become Mexican citizens like yourselves."

There was a restless shuffling in the audience. A few glanced at each other and looked away. They knew to a man that the governor had a foreign partner in a trading enterprise that even now was bringing goods across the Santa Fe Trail.

"So what can I say, caballeros? We too have heard rumors. We have our men listening at outposts. So far the Americanos have come as friends. But if they come as enemies, we have met them on the battlefield in the past, and if necessary we will defeat them again. So much for the Americanos."

"We come here, Your Excellency, with a petition," Don Francisco persisted.

One of the senior men rose and handed the scroll to the governor who unrolled it and read it quickly before he looked up. "The Indians, señores?"

"Yes, Excellency."

Here the expression on the governor's face shifted. There was no longer the expansive self-assuredness there had been with the American question. Only irritation. Pique.

"The Utes and Navajos," one of the senior men said. The governor nodded; he was well aware of the Utes and Navajos. "A rancho not six leagues south of Albuquerque was raided last month. The family slaughtered. The rancho burned. The livestock driven away."

"Yes. Yes," the governor said impatiently.

"It's the foreigners," another said. "Our boundaries are persistently assaulted by these foreigners. These Americanos. These Texans. They slaughter the buffalo herds so the Indians do not have enough to eat. Then they sell guns to these same Indians, who, because they have no buffaloes to hunt, hunt Mexicans instead. We are the ones who suffer because of this. Our families murdered. Our animals stolen. We work and work to make a living not for ourselves but for the damned Indian devils."

Again the governor nodded, the look of irritation growing deeper and his demeanor more solemn.

"We need help from the militia," another said. "Troops to put down these Indian murderers. Especially the Utes."

"Before the Comanches and Apaches find us so weak that they too begin to assault our settlements. Then all of the Indians will be at war."

"We need the militia with their horses and guns!"

All eyes were on the governor now. A stillness had come over the room, charged with apprehension and irritation. As if all, governor included, knew the inevitable outcome of this drama yet all had to play their parts to the end. Unchanged. Unresolved. Unsatisfied. Until something violent ripped apart the status of what was.

"I have been working on this problem with the Assembly," the governor said. "As always, the military is on the alert."

"With all due respect, Your Excellency. It is fine for the troops to be on the alert. But if there are not enough horses and guns. Not enough troops. What does it matter? Here in the presidio, in Santa Fe, only half of the company is available for action. Like in Albuquerque, there are administrative duties. In our town there have been desertions. There has been talk of more. The soldiers complain because they have not been paid. We need something more. Something drastic."

The governor sighed. "I have written to the War Ministry asking for men and supplies. I have appealed to the church for a loan of funds. Through your representatives in the Assembly you no doubt know of our problem. I can only appeal to you in person now. As loyal citizens of Mexico. As residents of Albuquerque. We need your help to replenish the treasury. Without money we cannot raise troops. Without money we cannot buy horses. Without money there is no gunpowder. No guns. Money. Money. Money!" he said in irritation.

The wall slid between them as the petitioners looked at each other with hardened faces. What did you expect? their expressions seemed to say. You come asking for help and the government holds out its hand like a beggar. The same old story. The same old hand.

"Your Excellency," Don Francisco said. "We have paid and paid. There is little we have left to contribute to the treasury—even if we wanted to."

"What about the government in Mexico?" another asked.

"I have made my appeal to the War Ministry. Now we must wait for the answer."

"In the meantime the Indians—"

"Yes. In the meantime the Indians."

There was nothing more to say. They would be riding back to Albuquerque with nothing accomplished. The petitioners rose, politely thanked the governor, and left. Most to find some cantina to drink off their anger and frustration.

The Indians were like a disease that lived off the bodies of the settlers, flaring in feverish attacks, then subsiding to a tenuous state of tolerance that was neither sickness nor health.

Carlos barely heard the dialogue between his father and Rudolfo Rivera during dinner. His eyes were drawn to the women of the house who served, then retreated to the kitchen. Eyes past his cousin, Celia, toward the other one, rebozo now gone from her face. She was more beautiful than he had imagined. A cousin of the Rivera's whose parents had just died in a little village north of Santa Fe.

His eyes followed her each time she brought something to the table. When she passed a platter of hot tortillas, it took all of his restraint not to reach out and touch her hand. Never had tortillas tasted so good. Like cake. But as she returned to the kitchen, the eyes that looked back at him were not her eyes, but Celia's. And when he heard undertones buzzing from the end of the room, it was Celia whispering feverishly with that sick cow look on her face, pointing at Carlos, while the other, the beauty, seemed disinterested.

"A little vino!" Rudolfo shouted toward the kitchen.

Quickly came the soft patter of feet on the adobe floor. The wooden tray, old and treasured, held a half-full bottle and the glasses. Ceremoniously, Rudolfo poured for his guests, holding the bottle up for their inspection. "The finest wine from El Paso. To your health, señores."

They sat on folded mattresses against the wall of the candle-lit room. It would be here that the two guests would sleep later, unfolding and spreading what now served as seats.

"Now to business," Don Francisco said.

Rudolfo smiled. "You are like an Americano, cousin. Ready to talk pesos even before the first sip."

Don Francisco relaxed. Carlos half drained his glass and listened for other sounds in the house. The two old men would ex-change polite talk now for God knows how long. Gentle chiding banter until the bottle was finished and there was nothing else to do but proceed with business. His father, he knew, was tired and ready for sleep, but even sleep waited for polite custom to play itself out.

"So you see how it is, cousin," Rudolfo finally said. Carlos' ears perked up. "With just a few wagons what can a man do? The Americanos dominate the wagon trains from Missouri. Even the caravans that go to Chihuahua are more Yankee than Mexican. A trader needs partners. Look at that governor of ours," he said in contempt. "He has a foreigner for a partner, control of the customs houses, and the ability to raise the tax on wagons to fleece whom-ever he wants. It seems the only way to get rich is to be governor or an Americano."

"Who needs to be rich?" Don Francisco answered. "We have our land and our livestock. We grow what we need. Attend to our families and our church. Who needs more?"

The wan smile on Rudolfo's face had an embarrassed, sick-ly tinge to it. "Not everyone has land like you, cousin. Some of us must make a living other ways."

"So you need partners," Don Francisco said.

Rudolfo nodded enthusiastically. "Or a loan. An investment."

Don Francisco snorted impatiently. "The governor just asked us for money. This is a country of borrowers with no one who has anything to lend."

"Even a guarantee for a loan would be helpful. With a few more wagons and a little credit we could make a haul from Missouri that would make us rich." Rudolfo looked at Carlos as he spoke.

"But what would you want of me?" Carlos asked. "I am in no position to make any guarantees."

"I need an active partner. Someone young and vigorous whom I can trust. Someone who could take charge of the wagons and the negotiations in Missouri. Who could bring the wagons back safely through the Indian territory. You have been on the horse caravan to California over the Old Spanish Trail. You've ridden the trail to Chihuahua. You served in the militia against the Texans."

Your father is a man of property. A rich man who could make guarantees against a loan, Carlos thought. But all he said was, "I am not a trader. I have been a soldier and now I am a ranchero. There is much to do on our rancho." But the thought of a warm smile on a pretty face weakened his resolve. He could envision trips to Santa Fe. Secret liaisons in the dark. Business and pleasure. Pleasure and business.

Carlos could see his father's narrow, sly eyes weighing the possibilities. But only for an instant. He saw the dismissal in the old man's yawn. Who would oversee the rancho if Carlos were on the trail? Yes. Don Francisco could still do that, but for how long? And what kind of guarantee was there that there would be a profit? None. Only the word of an unsuccessful storekeeper who had started out on a mule trading cheap rags with the Indians and had not progressed much beyond that.

"I could not guarantee my rancho," Don Francisco said. "There are claims against it already, and I do not want more."

"There is that land of mine," Carlos said. His father looked at him, surprised that he would show interest. Then the soft sound of girlish laughter soothed its way through the quiet, and Don Francisco's eyes met those of his son.

"Trading will take you away from your wife," he said to Carlos.

Carlos' face hardened, although he nodded in agreement. It was not as if he were really married. A marriage without children was no marriage at all. The excitement, the passion had faded through familiarity to indifference. The once happy smiles had turned to tears and nagging. He would rather be on the trail. Or up in the pasture lands herding sheep. Anywhere but with his wife.

"Well, think about it," Rudolfo said. "There is no hurry. This year's caravan from Missouri is not due for another three months.

The most we could do now would be to buy more than the usual supply of merchandise for the store."

"I will consider it," Carlos said, hearing again the echo of laughter from another part of the small adobe house.

Don Francisco yawned once more and nodded good night as their host left. Then he looked at Carlos, took a deep breath, and sighed.

3

The church of San Felipe de Neri dominated the plaza of old Albuquerque, as it had since the founding of the church—and of the town. It had been a bastion, an outpost, an oasis in the physical desert that was New Mexico and in the spiritual desert of another culture, another race—the aboriginal Indians—for one hundred and forty years.

Now, once again, thought Father José Antonio, the oasis was under attack. True, the Indians seldom raided a settlement as large as Albuquerque. But the neighboring villages and ranchos were not safe. And the spiritual oasis had atrophied from neglect since Mexico had won its freedom from Spain.

It had been twenty-five years since the Spanish Franciscan padres had been expelled and the secular priests under the Bishop of Durango had been given the responsibility. But then who in Durango really cared about the spiritual needs of New Mexico? Durango was four hundred leagues south and west across deserts and through Apache country. In the thoughts of the Church in Durango, it seemed even farther away.

When the Franciscans had left, only a handful of priests had taken their place. A hundred towns and ranchos and some two dozen Indian pueblos were without spiritual advisors. This lack was filled so slowly that even now, twenty-five years later, there were still churches without priests.

Tercero tethered his horse and knocked at the door of the parish house. The elderly housekeeper looked at him in wide-eyed surprise. Another priest? her expression seemed to say. That's impossible. Father Gallegos is the priest here.

28

"I'm Father Rafa," he said. There was a look of recognition in her eyes. "I'm to be Father Gallegos' new assistant."

There was a wariness, a suspicion as she let him enter. From somewhere out of sight came the giggling of female voices. The housekeeper answered his questioning look with, "The Father's nieces. He is not here now, but you can wait if you want. I don't know when he'll be back."

"Where can I find him?"

"I don't know." But something about the way she said it told him that it was a lie. Again the giggling, softly from another room in the rambling house. "Would you like some chocolate, Father? I'll have one of the girls bring it." He shook his head. "A glass of wine? Father Gallegos loves his wine." He smiled and shook his head again. "He might not be back for quite a long time."

Tercero almost said, "I'll wait." But there was something unsettling about the housekeeper's wariness. Was Father Gallegos calling on someone gravely ill? Administering the last sacraments? Perhaps counseling a family with problems: a husband who drank too much, a son who was a wastrel. There was no need to conceal such priestly duties from him, the new assistant.

He pulled a sealed packet of letters from a pouch. "Please give these to Father Gallegos. They're from the Bishop. I'll be back later."

The giggling changed to a low murmur as Tercero turned to leave. It might have been his imagination that heard a sigh of relief as the housekeeper let him out.

Mounting his horse, he rode east across the plaza. There had been an old man, an old friend, who more than anyone had guided him toward his vocation as priest. Old Jesús María Chávez. How happy he would be to see the old man who had once herded sheep for his grandfather.

Just past the plaza a roar of laughter from one of the buildings made him turn his head. "You win again!" someone shouted. "You can't leave now!"

"I have a baptism to prepare for."

"Just one more round of cards. Just enough so I can get even."

Then, laughing, the man in priest's robes strode from the adobe building. "I'll see you in church, amigo," he shouted, "but be sure you don't dip your hand into the poor box."

Tercero turned quickly away and spurred his horse rapidly

past. It had been five years since he had seen Father Gallegos, but he recognized him immediately, and he realized how little he knew about the man.

Jesús María Chávez lived among a cluster of shacks on a neighboring rancho east of the plaza. There were similar little groupings of hovels on some of the larger ranchos in the area. With perhaps one hut carrying the most meager of necessities. Another serving as a cantina. And in the larger placitas perhaps even a chapel where an itinerant priest might say mass on occasion.

Jesús María's little hut was simple and rude, even for an adobe. In its crudeness it bore a remarkable likeness to the Navajo hogan. All it needed was a round roof and corners.

Father José Antonio slowed his horse and stood looking across the small settlement. Dirt. Everywhere there was dirt. Not just on the ground but in the very construction of the little houses, houses that would have been little more than sheds on the Rafa rancho. There was dirt on the faces of the small children playing noisily among the hovels; they had not seen him yet. From open doors chickens and dogs casually entered and left the huts and a pig emerged from one and grunted at him.

The people here would be the flock he would have to serve as a shepherd of God. Here was where the need was. Where our Lord Jesus brought the word. To the poor, the hungry. For until God lived in everyone's soul, especially the earth's castoffs, God was really outside all men.

"The priest!" a small child shouted. "Who died?"

Tercero dismounted and peered into the open door of a familiar hut. "Señor Chávez!" A very dark, squat woman turned around in the one-room hut and smiled, greeting him with a gap of missing teeth. She padded across the room to the door, dropped to her knees, and grabbed his hand to kiss it. Tercero's first impulse was to pull his hand away, but then his better sense prevailed as he realized that the poor woman had probably never had a priest visit her house before.

"Have you come to marry us, Father?" She smiled almost demurely, keeping her lips closed so her gap of teeth could not be seen.

"Are you Señora Chávez?" Again the smile punctuated by

30

a demure shrug of the shoulders, but no answer. "Is Señor Chávez here?"

She rose to her feet and stepped out into the dirt. "Jesús!" Turning in several directions, she called toward the other huts. "Jesús!" A grumble answered her calls. "Here he comes, Father." Then once again that embarrassed smile.

Tercero smiled in return. She was a good-natured woman, he could see that. Even her shouting was good-natured, with more of the child calling to a playmate than a shrew nagging at a husband. If he really was her husband. He remembered the Señora Chávez of five years ago. A thin stick of a woman with white hair who went to church every day and when not in church went quietly and diligently about her work. One of God's quiet people. Had she died?

The old man approached briskly, his lips moving in a chewing motion as if he were munching on the words that he mumbled to himself. A cautious, suspicious look came over his face as he stopped outside the hut. He glanced at the woman questioningly, then back at Tercero. "Yes, Father? Can I be of service?"

The priest smiled. His old friend did not recognize him. In fact saw only the outer garments and not the man in them. "It's me. José Antonio Rafa!"

A dry old man's laugh burst forth. "Tercero! Little Father Tercero." He embraced the young man. Then turning to the woman: "Here. My old young friend. Like one of my family. Like a grand-nephew. Ay, Dios. Look at you. I'd recognize you anywhere." When Tercero laughed, Jesús laughed with him. "Except for the clothes. And you've shaved your mustache. Come in. Come in. My house is your house."

They stepped into the hut. The uncovered opening of a window, really a hole in the wall, let the morning light stream in. Still it was dim. The dirt floor was swept clean and neat. A rolled mattress stuffed with corn shucks leaned against a wall and a rude table with two unpainted rough-hewn stools crowded the tiny room.

Jesús pulled out a stool and placed it in the best light and bowed, offering the seat to his young guest. "Something for Father Tercero," he said to the woman. Then to Tercero. "Chocolate? A little vino?"

Tercero looked around the tiny room. There was evidence of very little there. No chocolate. No wine. An old pitcher filled with

31

well water with a dipper beside it. But the rules of hospitality, the ever precious rules of generations, made him nod in acquiescence.

From some dark corner the woman brought out a precious, almost empty bottle and two tiny glasses, treasures from some distant time when things had been better. She poured the tiny thimbleful of wine carefully, then disappeared outside.

"To your health," the old man said, lifting a glass.

"Your health."

"And your family?" he asked. "Your grandfather, Don José?"

"Fine."

"As you can see, things have changed." He swept his hand in a small semicircle, denoting the hut, then tilted his head back in a pointing motion toward the outdoors where the woman had disappeared. There were tears in the old man's eyes. "My darling María—" He crossed himself solemnly. "—dead three years now. She worked too hard for too long. And this one—" Again the head tilted toward the outdoors. "She cooks and cleans."

Tercero sat very still, but his eyes moved restlessly from the tiny glass to Jesús' face to the empty open door. "Have you come to marry us, Father?" she had asked. But he could not bring himself to say anything to the old man.

"Tell me," Jesús asked. "Have you come to help Gallegos at San Felipe?"

Not Father Gallegos. Nor the reverend. Nor the pastor. But Gallegos! Like another field hand. Another New Mexican of equally low status.

"I'm to be Father Gallegos' assistant." Jesús' smile was ironic. "Is there something wrong?"

"He is very popular," came the evasive answer. "Especially with the ricos."

"Something is wrong." Jesús rubbed his thumb across the tips of his fingers, indicating money. "Is that why you're not married?"

"The sacrament of marriage is for the rich. Like heaven."

"That's not what our Lord said."

"No. It's the Gospel according to Father Gallegos. Only the rich can afford to be married. The poor live in sin, which all the more condemns us to hell."

"It is easier for a camel to go through the eye of a needle than for a rich man to enter the kingdom of heaven."

"Except in New Mexico."

Tercero sighed. He did not know what to say, and Jesús sat

in embarrassed but smoldering silence. From outside could be heard the shouting of children and the clucking of hens. Inside their silence outlasted the tiny glasses of wine.

"Do you still repair santos for the church?" Tercero finally asked.

Jesús nodded. He stood and motioned his guest outside. "Let me show you something." They walked past the huts to a clearing. There under a giant cottonwood tree sat another rude stool with a partially shaped piece of cedar beside it. "Here," Jesús said, lifting the carved piece. His eyes glistened. "What do you think?"

The form of the Virgin was clearly blocked out. The hand-carved features were solemn, the way Tercero remembered the dead Señora Chávez. The robes flowed downward to about the knees, below which the carving had not yet progressed. After the carving would come the painting with native dyes.

Tercero sighed, feeling his eyes moisten. He remembered the holy statues in the rich churches in Mexico. Virgins gilded in gold. Life size. Smiling tenderly on the faithful who kneeled at their feet.

This little Virgin of cedar, barely three feet tall, was so plain and ugly in contrast. Yet this crude little wooden lady with a face like the carver's dead wife touched him in a way that the rich statuary of Mexico could not. Perhaps it was recognizing the labor of love by the old sinner who carved it—love that showed in his gleaming eyes, in the tender way his gnarled fingers held it. Perhaps it was the scarcity of the materials from which the Virgin had been carved. The soft cedar that one must go miles to find—wood itself being rare and precious in a land where the houses themselves were made of dirt. Perhaps the look on the little Virgin's face, like the looks of the thin, tough, sorrowful women who belonged to this land. Whatever it was, he could not help but be overwhelmed by its simple piety.

"It's beautiful," he said.

Jesús smiled, his face beaming in pleasure. Then his expression clouded. "Gallegos wanted it for Easter. That was two weeks ago. I told him I could not promise. It would be ready when it was ready. No sooner. No later. He was angry and said he would not pay me for my work. The statues in the church had been covered on Good Friday and he wanted a new Virgin to appear on Easter Sunday. Like his own personal miracle. I said it would be ready when it was ready. He called me— Never mind what he called me. I told him that if he wanted a miracle for Easter Sunday he should have had a new Christ carved. Even then there would have to be time enough to do it right. Some things cannot be rushed. You understand that, Father Tercero?"

Tercero nodded. "What will you do when the Virgin is finished?"

A shrug as he set the wooden statue down. "I suppose Gallegos will pay me for it. If not— well. If it were not for him I would give it to the church. As it is there are other churches that would treat the Virgin properly."

They walked back slowly to the hut. Tercero had been on the way from Durango during Easter. The group had stopped in El Paso del Norte on Easter Sunday. There, like here in Albuquerque, the services had been elaborate. The most holy of holies. He could imagine how Father Gallegos must have felt about a new statue of the Virgin. She was the special patroness of New Mexicans.

"Do you still sing?" Jesús asked.

"Only rarely."

"Would you sing me a song?"

Tercero flushed. It had been his voice that had first brought him to the attention of the Church. There had been times when they would even send boys with especially beautiful voices to Mexico City to study. Seldom anyone from the northern province, but certainly many from the interior of Mexico. Not just the criollos, the Spanish born in the New World, but also especially pious Indian boys. There had been talk back then about sending Tercero to school in Mexico City, perhaps even to the university. As it turned out it had been the seminary instead.

When they reached the hut Tercero calmed his breathing, then softly started to sing. The old man stood enraptured, his mouth open, as the sounds filled the tiny room. Then, when it was over, he remained silent, his heart so full of music that he did not see Tercero's embarrassment nor the crowd gathered outside the door.

"It's just like being in church," someone outside said.

"Like high mass," another said.

"Or Easter."

"Or Christmas."

The voices roused Jesús from his rapture. When he turned with annoyance toward those whom he considered intruders, Tercero put out a restraining hand. The crowd of children and adults remained just outside the open door smiling shyly. Slowly they drifted away without another word. Only then did Jesús turn back to the priest.

"It is a gift of God," Jesús said.

Tercero took the old man's gnarled hands and turned them palm up. "As are these," he answered. He stepped from the room into the midday light. "I should be going," Tercero said. "If you want I'll talk to Father Gallegos about your marriage. If we cannot agree, I will marry you anyway."

There were tears in Jesús eyes. "Gracias" was all that he could say.

"Adiós, my dear friend."

"Adiós, my little Father Tercero."

Everyone was there. From neighboring ranchos. From the town. Aunts. Uncles. Cousins. Godparents. Friends. Old and young.

The large parlor had been cleared of furniture and a lively polka bounced from the strings of the two guitars and fiddle. Almost everyone was dancing. Little girls were dancing with their grandfathers. Young girls with their swains. Women with their husbands or brothers or family friends. Grandmothers with each other if necessary or young grandsons if available. The dance was everything. Joy. Laughter. A display of energy and skill. A release from the everyday into festivity that made life worth living. A glorious welcome to young Father José Antonio Rafa.

Outside in the patio spits were turning with roasting kid. In the kitchen the servant girls were going mad trying to make enough tortillas, enough chili, enough of everything for the guests whose energetic dancing required refueling. When stuffed, the guests would groan for a while before going back to their dancing to work off the excess food.

Tercero led his sister, Andrea, back to the edge of the hard-packed, earthen floor where she joined her mother and older sisters. In the near distance one of the Griego sons watched her closely, waiting for a decent interval before he rushed to claim her for the next dance. Tercero smiled at her feigned indifference, but he could see her bright eyes gaze slyly toward young Griego. He drifted toward the family men who, wine glasses in hand, were talking with neighbors who had gathered around Don Francisco and Father Gallegos.

"We no sooner return from Santa Fe," Carlos was saying, "than the governor proclaims a militia. All men between the ages of eighteen and fifty. He must have known while he was talking to us. The proclamation must have been in process on that very day."

Father Gallegos' eyes were bright and hard. Energetic. "So he asked for money again. Governors are always asking for money. There is some feeling that the Church is an endless source of riches."

"The same with the ranchos," Don Francisco added.

"I have heard," said Father Gallegos, "that the caravan from Missouri will be delayed. In the past the government in Santa Fe has borrowed money against the taxes they are to levy on the wagons. But if there is no caravan—"

"Sometimes," said Don Francisco, "I wonder if it would be any worse under the Americanos." Eyes turned and there was a fleeting moment of silence. "I'm serious," he added.

"They are a strange breed, these Yankees," Tercero said. He felt the hard gaze of his superior, Father Gallegos. "I have read of the independence, the liberty that they treasure more than life. At times I think a little of that would not hurt us New Mexicans."

"But crude, hard men," Don Francisco added. "What few of their women I have seen out here have been prostitutes. There is no tradition with them. No respect for family and church. As if every man were a government unto his own who owed nothing to anyone."

Father Gallegos' eyes glistened. "But they know how to make money. They do things. They work hard. And profit by it."

"Work is for peons and Indians," Carlos said. "Not for hidalgos."

"At any rate," Father Gallegos continued, "the Americanos are heathens, infidels—blasphemous Protestants. Almost as bad as Jews. It would be another holy war, with Catholics fighting for their lives against the invaders. Who knows what outrages our women and our churches would suffer at the hands of those barbarians."

"But some Americanos are Catholics, too," Tercero protested. "An Americano can belong to any church he wants." He felt their

36

eyes turn on him now, especially the hard eyes of Father Gallegos, like those of a lizard watching a fly. "I do not believe," he continued, "that there could be any holy war."

Father Gallegos sighed. "Is that what they teach now in the seminary in Durango?" The older priest frowned, then caught the eye of the señora from a neighboring rancho and excused himself to join the dancers.

"There is one thing you can say for the Yankees," Carlos said, "they probably would not ignore us any *more* than the government in Mexico. And their soldiers could protect us against the Indians."

Don Francisco had turned to watch the dancing. "Look at him," he said, meaning Father Gallegos. "That man is a true caballero. He dances—if you'll excuse my saying so—as if the devil himself possessed his feet."

Tercero looked at his dancing superior, moving gracefully to the tune, smiling and talking with the señora. He had spoken to Father Gallegos about marriage for old Jesús María Chávez. No! had been the answer. Definitely not! Chávez must pay like all the others. What would happen if every peon in New Mexico could receive God without paying the price? Especially an old sinner like Chávez. Did you know about the statue of the Virgin? It was to replace an old image and was to be ready for Easter. First Chávez went north for a proper piece of wood. Cedar. Local cottonwood was not good enough for him. He had to go himself and pick out the piece. Borrow a mule. Look over the wood so that it was just right. Cedar? After the statue was painted, no one would know what kind of wood it had been made of. Then the work was just now being completed, but Easter had been a month ago. It had ruined Easter service for Father Gallegos.

Render unto Caesar the things that are Caesar's, Tercero thought, watching the older priest prancing a lively polka. And unto God the things that are God's. Thinking of the marriage ceremony he would perform for old Chávez and his woman.

A new group, late arrivals, was ushered into the house by one of the servant girls who led them to their host. "Don Francisco," the señora gushed. "Such a lively fiesta. And the guest of honor. Little Tercero. Only it's Father José Antonio now. Such a handsome young man. The Church was lucky that some young lady did not snatch you away."

Tercero nodded indulgently while his mother drew aside the

señora and her daughter. Don Francisco led the señor to the wine. The evening was young, and the dancing would go on until the early hours of the morning. It was good to be back, Tercero thought. Among friends and family. In familiar circumstances.

As he watched, his brother Carlos danced by with a pretty young lady from a neighboring rancho; Carlos' wife stood with the Rafa family women, watching her husband's flirtations. Across the room Father Gallegos took another partner and was first on the floor for the next dance.

Americanos? Indians? Tercero thought. Who needs to worry about them? What with our own New Mexicans, there is enough to worry about. He crossed the room to ask his sister-in-law, Ana María, for a dance.

4

Carlos Rafa had been born ten minutes before his twin, José Antonio III, so therefore he was the "older" brother. This was of the utmost importance. Although there had been gradual changes in the customs of inheritance in New Mexico, a procession of generations had so subdivided what had once been large tracts of land that many families thought more of preserving their ancestral property than of equal division among their offspring. Thus it was with the Rafas in 1821 when the twins had been born. The oldest son would inherit the greatest share, carrying on the family tradition of farming on the rich land of the Río Grande Valley and sheepherding on the pasture lands some distance away. Ten minutes, under the circumstances, might as well have been ten years.

The birth of twins was an event of great joy and mystery. A sign of good fortune. Of bountifulness. God's gift to the woman blessed with a double womb. It was also a tradition in the Rafa family. In some mysterious way, there had been twin sons born every other generation. Don José Antonio II, the boys' grandfather, was a twin; his brother, José María, had become a priest and died at the hands of Indians in one of the obscure pueblos in

Zuñi land. The grandfather of Don José Antonio II, in turn, had also been a twin. It had been this Rafa, José Antonio I, who had settled in Los Rafas with his widowed mother, twin brother, and four sisters. José Antonio I's twin, José Blas, had also been a priest—initiating a family tradition that had been carried on now for over one hundred and fifty years.

So their roles in life had been settled for Carlos and Tercero ten minutes after Carlos' birth. A don and a padre. With life flowing on the way it had for generations. With a predictability that could have been boredom but instead became tradition.

Carlos was pleased that his brother was home. Even more than he had been pleased when his brother had gone to Durango. For at that time, five years ago, his naturally rebellious soul had wanted to be rid of this alter ego—had wanted to be his own man, not half of a pair. And their temperaments begged comparison. As if nature had known what roles they were to live out and had made adjustments accordingly. Perhaps it had been the terrible fever that had struck down Tercero in their boyhood, leaving Carlos untouched. Perhaps the weeks in bed, hovering between life and death, had given Tercero a glimpse of heaven or hell—a sense of the mystery of life when he awoke one day completely cured although a changed person.

It had been months after that before Carlos had a close companion again in all his riotous boyhood activities. Horse racing along the flatlands, with all manner of daredevil showmanship. Fighting. Deadly, serious quarrels where knives might flash and leave red trails where they had traveled. The cold, hard nights off in the distant grazing lands around a shepherd's campfire, learning to be about the family business. With the bright, distant stars winking at him as, wrapped under a sheepskin, he stared into the black sky sprinkled with the magic light of other worlds and wondered—not about the mysteries of the universe, but about when the work at this wretched sheep camp would be over so he could get back to the music and warm female bodies of a fandango.

Through the years they had drifted apart—different souls on different paths—until the difference had led Carlos to a deep resentment of his brother.

"Look at what a nice boy Tercero is."

"A voice like an angel. It was as if the church were part of heaven when he sang."

"A bright, intelligent young man, Tercero. Smart!"

Carlos would turn away when he heard such comments, the implied criticism stinging him to anger. Until that day when Tercero had gone to the seminary in Durango, having finally succumbed to all the pressures to pursue the priesthood. That had been when the good part of Carlos' life had begun. Alone. Unencumbered. With no comparisons to goad him to jealousy.

Now, as they rode together, east from the rancho up the gradual slope to the foothills, Carlos felt free of his twin. He laughed and spurred his horse faster.

"I can see it now!" Tercero shouted at him. "There. That landmark is the boundary. I'll race you to it."

Laughing, they spurred their horses toward their goal, a huge boulder at the foot of a steep slope with the word "Rafa" scratched into it. With a last cruel dig of spurs, Carlos propelled his horse forward, arriving at the boulder first.

"I won!" he shouted. He laughed, reining in his excited mount and turning to face west toward the valley and the river.

"You had the pick of the horses," Tercero shouted back.

Again Carlos laughed, shaking his head. "You've been on your knees too many years instead of on your behind in the saddle." Tercero made a mock blessing to the air, waving a hand in the sign of the cross, and smiled.

Quieting their horses they drew closer together. Carlos pointed down the slope toward the settlement along the Río Grande, some ten miles distant. "You can see it all from here," Carlos said. "The villa. The farms. Over there. To the north. Comanche Trail runs out toward the pass between the mountains. That's where they sold the grazing rights. We can ride back that way. Only we'll have to be careful. They call it Comanche Trail for good reason. And sheep draw Indians like horses draw flies."

"So that's what they sold." Tercero became quiet and pensive, looking out across the sparse country.

"Good riddance. The Indians will steal the new owners into poverty. They'll want to give it away before too many seasons. Besides, we have plenty of land left." Carlos was thinking that there was more than enough for him. More than enough to sell off a little when Andrea married. More than enough—

"Couldn't they have raised the money some other way? There is only so much land."

Carlos laughed. "So much? it goes on forever. If we want more, we take it. Besides, they wanted you to be a priest. Mamá herself picked out the vestments with Father Gallegos. Silk. Satin. Damask. Brocade. From Spain and Mexico and Peru. From China even. She spent the happiest year of her life sewing altar cloths for you. And old Gallegos would come over and advise, licking his fat lips because he knew there would always be a feast afterwards. Like a pig lining up at the trough."

"There could have been some other way."

"Oh, don't be so damned hand-wringing holy. Yes. They could have sold sheep, but Papá wasn't ready to do that yet. So what else is there? In this God-forsaken land there is no money. Only land or sheep or cattle. And they wanted to do it for you. My God. Be a gracious son. If it is better to give than to receive, let them give. They're ecstatic that there's a priest in the family. Especially Mamá."

"Just the same—"

"You're stubborn. You know that? Mule-headed. Take it as your due. The way that in time I will get mine. All the land that's left."

Finally Tercero smiled. "You're right." Then he turned his horse north along the base of the foothills toward Comanche Trail.

Carlos urged his horse into the lead. "Let's have a good ride." he said. "Tomorrow I go back to the militia and you go to your heavenly duties. Today we enjoy."

5

The concern about marauding Indians faded before the ever increasing rumors about the Americanos. Developments had moved quickly these two months since Tercero had come home. Carlos was an officer in the militia, training for the impending battle with the Yankees, his trading venture in Santa Fe put aside for the more pressing business of war. The governor had come to Albuquerque to escort his family to the capital in Santa Fe. With the Indian problem ignored and many of the able-bodied men in the militia, Don Francisco was hard-pressed to find the extra guards he needed for his sheep. As for the family women, life went on much as always. There were the servants to supervise in the constant cooking and cleaning and sewing—the humdrum endless undercurrent that made other activity possible.

Tercero bid them goodbye to take up his new duties. They might not be the most pleasant of duties, he thought to himself, but he had not entered the priesthood because the duties would be pleasant. Those were not the concerns of God and Church. Their concerns were souls. Souls to be guided on the right path. Souls to be saved. Indian souls to be brought into the faith. Santa Fe—holy faith. New Mexico had seen its share of Catholic martyrs in the three hundred years since the Spanish first came. Some of them Rafas. For it was duty to God above all. Above pleasantness. Above death itself.

But that Father Gallegos, he thought, shaking his head. It was more than the differing views of age and youth. It was a different attitude toward the souls they supposedly served. A weighing of souls on different scales—one by a human measure of ability to pay, the other by the more humane measure of what was needed to reach God.

The only thing that made it bearable was that Father Gallegos was close to the Rafa family, so that he tolerated certain differences that in any other assistant would have called for the strictest discipline. However, there were still other differences. There would be little of the comfortable parish house with its comfortable beds and exquisite meals served on china. For Tercero there was the horse and campfire, serving the surrounding territory where the word of God needed to be taken. To placitas with rude chapels where a priest might not have been seen for months, even years. To more distant villages that somehow tenaciously survived the onslaught of Indians, the ravages of weather, and the neglect of the Church.

Everywhere it was the same. Simple people who hardly knew their prayers, much less their other Catholic duties. People too poor to pay for baptisms or marriages, so they lived as they could in the simple innocence of Adam and Eve who first propagated the world without benefit of clergy. Fervent, devout people who greeted each other with pieties, words they felt but which they did not exactly understand.

Father Gallegos said make them pay—or no marriages, no baptisms, no communions. Tercero accepted whatever humble donations that were made, neither soliciting nor refusing. And he performed his priestly duties whether paid or not, not so much to defy his superior's orders as to follow his own feelings about what was truly God's will.

Tercero had been away from the villa of Albuquerque for a month, visiting a succession of settlements while moving slowly from this center toward ever more distant areas. He headed south now, paralleling the Río Grande River, past the Indian pueblo of Isleta toward the more sparsely populated area that lay along El Camino Real from El Paso del Norte. West, joining the Río Grande, was the Río Puerco, the dirty river. East, a branch of the trail led past Tomé toward the foothills where a tiny village might or might not still exist. Behind him was the Río Grande and vast expanses of land used for grazing cattle.

There had been a tiny chapel in this little village that he headed for. Father Gallegos had told him that it lay in dangerous territory frequented by bandits who would raid small, unprotected caravans going up the river trail to Santa Fe, then retreat to the hills to divide their spoils and wait for their next victims. There would be Indians, too. The village was too distant from the main trail to be a stopping place for caravans heading north, yet it was not so far distant that it could not be a refuge when necessary. Who knows why someone picked that place to settle? Yet, for whatever reason, there were Catholic souls there who had been waiting a long time for the word of God. If the village still existed.

It was late afternoon when Tercero reached the trail that led east. There was a hacienda not too far south from here, a hospitable place on the main trail where the Bishop of Durango had stayed on his last visit to New Mexico. He stopped his tired mount and looked south, thinking of a soft bed, perhaps a warm bath, certainly food to warm the insides of the weariest traveler.

"What do you think?" he said to his horse. No answer. Not a whinny. Just heavy breathing, almost like a sigh.

Tercero turned his gaze east. The foothills still glowed in the afternoon sun. Up there, winding through the gentle slopes, the trail would lead to a simple rude village where they had not seen a priest for two or three years. Simple folk with simple fare. Beans. Tortillas. Perhaps a rude mattress stuffed with straw or corn shucks. Waiting. He took a longing look south, then stirred the tired horse east against the overwhelming temptation of comfort.

"Come along, little brother," he said to his horse. "Perhaps we'll get there before dark. If not, we'll find ourselves some nice soft ground."

Darkness closed in among the hills earlier than it did in the flat open country. It was not long before Tercero found a campsite for the night. There, in the quiet, he listened to the night sounds in the darkness. A comforting silence broken by the occasional sounds of distant animal life. His dinner was a handful of jerked buffalo meat and a dry tortilla, washed down with a few swallows of water. He wrapped himself in a serape and stared up into the wondrous black sky sprinkled with stars as he said his rosary.

Just as the evening sun set early in the foothills, so the morning sun rose late. Even the horse seemed refreshed as Tercero packed his few belongings and started without benefit of breakfast. He had been on the trail but a short time when he crossed a stream and stopped to water his horse and replenish his own supply.

There was a rustling in the trees. The first time Tercero barely heard it and dismissed it with hardly a thought as a bird. The second time it crossed the threshold of his awareness and he stood very still and listened, moving his eyes slowly to look for movement in the foliage. Then he saw it almost before he heard it again. A slight movement not fifty feet distant.

"María santísima," he whispered. But if it were bandits or Indians, why didn't they attack? And if it were more than one, they outnumbered him. Even one hidden person with a weapon had the advantage.

"Hello!" Tercero called. No answer. "Hello! You there. In the bushes."

A frightened groan. Then the impassioned cry, "Diablo! Devil. Son of Satan."

Diablo? Tercero reached into his shirt, grasped the crucifix on the end of his rosary, and walked cautiously toward the screen of brush. The frightened groans grew louder, leading him to one particular bush. There, on his knees, his hands gripped more in terror than in prayerful supplication, was a wretched old man beside a tiny burro. The man prostrated himself before Tercero, crying loudly, "Have mercy!"

Tercero placed a hand on the man's back to calm him. "Have no fear," he said. "I won't harm you." A wild, tear-filled red eye peeked up at him from the crook of the man's arm. "I'm no devil," Tercero assured him. "Quite the contrary."

"Diablo," the wild-eyed man said. "She told me you would come in disguise. She saw it in the chicken feathers."

But at least the man was talking now—a dialogue with the devil. "I'm a priest."

A sly smile, a braver presence. "What better disguise. Who would think that a priest was really the devil?"

"But I am a priest. Father Rafa from San Felipe de Neri in the villa of Albuquerque."

The old man shook his head. "We already have a priest in our village. There can't be two."

Already have a priest? The old man must be mad, Tercero thought. There were no priests in these outlying areas. He had been to many such places in the past month. Everywhere he had been welcomed. They had lined up outside their little adobe huts to see him pass by. There were many who had not seen a priest in years. Children who had never seen one. What was this nonsense about already having a priest?

"Where is your village from here?"

The sly smile again. The old man picked two small dried sticks from the ground and held them in front crossed like a crucifix. "You can't trick me," he said. "I'm wise to you."

"I'm a priest!" Tercero insisted in exasperation.

The old man was backing away from him now, toward the burro who munched contentedly on wild grass. "Prove to me that you're not the devil."

"I'm riding a horse. If I were the devil I wouldn't need a horse. I would just fly through the air."

The old man scrutinized him with a puzzled look on his face. "No," he finally said. "Not good enough. It's a trick. That's not a real horse. It's just an illusion."

Annoyed, Tercero led his horse toward the man. "Here," he said. "Stick your hand in the mouth of this illusion." Thinking: I hope he bites you good.

Backing away, the man thrust his crossed sticks vigorously forward. "Diablo!" he hissed. "Diablo!"

"Touch him."

The man bumped up against his burro, unable to back away any further, and Tercero's horse walked to him and nuzzled against his chest.

"It's real," the man said. He looked as if he were going to faint.

"Here." Tercero finally realized what would once and for all convince this old fool. "Here is my rosary with the silver crucifix. Satan could not even look upon this without shriveling away in terror."

Once again the man dropped to his knees. "Oh, Father. Forgive me. The weed woman of our village had warned me that it was the time of the devil. That strangers would enter my life bringing trouble and downfall. That I must be on guard. She saw it in the feathers of the chicken that I paid her with. For another chicken she could have cast a spell that would protect me, but I didn't have another chicken. Only my poor burro. Without him I could not even earn a miserable living selling wood."

"The devil comes in strange ways. Not always as a man, but more often in men's hearts. I will pray with you. That way we will both ask for protection from the only true source, Almighty God."

"Yes," the woodcutter smiled. "You even sound like a priest now. When I saw you come up the trail through the early morning shadows, I was terrified. I was certain some monster devil had come to destroy me. I wished that I had stolen another chicken to pay to the weed woman. But I see now that you most certainly are a priest, and you speak our language. Not like that other one who speaks mainly in some strange tongue—the tongue of angels is what one of the villagers called it."

Tercero nodded in agreement although he did not understand. A strange priest who did not know our language and who spoke in the tongue of angels. He wanted to stare hard into the man's eyes and look there for truth. The woodcutter was a superstitious old man. With devils and weed women and chicken feathers. Perhaps all of this talk of a strange priest was his imagination.

"What is the name of your village?" Tercero asked.

"Los Bacas. It used to be Santa Clara, but then so many people who lived there were named Baca that we changed it."

"Show me the way, woodcutter. I have come to say mass in the chapel at Los Bacas."

An excited smile. "It has been a long time, Father, since we have had a mass in our chapel. Oh, glory. This must be my lucky day."

A strange priest, Tercero thought. Who speaks with the tongue of angels but cannot say mass. No, he thought. The old woodcutter is dreaming while awake.

* * *

Even following the slow little burro, the ride did not take long. In less than an hour the trail broadened into a gentle valley with a handful of rude adobe houses scattered along both sides of the trail. The fields extended back from the houses toward the slopes that rose sharply to the hills.

"Hey! Hey! Los Bacas! Look what we have here!" the woodcutter shouted.

It seemed that from every house at least one head peeked out. Hadn't the woodcutter said that almost everyone here was named Baca?

"Look," a woman said in a high-pitched, excited voice. "Another priest."

"Where are you taking him?" another shouted.

"To Don Ignacio's!" Then, aside to Tercero. "Don Ignacio is our alcalde and the richest man in the village. Rico. Muy rico. He even owns two horses."

Don Ignacio's house looked no different from those of the others. It was no taller nor did it have more than the one simple room. There were no more chickens or goats either in or outside the house. And the fields behind looked no more nor less productive than the fields of anyone else. Yet Don Ignacio was a man of substance. You could see it in the respectful way the woodcutter approached him. Though the white-haired Don Ignacio was stooped with age, one could see that in his time of full vigor he had been a tall, powerful man.

"Don Ignacio," the woodcutter said. "There is another honored guest in our village."

"Welcome, Father," Don Ignacio said. "My house is your house. It is a rare pleasure for us to be visited by a man of the cloth. We are simple people who have not seen a priest in several years—ever since the time of the heavy rains and the flood. But now. All at once. Two priests. You are doubly welcome."

There it was again, Tercero thought. Two priests. It had not been the woodcutter's imagination. Who was this unauthorized priest? Was he truly a priest? Had the Protestants invaded this Catholic New Mexico, hoping to wrestle away souls from the only true God? The French, he thought. That would explain the tongue of angels. A Yankee perhaps? But surely someone in this village would recognize the American language.

He was ushered into the one-room house and seated at a table not unlike that of his friend José María Chávez in Albuquerque.

"Have you eaten today, Father?" Don Ignacio asked. Tercero shook his head, and quickly a thin, white-haired little woman set a plate of beans before him with a cold tortilla and a cup of hot atole, ground toasted cornmeal boiled in water.

"Where have you come from, Father?" He told them—not just the woodcutter and his hosts but also the small crowd that gathered outside the house. The lucky few stood in the open door and relayed the conversation back to those who stood more distant.

"These are all my family," Don Ignacio said, pointing to the crowd outside. "I came to New Mexico many years ago from Zacatecas. I was a miner in Mexico. I thought how nice it would be to find my own mine in this northern territory. But no luck. So I did the next best thing. Started my own village. A family had grown along the way. Children. Grandchildren. Great-grandchildren. A whole village full. This had once been the little village of Santa Clara. But the Apaches destroyed it, so we rebuilt it and renamed it. Begging your pardon, Father, but if a saint could not protect it from the Indians, we would name it after someone who could. Ourselves."

Tercero pushed away the empty plate and shoved the last piece of tortilla filled with beans into his mouth. He had seen nothing in the village to fill him with confidence regarding safety from marauding Apaches.

"How long have you been here?" Tercero asked.

"Three years now. And by the grace of God, three hundred more."

Tercero tried not to show what passed through his mind. It would not do to discourage those who would put down roots in dangerous new places. After all, what had brought their forebears across the ocean to this new world, across the deserts to New Mexico? It had not been fear of danger.

"Don Ignacio, I would like to meet this other priest that you speak of."

"He is at my grandniece's house. He is like you, Father. Young. With clothes like yours. He looks like a Yankee, but speaks mostly a strange tongue, although he knows some Spanish. We found him wandering in the foothills two days ago. Delirious. Feverish.

With terrible wounds. It's a wonder the Indians had not killed him."

"Our grandniece is the midwife," the señora explained. "She knows the secrets of plants that cure all manner of illness. She is a doctor of wild weeds."

They walked down the trail to the furthest edge of the little village, the crowd following. Don Ignacio entered the little house, calling softly, but there was no answer. Around the room could be seen dry flowers and plants and roots, exuding a faint aroma that was both medicinal and fragrant and not at all unpleasant. From a corner came a low moan. Quietly they crept to the mattress on the floor and peered at the figure wrapped in an old Indian blanket.

"He's asleep," the woodcutter whispered.

"Muy infermo," Don Ignacio whispered. "Very ill."

The damp black hair was stuck against the pale forehead. The face was thin and drawn, almost like the faces on statues carved in wood by New Mexican santeros. He was a Yankee for certain. Pale skin, mouth thin and very unIndian-like. On the earthen floor was a carefully folded cassock identical to his own, yet Tercero knew that this could not be a Mexican priest.

"I will come back when he is awake," Tercero whispered.

The crowd outside looked expectantly from one face to the other when they came out. Don Ignacio shrugged. "Asleep." Those in the crowd nodded and fell back into a column as they went back along the trail.

"Are you going to say mass, Father?" someone from the crowd asked.

"Over there," another said. "The chapel."

They stopped in the middle of the trail to point out their beloved chapel to the priest. It was a miserable, squat little building, adobe like the rest. There was one difference. At the front the flat roof had been built up with adobe bricks to form a triangular steeple on top of which was a crude, weathered wooden cross. The villagers turned to each other and to Father Rafa and smiled shyly, pleased and modestly proud of their little chapel.

"I will say mass tomorrow morning," Tercero said. "I will come early and hear confessions so you can receive communion."

The shyly smiling faces beamed even brighter, for tomorrow would truly be a memorable day.

Mass had been celebrated and the chapel had emptied. It seemed that everyone in the village had gone to confession. It was late morning now, and Tercero stood behind the altar quietly musing over this tiny congregation. Men were not so different after all. There were the same sins in Durango, Albuquerque, and Los Bacas. The same asking for forgiveness. The same fervent penances. The size and grandeur of the church made no difference. Neither did the education or wealth of the people. It was all much the same.

There would be other important things to do in his brief stay here. A group wedding for those who lived together without benefit of the holy sacrament of matrimony. Baptism for the offspring of such marriages. Classes to at least teach a few prayers to older children; there was no time for more. Even if he had a catechism to leave for some adult to teach, there was no one in the village who could read.

He collected his few things and placed them neatly on the altar for use later. A week perhaps, he thought. That was enough to do what he had to do. When he left the chapel, Don Ignacio and a heavy-set, middle-aged woman were waiting for him.

"My grandniece and I thought you would want to visit the other priest," Don Ignacio said.

Slowly they walked along the trail. Was she a bruja—a witch? Tercero thought. In many remote little villages the use of herbs was mixed up with the practice of witchcraft. But the woman seemed a fervent Catholic, and her contralto had a soothing quality to it that must reassure and comfort the sick as well as the new-born.

"He was on foot when they found him," she said. "In his priest's cassock, wearing Indian sandals that were no better than bare feet. There was no sign of a horse or burro nor of any caravan. The caravans usually go along the river trail whether north or south, and the foothills are almost half a day's ride from the river.

"A person could not survive out there on foot for long. So his horse or burro must have run away. He had come from El Paso del Norte. That's all I have heard him say in his delirium. 'El Paso. El Paso.' Then he slipped into the tongue of angels, staring with wide blue eyes as if seeing the devil himself, although he must have been asleep. He does not hear what you say.

"He has the fever. That's because of the wounds. Like knife or sword wounds. Maybe even a musket wound. He was so thin when we found him. Almost starved. I don't know what had weakened him most, hunger or thirst. If he had not been so young and strong, he would have been dead by now.

"One more thing. The satchel. He has a locked satchel almost like that used to carry the mail to Santa Fe. He keeps it with him always, sleeping with it under his head like a pillow. He will not let anyone touch it. I have not seen the key nor have I seen the satchel open."

Don Ignacio looked solemnly at Tercero. "He does not know that he is among friends. Perhaps he thinks we want to steal the holy things he carries."

They were at the edge of the village now. The grandniece led the way into the house. Although it was almost noon, it was dark inside, the only light streaming in from the open door and the narrow slits that served as windows. The fragrance of herbs greeted them. That and a metallic clicking sound.

When they turned their gaze to the pallet in the corner, they could see the priest sitting up. Pointing at them, grasped shakily in his two hands, was a huge pistol. They could not translate the words that gushed feverishly from him in a strange language, but they understood the meaning and raised their hands. Then his eyes rolled in their sockets, the whites glistening in the dim light, and he pitched forward in a faint, still grimly clutching the pistol.

6

The training of the Albuquerque militia seemed hopeless to Carlos. The few regular troops acted as drillmasters, trying to shape two companies of citizens into a fighting force potent enough to repel the Yankee invaders.

Of their bravery there was no question. And the dragoons'

horsemanship was unsurpassed. New Mexicans had always been superb horsemen and even the Yankee traders who had found their way to this territory had always expressed surprise and admiration for the skill and daring with which even the youngest boy or oldest man rode.

The horsemen's skills with wooden lance and saber were on a par. If horsemanship alone won modern wars, the Yankees had better surrender immediately. But there were not enough horsemen. So the bulk of their defense would rest with their foot soldiers.

Intent was not enough to shape this mixed crew into an army. While their marksmanship with bow and arrow was at a high level, it would be no match for the rifles of the Americanos. They would have to rely on those few who were armed with modern weapons. At least modern compared to the lance and bow and arrow.

Even so, among the many rumors whirling in the air were those of superior new weapons carried by the Yankee soldiers. Rifles even better than those weapons they had seen used with such devastation by American trappers. New pistolas for close range fighting that fired several bullets in succession without reloading. As for artillery, who knows what new monster weapons the Yankees were dragging across the Indian country to New Mexico.

The best horsemen with all the skills of lance and sword and bow and arrow were no match for the rudest idiot with superior weapons. They were unfair, those Yankees. Not even acknowledging the age-old tradition of chivalrous warfare, but using their ungodly science to forge new weapons of destruction.

Rumors came from all quarters and with such consistency and repetition that they took on the substance of fact. Carlos and the other officers of the Albuquerque companies kept these rumors within their own group. There was no need to add to the fears of the men in the ranks. The one rumor they acknowledged was that the American army was on its way and that it was a race as to who would arrive in Santa Fe first—the army or the wagon caravan from Missouri.

Their first payday was approaching and once again only the officers heard one of the more discreet rumors: There would be no pay. The treasury was without funds. The little paper slips of credit that they would pass out were useless since the local merchants no longer believed in government promises.

A few days before payday the militia was roused early one morning with orders to march. Destination: Santa Fe. To join the governor's other forces and train together for the valiant defense of their homes and families.

What did one payday more or less mean compared to the defense of all they loved? Nothing. Not one centavo. So they marched with enthusiasm, looking forward to their chance for glory in repelling the invaders. There was even more to entice Carlos. He thought also of dark eyes and voluptuous flesh at Señor Rivera's house, and he mounted his horse eagerly.

After the first few days Santa Fe was a disappointment. There was the same continual flow of rumors. Training seemed haphazard and sporadic. With idle time on their hands some troops bartered with each other and the local citizens, while others gambled and drank if they had the money or could obtain credit.

One morning Carlos decided that it was time. His duties had been such that he had been able to watch the promenade at the plaza only one day. His cousin, Celia, had acknowledged him with a nod and an unrestrained smile. Her cousin was there, still distant and beautiful. María Dolores Montoya was her name, he learned. Those who knew her called her Dolores. But Carlos would have nothing of the simple promenades of the adolescent. Nonsense! he thought. Who wants to watch a parade of flirtations? Give me the real thing.

So this morning, since he had no duties for some hours, Carlos groomed his horse, dressed carefully in a clean uniform, and rode to the little store.

The proprietor looked up and smiled broadly. "The blessings of the Holy Mother on you, Cousin Carlos. What a surprise! And in an officer's uniform. When did you arrive? Celia. Dolores. Come here."

The two young women rushed in from the back of the store. Señora Rivera followed them. Heavy-set. Plodding. Placing herself between them and watching with the stolid protectiveness of a defender of the faith and guardian of virginity.

"We have company," Rudolfo said. "Can you stay for chocolate, Don Carlos?"

Carlos watched the man smile and rub his hands, then turn to the two young women and nod as if to some silent agreement.

Treat him nice, Carlos could imagine him saying. He will be the making of our fortune. His father is rich.

"Come greet your cousin, young ladies. Come. Come. Mamá? How about some chocolate for our guest?" Celia and Dolores kissed the air alongside Carlos' cheek. Mamá grunted and slowly led the way into the kitchen.

Well, Carlos thought. Even better than I expected.

The visits to the Rivera house were stilted and cautious and very familiar to Carlos. A fleeting recognition would pass over him at strange, unrelated moments. A familiar look on Señora Rivera's face as he smiled at one of the girls. The warmth with which Celia would greet him. The cool reticence from Dolores. In that instant when this feeling would come over him it was as if he were re-enacting a drama in which all of the participants but he had changed.

Then one evening at dinner, as he peered through the candlelight, he caught a glimpse of Señora Rivera. She was leaning back in the shadows unaware of being watched, looking toward her daughter. The expression on her face was at once protective, puzzled, and angry. The look of a mother who does not approve of her daughter's infatuation and is beginning to wonder about her daughter's virtue. Although Carlos had no interest at all in Celia, it was a look he remembered. Another time. Another place. His mother-in-law before his marriage to Ana María.

He did not want to be reminded of Ana María nor of his mother-in-law, Señora Gutiérrez. Reminders weighed him with guilt and angered him, and it was anger that was his downfall. That drove him to those desperate acts that continually got him into difficulties. From direct angry quarrels with Ana María to those displaced fits against innocent people—crazed fights with someone in a cantina, angry striking out at one of the workmen on the rancho, quarrels with his father or his brothers-in-law, savage riding of a good horse until the poor beast was at the point of breakdown. Then from these, more guilt. More anger. A ceaseless corrosion that found its moments of forgetfulness in sex or drink or a glorious opportunity for war against a hated enemy.

Ana María's courtship, Carlos remembered, had started in much the same way as these visits to the Riveras. Six, no seven years it had been. He had seen her first in church one Sunday.

Shy. Aloof. Not yet knowing that the shyness was but a mask.

"That one," he had said to his brother Tercero.

"Oh, my God. Ana María Gutiérrez? We've known her for years. Their place is across the acequia madre east of the river."

"I've never seen her before. Not like this."

"You're crazy. If you'd come to church more often, you'd see her. She looks the same as she's always looked. Stuck up."

"She needs protection. She needs someone who is kind to her and can melt through that shyness to the real woman underneath."

"Jesus save us."

At home it was no better. "I have nothing against the Gutiérrez's," his father had said, "except that they are not people of the first order, people of reason. They are not poor, but they are not rich either. They own good land but not much of it. There are four sons and five daughters, so there will not be much there for a dowry. And besides—the girl. I hear this is the pious one. At one time they say she wanted to become a nun."

"Anyway," his mother added. "One of her eyes is slightly crossed and she cannot cook."

"Oh Mamá. Papá. I love her. I can't live without her."

His parents had looked at each other as if to say: "I told you so. The wild one has fallen in love with a nun."

After a few months of such repetitive scenes, Don Francisco and Doña Estela agreed. Who knows why? Usually children had nothing to say about whom they would marry. But with such a wild son perhaps marriage might tame him. Better a proper marriage than an improper scandal. So Carlos' father and godfather paid a call on Ana María's parents.

A week later, to the day, came the answer. "We would be pleased and honored that these beautiful young people be betrothed in the eyes of God and of their families. The holy sacrament of matrimony will thus join not only our beautiful daughter and your handsome son, but two illustrious, pioneering families of New Mexico. By the grace of God."

That had been the beginning of a short engagement. Carlos would visit each night accompanied by his father or godfather, sitting in the sala with a family overseer—usually Señora Gutiérrez—who would be sewing endlessly, while the older men withdrew into another room to smoke. Carlos would talk stiltedly of everything but what he really wanted to talk about: his suppressed passion that made their overseer more intolerable, yet more necessary.

There were those piercing looks from Señora Gutiérrez. As if her slightest relaxation would give them opportunities for impropriety. Luckily this situation did not last long, for the wedding preparations moved rapidly at both houses. Then one day the entire Rafa household, wagons loaded, made the trip to the Gutiérrez house for the ceremony. Carlos brought a trunk with gifts for the bride-to-be, including a white silk wedding gown. On the carretas was food for the festivities. Carlos' godfather was dressed in his finest, for he was to be the best man.

The engagement ceremony was solemnly completed that first afternoon. The next day was the wedding, with the pastor from town officiating. And what a wedding it had been! Food. Wine. Dancing. A festivity to rival a holy day in church.

Then later the bride retired to their wedding chamber. Still later, Carlos followed—while the festivities continued undiminished across the patio. Dancing. Laughter. Sounds of voices in human accord. While in the wedding chamber the beginning of the end.

His young bride had bolted the door, and he could hear her sobs through it. "Let me in," he had whispered. "The shame!"

Finally his entreaties brought her reluctantly to the door, still weeping. "Only if you promise not to do anything." He promised.

In later years other young men had told him similar tales. However, most of them told the story as if it were a joke. After all, if things got better—and soon—one could afford to laugh. Then the teller would wink and his listeners would look around at each other as if saying: What a fellow! What a man! ¡Qué hombre!

With Carlos it had never gotten much better so there was nothing to laugh at. Only anger and resentment, and finally a furtive trip to one of the girls who lived on the edge of town where he relieved his frustrations.

"Well, Carlos. It's nice to have you as a member of our little family here," Señor Rivera said. "Your father and I are more than just cousins. And you. You are your father's son."

"Thank you, Cousin Rudolfo." But underneath, Carlos' blood was pulsing rapidly, and he kept saying in his mind: Look at me, Dolores. Can't you see what I feel? Smile at me. Just a little. The

56

way that lovesick cousin, Celia, smiles. It's you, Dolores. Can't you see that? You.

One evening a week Dolores visited the church of St. Francis to make a novena for her dead parents and brothers and sisters. Carlos did not understand why, but she was allowed to go out alone. If she had been a daughter of the family, she would have been accompanied. Celia would never have been allowed to go out at night without an escort. But then Dolores was only their ward and perhaps they needed time to be alone as much as she needed to be away from the confines of the house.

Carlos discovered this one evening as he idled in the plaza, trying to decide whether or not to go into one of the cantinas and try his luck at cards. A familiar figure, head and face hidden in a rebozo, came along the plaza with a walk that was impossible to disguise. He ground his cigarillo into the dirt and stepped from the shadows toward her.

"Good evening, Dolores."

She turned, startled, from the determined path she had been walking. "Who—who is it?"

"Carlos."

He could almost hear her next thoughts aloud: Carlos who? But she answered, "Oh, Señor Rafa."

The formality in her voice irritated him. How could one be formal when speaking just three words? "May I walk with you?"

She had barely slowed her pace, and Carlos was already alongside her as they drew nearer to the church. "But Señor Rafa. You are a married man."

The shock of her answer brought forth an unexpected guffaw. "I am a cousin," he finally said. But she had turned into the adobe building, and he could not bring himself to follow.

Carlos sulked in the shadows watching the entrance. The words: But you are a married man! echoed in his mind over and over, feeding his anger. Then he saw in his mind the soft curve of her breast, the turn of her hip and thigh, and another passion came over him. He waited almost an hour before she came out. The shadowy figure in the dark stopped before entering the dirt street—but there were two of them. He could not see well enough until they moved slowly into the moonlight. That was Dolores. He was certain. The other one? A man. He could not see clearly, but from the clothes and a brief glimpse as the man turned his face toward the moonlight, Carlos was certain he was a Yankee.

A blind rage paralyzed him. He saw them hold hands, then lean gently toward each other for a light kiss before they each went their separate ways. Carlos did not know which one to follow and assault, so they were both out of sight while he stood in confusion in the shadows.

Two evenings later, when Carlos was once again a guest at the Rivera's house, Dolores' distant coolness made him more angry and yet made her all the more desirable. Neither mentioned their chance meeting outside the church. Perhaps it was nothing, Carlos finally told himself. It was dark and the moon was thin that night. It could have been my imagination.

Yet the next week on the same night, Carlos watched outside the church, keeping himself hidden, and saw the same little drama. Only this time he controlled his anger and followed the man through the dark dirt streets of Santa Fe to one of the cantinas.

Inside was the usual motley assortment. Trappers, traders, and prospectors. Local rancheros and storekeepers. Shepherds. A mixture of local New Mexicans, an occasional Indian, and a few Americans. Even though the rumors of war were everywhere, noise and gaiety blotted out any thought of the approaching conflict.

Carlos saw him join a group at a card table. He was a tall man. Most of the Yankees were taller than the local New Mexicans. His light hair and fair skin were animated by a ready smile as he picked up the cards. A young girl might have thought him handsome. He was young, perhaps a year or two younger than Carlos, and his youth showed on his boyish face. He had money. The neat stack of chips he bought attested to that. Carlos ordered a drink and watched. Players came and went. An older Yankee came and talked to the young card player who nodded. A short while later they both left. Partners? Carlos thought. They had the look of successful businessmen in collusion.

"Hey, Carlos!" one of the players at the card table called. A fellow officer in the militia. "How about it?" he asked, dealing an imaginary hand of cards.

"Not tonight."

"Tomorrow then?"

Carlos nodded and left. Perhaps tomorrow the young Americano would be back.

It was two nights later that the young Americano returned. His older partner had been there through the evening playing cards. Carlos had drunk more than he should and had been losing steadily. He had just thrown down another losing hand and was ready to leave in disgust. He was out of chips and he had already borrowed from the big winner, the older Yankee.

"Evening, gents." The casual friendliness was matched by the boyish smile. The older Yankee looked up while scooping the chips from the center of the table. "May I join you?"

He did not wait for an answer but took the chair that one of the local rancheros had just vacated. Carlos' eyes narrowed as he studied his adversary. If he had been more sober he might have sensed the absurd irony of sitting at a gambling table with two Americanos while he was in the uniform of the militia waiting to do battle with their countrymen. But it was the personal enmity rather than the bigger prospect of war that enflamed him now. This was the one, he thought. She prefers him to me. Pale skin, pale-eyed chingado. Less than a man. Barely a boy.

Carlos leaned toward the big winner. "I'd like to borrow some more chips. I sense that my luck is changing."

He felt the hand on his arm and tried to ignore the accompanying words. "It's late, compadre. It's time for us to get back to camp."

"Is he good for another loan?" the older Yankee asked.

"His father is a big landholder near Albuquerque," someone in the crowd said. "He's good."

"I think it's time," Carlos' companion repeated.

Carlos threw the hand away viciously. "My luck is changing!" he said angrily. "I'll decide when it's time." His companion drew back, a confused expression in his eyes, and looked around the table helplessly.

"Well. Are we going to play cards?" the young Yankee asked.

Cautiously, the older Yankee shoved across another stack of chips. "Here's the count so far," he said, showing Carlos the slip of paper. "That's enough to buy twenty good horses."

"My luck is changing," Carlos said. "Let's play cards."

Two hours later he threw his last chip in the center of the table and turned up his hand. The young Yankee smiled and turned his cards up. Everyone else had dropped out. "¡Chingada!" Carlos spat, watching the Yankee scrape the chips across the table.

"Now it's time," Carlos' companion said.

Docilely Carlos rose and followed him out after a brief glance at the slips of paper the older Yankee held. "I will pay you, señor," he said. "By the end of the week."

Only when he was outside did the enormity of his losses hit him. How many times twenty good horses had it finally turned out to be? Too many. ¡Jesús! His father would kill him—losing what he did not have. A panic seized him. How could he have lost so much? There must have been something wrong.

"They cheated me," he finally said, as if a great realization, a way of salvation, had been revealed to him. "Did you see that?" he asked his companion. "They cheated me."

His friend's eyes were troubled, sad. "I don't think so, Carlos. I was in the game and came out all right. Besides, the Yankees don't run the card games in this town. We Mexicans do."

"How else?" Carlos asked. "Did you see that last round? Did you see my cards? How could anyone have beat them unless they were cheating?"

"Luck. The young Americano had been losing most of the night. Almost as much as you. That last hand just saved him from losing too much."

"¡Chingada!" Carlos spat. "It was him. That young Americano." He turned to re-enter the cantina, but his friend pulled him away.

"Don't be a fool. Did you see the revolvers those Yankees had? Six shots before you could even get two from that old pistola of yours."

"I was cheated!" His voice was loud now. Belligerent. A few men in the street turned and looked, then moved along quickly about their business.

"Carlos."

"I will fight you if you don't let me pass. That son-of-a-bitch. Chingado cabrón. There is no honor if I do not settle with him."

"Carlos."

But he had broken loose in his drunken fury and stomped noisily into the cantina. They were gone. Both of them. With their cheater's money and their cheater's signed pieces of paper. Several men turned and fixed their eyes on him, then watched with indifference as Carlos turned on his heels and left.

"The cowardly bastards ran away!" But, he thought to himself, I know where to find that young Yankee. I know.

60

* * *

Carlos watched the church of St. Francis with furious impatience. He had been waiting too long to settle his score with this young Yankee. He had watched Dolores enter and knew that soon this . . . this interloper would come to meet her from one of the narrow alleys between houses.

Carlos stood back quietly in the shadows and began to scrutinize the dark streets. It would probably be that little alley on the right, closest to the church. El Güero, "The Blonde," as he now thought of his rival, had waited there the last time.

After long impatient minutes there was the quiet shuffling of boots and the nascent aroma of tobacco smoke. El Güero was late tonight. The other times he had come early, waited a few minutes until the entrance to the church was clear, then gone in to commit unthinkable blasphemies with the girl.

Better get to him now, Carlos thought, before El Güero moves from the alley. There would be even less chance of being seen there. He patted his waistband and felt the comforting hardness of his pistola and his knife—if it came to that.

But it would not, he thought. Somehow the rightness of his position would be recognized and the money he had lost would be returned to him. Without a protest. Because after all, it was he, Carlos Rafa, who had been wronged and in the sight of God and St. Francis even a crude Yankee would be able to see that. As for the other—the notes— El Güero would merely tell his older friend who would see the justice in it all and return them. Carlos' father would never know.

Comforted by his delusions, Carlos walked quietly in the darkness until he stopped a few feet from the glowing tip of a cigarillo.

"Señor."

"Stay where you are, mister. Who are you and what do you want?"

"I have some unfinished business we have to discuss, señor." No response. "The card game in the cantina two nights ago."

The lighted cigarillo came closer. "I lost twenty dollars," El Güero said in disgust.

"I lost much more than that, señor."

"Then we're both losers. What do you want from me, amigo?"

"My money. And those notes I signed for your friend. I was cheated!" Carlos' whispering voice rose in anger.

"You're crazy! What is this? A hold-up?"

In the darkness, Carlos saw the lighted cigarillo drop and the man's arm move quickly to his side. This was not supposed to happen. The man was supposed to answer: "Certainly, señor. I see the honor in your cause. Here is your money. Tomorrow I'll bring your notes." But quick as the man's motion was, Carlos' knife was quicker.

"Yankee bastard," he hissed.

The answer was a look of astonishment on the man's face. In the dim light, Carlos saw the hand go slack before the revolver was out of its holster. Then he withdrew the knife and stabbed again, keeping enough distance so he would not be splattered by blood. He withdrew the knife and wiped it in the dirt before turning and running from the alley. He knew El Güero was done.

As he crossed the dark street, Carlos looked back at the church. Dolores was standing outside the entrance waiting. She turned this way and that, looking, and while he could not see her face, Carlos could imagine her puzzled concern.

He disappeared between adobe houses, dropped the knife into his horse's saddlebag, and made ready to enter the cantina. From the distance came a scream, but it was too far away and no one seemed to hear or care. The cantina door closed behind him. He felt as if he would explode. It was as if everyone in the place was looking at him and knew what he had done. It took all his control to order a drink to try to drown out his guilt.

Enough, Carlos finally told himself after the third drink had no effect on him. He was only a cheating Yankee and, besides, we are almost at war.

7

Toward the end of the second week at Los Bacas, Tercero was suddenly overcome with a heightened sense of anxiety. Something was wrong somewhere. He felt it as a powerful physical presence that focused within his breast. It struck him late one night as he prayed in the dark, as if his prayers were being answered by God's perversity that threatened plagues not unlike Job's. But all went well here in Los Bacas. The people were devout and receptive to the word of God. And the feeling somehow did not belong to this place. It came to him from a distance. Calling to him from far away.

Thoughts of his mother and father flooded in on him. Of his grandfather. They were old and— No, he realized. It was not them. It was more like that recent time when he had been in Durango. Like those other times going back to his boyhood. As if some part of himself needed help. And it dawned on him that something was wrong with Carlos. He should have known!

"Tercero!" He could hear the boyish whisper as if it were palpable. The sound had come through the shuttered window in his room those many years ago. It had been dark, like now. Deathly still. That hour when it was still night and not yet morning, when even the earth seemed to stop in transition as if its heart missed a beat, unable to decide between life and death.

Tercero had roused himself from a sleep made restless by an ominous foreboding. A feeling that part of himself was in some dark labyrinth trying to find the way out.

Quickly he moved to the shutter. "Who is it?" he whispered back. But he already knew.

"Carlos."

Tercero put aside the knife he had carried with him and lit a candle before he opened the strongly bolted shutter. Carlos leaned against the adobe wall, his left arm held against his stomach while his right arm hung loose by his side. In the flickering light his boyish face was pale. The left sleeve of his jacket hung wet and dark, and drops fell thick to the patio ground.

"My God," Tercero said. "Let me unbolt the door." He led his brother past the fortress-like walls of the room and closed the door behind. "I better call Papá."

"No! He's not to know. Nor Mamá."

"My God, Carlos. You'll bleed to death."

"It's nothing. Just my arm. I don't want to alarm them."

"I'll get the curandera." He led Carlos to a hard bench and sat him there. What had Carlos been up to? But there was no time for questions. It was time to stop the flow of blood and clean and bind the wound.

63

The servant had come quickly, quietly. With a vow of silence about her patient. When she had gone back across the patio the first traces of morning had lightened the sky.

"What happened?" Tercero had asked.

Carlos shook his head grimly. "I can't talk about it."

"You come knocking on my window hours after you should have been in bed, your arm bleeding like it's been severed, you ask for help, and now you can't talk about it. That infuriates me, Carlos!"

Carlos stiffened, his head rearing back with nostrils flaring. "I don't have to tell anybody anything. Least of all you."

"If your arm were healed, we'd settle it right now. *Least of all me!* I'm your brother. The closest person to you."

"I'm myself. I don't have to answer to anyone."

In his anger, Tercero could have thrashed him. Certainly they had fought often enough before. But Carlos' last few words articulated what Tercero had so often said to himself. "I am myself. Me! Not half of a pair. Not part of someone else. All me! A whole me."

And Tercero did not really have to ask Carlos what the knifing had been about. He saw his brother's ashen face, drained of blood, with the hard eyes and the tight thin lips. It was almost as if he could read the other's mind. "You were fighting about honor again," Tercero said matter-of-factly.

"I better go to my room before the servants start getting up for the day."

"What good is honor if you are dead?"

But Carlos had risen shakily and walked to the door. Tercero had not said what else he had read in his brother's mind. That they had raced horses. That there had been a quarrel over who had won. That in this quarrel honor had been impugned. It was as if he had been there himself. It frightened him to have such secret thoughts and to know that they were true.

Carlos had hesitated at the door as if he did not have the strength to open it. "Let me walk with you to your room," Tercero said. Quietly, Carlos acquiesced.

This has not been the first time, Tercero had thought. Nor will it be the last. It's as if Carlos' soul were wrestling with devils he could never quite defeat. Pray, Carlos, he thought, hoping that this silent message would be heard by his brother. But the only answer was, "Thank you, little brother. I'm so tired."

The arm had healed in due time, though not without discovery by their father who could not decide between being angry and being proud. For Tercero there had been admonishment for not telling and he had been confused and angry at this injustice.

"You should have known better!" he had been scolded. "What if he had taken infection and died?" All this did was harden his feeling of separateness and his resolve to go his own way as soon as possible.

"You are pensive, Father." Tercero looked up at the lighted candle in the partially open door. He was still on his knees on the earthen floor of the hut but his attitude was obviously no longer one of prayer. "Is it our sick one?" Don Ignacio asked, nodding toward the sleeping figure in the corner. Tercero shook his head; he could not quite bring himself to smile even though the reality of Don Ignacio had dispelled troublesome memories. "You are thinking of something far away?"

"Yes."

"Heaven, perhaps?"

Now he smiled. "Far from it."

"Then some other holy thoughts." Tercero continued to smile. "I have come to see how he is," Don Ignacio went on. "My grandniece said that he is coming along well but that he still hardly speaks, even in that strange language."

"He is much better. He could talk if he wanted to, but he is not ready yet."

"Then I'll go. Now that my grandniece is staying with me, she scolds me for being out alone after dark. 'You'll fall into the ditch,' she says. Imagine."

"Buenas noches, Don Ignacio."

"Buenas noches."

There had been a chance to observe this sick young man for several days now. He was, Tercero judged, barely past twenty years of age. Stocky and taller than the average New Mexican. His hair was black and his skin more ruddy than the tan of the local people. Startling, piercing blue eyes followed the movements of anyone in the hut. In his more lucid moments silence was his shield against their questions. Yet when he lapsed into a fitful sleep he spoke volubly in the strange language that many of the villagers referred to as the tongue of angels.

65

In the nights, after busy days directing the repair of the little chapel, of teaching prayers to children and adults alike, of counseling the sick or troubled, Tercero would often sit in the dark of the hut listening for a clue.

"Skihanach. Ballyshedy. Cork," he heard one night, mumbled repeatedly over and over again.

The word "cork" he recognized from his smattering of the American language. He listened carefully. "Cork." There it was again. Distinctly. Clearly. Was he thirsty, needing someone to remove the cork from a bottle of water?

"Skihanach. Ballyshedy." What did those words mean?

Two nights later, Tercero knelt in the flickering candlelight praying aloud because he felt the need to hear a human voice in the silent hut, even if only his own. His fingers had slipped over the beads of his rosary absentmindedly and his voice droned through his inattention, so that it might have been the murmur of the wind outside when he heard another voice in Spanish join him in an Ave.

"María santísima. Madre de Dios—"

In his surprise he almost stopped praying, but quickly he forced himself to continue as if nothing had happened. He dared not look toward the pallet. It was a pleasant tenor voice that spoke Spanish with a lilt instead of the more typical syncopation of one whose native language it was. Yet it was passably decent pronunciation. Better than most of the Anglo traders one saw in New Mexico.

The two voices continued in unison through the cycle of beads. It was as if in common prayer they were coming to some agreement. When the rosary had been completed, Tercero crossed himself and stayed still in the silent room, waiting for the other one to speak. Finally it came.

"Are you praying because I'm going to die?"

Tercero rose and turned toward him. The piercing blue eyes followed him. Not hostile. Just wary. "No," he answered. "You're healing very well."

A deep sigh. Then a certain tightness around the chin and jaw. "You have taken my pistol."

"You will get it back when the time comes."

"When what time comes?"

"When we learn more about you. What you are doing here. A

pistol is a dangerous weapon in the hands of someone who would do another harm."

The stranger looked around quietly in the dim interior. "Where am I?"

"In the hamlet of Los Bacas. Province of New Mexico. About a half day's ride from the Río Grande River along which is the trail to Santa Fe."

"Mexico."

"Yes. Mexico." The stranger looked once again into the sparsely lighted room, then sighed and closed his eyes. Tercero watched him drop quickly to sleep, then stood watching as if there might be some clue on his sleeping countenance. Now you know where you are, he thought. But we still know nothing about you.

Tercero thought about the stranger when he awakened during the night. There was no question that the man was a Catholic, but he was obviously no priest. His knowledge of Spanish was good, yet there was that strange tongue he spoke in his sleep. It was none of the common European languages—French, German, Italian; these he would recognize. There were few Catholics in Russia but some in Poland. As for Scandinavia, heathen Protestants there, while there were Catholics in southeastern Europe in Bohemia. "Skihanach. Ballyshedy. Cork," he thought. Portuguese? Could it be Portuguese? But why the American word "cork"?

The next morning they prayed together again, then exchanged a few words before Tercero went about his duties. "I am Father José Antonio Rafa," he said as he was about to leave. "Do you have a name?"

The stranger hesitated, perhaps deciding whether or not to tell his real name, though God knows what it would matter in this place. "Miguel," he finally answered.

"Do you have another name?"

"Not for now."

"Where do you come from, Miguel?"

"I would like my pistol back," was his answer.

"We will talk about that another time."

Two nights later, during another of his restless nights, Tercero felt a second attack of anxiety and his thoughts carried him far away. Carlos! he thought. What is it, Carlos? Drawn into himself, he did not hear the faint rustlings from the adjacent pallet.

Even the opening and closing of the door made no impression on him, until suddenly his eyes popped open, and he knew that he was alone in the hut. Then the memory of the tiny noises came to him.

"Damn!" he thought. "What is that crazy fool trying to do?"

Quickly he slipped into his clothes. Unable to find his sandals, he ran barefoot into the night. The slightly waning moon was high and bright so that it was easy to see. Across the road and two houses away a dark figure moved stealthily toward the pasture, then stopped at the braying of a burro. What few horses there were, Tercero knew, were down the trail in Don Ignacio's pasture. A burro was not going to take anyone very far very fast.

Quickly he ran in the shadows, his bare feet padding softly in the dirt. The figure ahead leaned against a tree. Miguel had gone a long way in his weakened condition. Then he pushed off from the tree toward the burro who was now making a fearsome racket. A lighted candle shone in the window of the nearest hut. Tercero crossed the road in a rush and grasped Miguel, just as he had turned away from the burro to head further down the trail.

"Let go of me!" he snarled. Then the excitement and the fatigue overcame him and he sank slowly and softly to the ground.

"Crazy fool," Tercero said. "How far would you get before the Indians killed you? Or you died of thirst or hunger, not to mention fatigue?"

"Who is that?" came a shout from the candle-bearer who stood in the door of the hut.

"Father Rafa."

The man came forward, and the two of them lifted the fallen Miguel and carried him back to the hut. Tercero covered him and then lay in bed thinking. The stranger would soon be strong enough to leave. He did not have to run away. Although there was always the matter of a government passport, the man was free to go wherever he wished provided he did not steal a horse or mule or burro. Yet he did not seem to know that. His behavior was that of a fugitive. There had to be a way to get him to talk so that something could be done.

"We could turn him over to the authorities," Don Ignacio said the next morning.

"How long since you've seen an Army patrol here?" Tercero asked. Don Ignacio shrugged. "How long since anyone from here has gone to a villa where they have troops and government officials?"

"We could just let him run away."

"He would not last long on foot."

"That is his problem, Father. If he's fool enough, let him."

"I have to go back to Albuquerque soon," Tercero said. "I could take him with me." When he had said it, he realized the eminent sensibility of it. All he needed was Miguel's cooperation.

"You are a problem." Miguel sat up on his pallet and looked hard as Tercero spoke. "I have to return to the villa of Albuquerque. I should have left yesterday."

"Why tell me?"

"Do you have a passport?" Miguel shook his head. "It is my duty as a citizen of Mexico to turn you over to our government. You are in the country illegally."

"Not if I'm a Mexican citizen."

"You are no more Mexican than you are a priest." Sullen silence as Miguel turned his face to the wall. "You could stay with these poor people. Soldiers may not come here for months. Perhaps years. They took care of you here while you were injured. They would certainly welcome you when you are healed." Tercero could see only the back of his head. "You could go back to Albuquerque with me and there make your peace with representatives of the government. Then you would be free to do whatever you want."

"Where is my pistol?"

"What is a priest doing carrying a pistol? They tell me it is an American one. Are you a spy?" Silence. "But you are a Catholic."

"My brother is a priest."

"A Mexican priest?" A rueful smile and shake of the head. "How long is it since you have been to confession?"

Miguel turned his gaze back. His face was troubled but still set in that stubborn way of his.

"Would you like to make a confession?"

"I cannot, Father."

"You would have to say too much." No response. "Do you want to go with me to Albuquerque?" Again there was no answer. "I can wait one more week until you are stronger. But then I have to go."

Silence was Miguel's answer. But during the next week he did not try to run away, even though he went on daily walks to build his strength. Each night he joined Tercero for prayers, and the priest sensed a subtle shift in the praying. It was less the rote of duty and long habit and more as if they were urgent, spontaneous pleas for guidance. They were the same words but said for different reasons and so they sounded different. One night Miguel asked if he might accompany Tercero to Albuquerque. The next evening, after supper, he asked about confession.

"You are an honorable man, Father Rafa. You are bound to keep the secrets of confession."

"Yes."

"Before we go then, I want to confess. Bless me, Father, for I have sinned. My last confession was in March of this year—some four months ago."

8

"My name is Michael Dalton," he began. "Miguel in Spanish. I was born in the townland of Skihanach, parish of Ballyshedy, County Cork, Ireland. I tell you this not because it has any relevance to the sins I have committed against God; for those sins I am just another nameless soul. I tell you this because I am a stranger in a strange land and must throw myself on the mercy of strangers who, thank God, share a common belief in Jesus Christ and the holy Catholic Church. Whatever the tongues we speak or the shades of our skin, we are truly brothers in the sight of the Almighty.

"I have lived in fear and trepidation over the past months. I will not delve too much into my origins. That is another world across the sea. I will only say that I come from a large and devout family. My father was an honest, hard-working man who farmed another man's land. My mother, God rest her soul, was a saint.

"Of my brothers and sisters there are four each. Nine children altogether. And I must mention my favorite uncle, Harry. He had served as a mercenary soldier for other armies in other lands. A world traveler. A man who has seen the Holy See in Rome and the bloody battlefields of Europe. It was from him that I learned the Spanish language since he served with the Spanish, among others. It was from him, too, that I learned that many Irish are descendants of Miletius, an ancient Spaniard from the Iberian peninsula. That the Irish and Spanish have more in common than their religion. But it was not the Spanish that brought me to this New World but another country. The United States of America."

The Irish Poor Law had pointed the way to salvation for many destitute farmers like the Daltons. As if the clouds had parted and a ray of sunshine had shown the way to heaven. The lord of their estate had shipped a goodly number of tenant farmers to America, including Miguel's father, who planned to send for the family as soon as he saved their passage money.

However, his mother had taken ill and died shortly thereafter. His brothers and sisters, all older, had reassessed that call to a far-off land in the light of their mother's death and all had decided to remain in Ireland: the brother who was a priest, the two sisters who were nuns, and the others who survived the best they could in a land of hopeless poverty.

Thus, when the first hard-earned funds for passage to America came, they all agreed that it should go to Miguel now that their mother was dead.

It had been a send-off, Miguel remembered, to rival the wake of the beloved patriarch of the largest, richest family in County Cork. America! My God, America! Friends would come up and shake his hand and slap his back and gaze at him in awe as if he were ascending body and soul into heaven the way the Blessed Virgin herself had been called.

The ship had sailed in early spring for Philadelphia where he was to join his father. He had not minded the crowded decks, the poor food, and brackish water. The misery was leavened by singing and dancing—even more intense when a fellow passenger died before reaching the promised land.

In Philadelphia another shock. There was no father to greet him. Bewildered, he wandered through the city searching for the last address he had, only to find that his father had died while he had been crossing the Atlantic Ocean. All that was left was a small bundle of worn-out work clothes, a pair of boots that needed re-soling, and a packet of old letters from his dead mother, full of endearment and cheer and hope for their coming reunion in the brave new world. Neither had expected it to be the hereafter instead of Philadelphia. Miguel had sat on the steps of the boardinghouse in the poor section of the city and cried as if his heart would break.

But tears or no, loneliness or no, one must still eat. So he looked for work. Jobs were hard to find. There had been riots in Philadelphia the year before, protesting the influx of immigrants and the lack of work. The Catholic Church too had been the target of reactions.

Why did I leave Ireland? Miguel had thought in despair. I am just as unemployed here as there. I hear as much anti-Catholic raving as I would from an Irish Protestant. And if I want to fight my neighbor, I can fight the same Englishmen here. Though they may be masked by the faint veneer of having become new, free men—Americans—they carry the same old prejudices. For all of this, at least in Ireland I would be among family and friends. And yet, he thought, here there is still hope while in Ireland there is none.

If he had had the twenty-five dollars passage money or could have obtained a job on board ship, he would have sailed back to the Emerald Isle during those first few months. But somehow he survived. And when the Army sought recruits, there was none more eager than the hungry and homeless young Irishman who still hung on to a thread of hope.

"Oh, say were you ever in the Río Grande? Way, you Río." It was his destiny to be an American even if he had to fight for that right on the far shores of another alien country. "It's there that the river runs down golden sand. For we're bound to the Río Grande!"

Well, where General Taylor's forces landed was nothing like the Emerald Isle. It was a place called Texas, which Miguel had never dreamed existed even in his most despairing nightmares.

They had camped on the river, on the Río Grande across from the Mexican town of Matamoros. "Mata moros," he had translated for his non-Spanish-speaking comrades: "Kill Moors." Who were the ancient enemy of the Spanish people and from whom King Ferdinand and Queen Isabella had freed their country even as Columbus was on his way across the ocean sea to discover a new world. Matamoros.

War had not been declared. The two armies were like lolling

giants observing each other from opposite banks of the river. The American army was a motley collection of regulars. Almost half were immigrants from other countries. Mostly Irish like Miguel. But German, English, Scottish, and others too. A polyglot of languages and temperaments.

"If we can make an Army of this sorry crew," his sergeant said over and over like a litany, "we can make a country out of this Godforsaken land!"

Then, as salve for the fleas and the dirt and the changeable weather that could be mild, hot, windy, or wet, came the enticements from the Mexicans across the river to the occupants of Fort Texas.

"The Commander-in-chief of the Mexican army, to the English and Irish under the orders of the American General Taylor: Know ye: That the government of the United States is committing repeated acts of barbarous aggression against the magnanimous Mexican Nation; that the government which exists under 'the flag of the stars' is unworthy of the designation of Christian. Recollect that you were born in Great Britain; that the American government looks with coldness upon the powerful flag of St. George, and is provoking to a rupture the warlike people to whom it belongs; President Polk boldly manifesting a desire to take possession of Oregon, as he has already done of Texas. Now, then, come with all confidence to the Mexican ranks; and I guaranty to you, upon my honour, good treatment, and that all your expenses shall be defrayed until your arrival in the beautiful capital of Mexico.

"Germans, French, Poles, and individuals of other nations! Separate yourselves from the Yankees, and do not contribute to defend a robbery and usurpation, which, be assured, the civilized nations of Europe look upon with the utmost indignation. Come, therefore, and array yourselves under the tri-colored flag, in the confidence that the God of armies protects it, and that it will protect you equally with the English.

> *Headquarters upon the road to Matamoros*
> *April 2, 1846*
> *Pedro de Ampudia"*

One was not certain exactly where these pieces of paper came from. There was all manner of opportunity. After the initial landing of the American forces, when most Mexican farmers on the Texas side of the Río Grande had fled across the river to

Matamoros, there had been a settling into a tenuous but friendly tolerance. A few Mexican farmers came back across to their homes with their goats and fighting cocks and children. Others from Matamoros would cross daily by ferry to sell milk and cheese and fresh fruit, returning at the end of a busy day of commerce.

So there was ample opportunity for the notices to be surreptitiously left for a soldier to pick up. Other information came by word of mouth. That the Mexican government would pay the way of American soldiers to Mexico City where they could enlist in the Mexican army and form their own battalion.

There were other enticements. More meaningful ones to young men far from home. At times the army bands would serenade each other across the river, like lovers separated by the irreconcilable feuding of their families. It was like a summer picnic where one would speak loudly so as to be heard at a distance by the object of one's attention, yet one could not mingle intimately. Thus it was one morning, with the Mexican army band playing, that Miguel and his closest friend had meandered along the river north of the fort.

"I tell you, Mike," his friend had said. "If that sergeant of ours picks on me one more time, I'll—"

"Now. Now. He's just one of those bigoted Ulster anti-Catholics. You should try to ignore him."

"We're supposed to be Americans. Every man jack of us. Catholic or no. Ulster or Dublin. Irish or German. Jesus! We're here to fight the Mexicans, and the man I hate most in the world is one of us."

"Just keep calm, Brennan. When the Mexicans start thumping that artillery across the river, there won't be time for privates to worry about sergeants or vice versa. Come on. Let's find a nice place and take a swim. That will cool you off. We can lie in the sun and listen to the band. Like a grand Sunday after mass with nothing to do but enjoy."

"I'll kill him!" Brennan hissed.

"After we take a swim."

As they walked silently along, Brennan brooded about his lot in life. It was true. Their sergeant was a bully who had already been shot at one dark night by an unknown assailant. Missed, worse luck. And Brennan had a penchant for arguing, for talking about his rights as a free American. He had never been hungry enough, Mike thought, nor lonely enough to let these things pass—like the night rumblings of one's stomach protesting a miserable meal, but a meal nonetheless.

From across the river drifted the faint sounds of laughter distorted by the distance. They were played with by the wind as if the sounds were a flock of birds moving this way and that on the currents of air. At once unified, yet separate and distinct, alternately coming into the focus to stay a moment, then disappearing.

Brennan looked up, eyes alert. "I think I hear the cooing of doves."

Mike smiled as they slowed their pace and kept under cover, moving along the bank. "Ahh," Mike sighed, holding Brennan back with an outstretched hand.

There across the river four brown-skinned young ladies were demurely bathing, laughing and splashing each other playfully. The two young soldiers squatted on their haunches and watched silently through a screen of brush. The girls had waded out waist deep, their long hair pulled and tied behind their heads, their breasts shiny from the reflection of sun on water.

"Those poor dears," Brennan whispered. "It must be colder than a sergeant's heart out there."

"And you have the remedy, I suppose."

Brennan smiled. "Look at that one. The little one on the right. Oh, I love you, darling," he whispered across the river. "I've only seen you once and more than modesty allows, but I love you anyway. Maybe more because I've seen more of you."

Mike had continued to look in silence, thinking his own private thoughts. There were no favorites. He watched them all in turn. Brown-skinned honeys whose complexions shaded from palest tan to deepest brown.

"Would you ever think," Mike finally said, "that there could be such variation in shape and color. And all girls from the same town in the same country."

"Let's go down there. Let's go take our swim before they go away."

Without responding, Mike crawled away from their vantage point and waved his companion to follow. He led the way back up the trail to that invisible point where they had first heard the laughter.

"What the hell are you doing?" Brennan asked.

"We've got to give them a warning," Mike answered softly. Then he started to whistle, and he let out a shout in sheer exuberance as he turned and walked noisily toward the river. The laughter seemed to be louder now, more shrill, faster.

When the young soldiers turned past the last cover of foliage onto the open riverbank, they slowed their pace, not knowing what to expect. It was silent now. Only the faint sounds of the Río Grande flowing toward the Gulf of Mexico. Even the Mexican army band was silent. Mike stopped on the slight rise and felt Brennan stop beside him. The four young ladies had all turned, still waist deep in the water, unashamed in their nudity, frozen like beautiful brown statues.

The two young men and four young women looked at each other for a moment in silence from opposite banks of the river. Then the girls turned, almost in slow motion, and in low voices that carried soft as a whisper, held an undecipherable conversation that no doubt centered about what they were to do.

"Halloo!" Brennan shouted, waving in what he hoped would be seen as a friendly gesture. "Don't be afraid! We won't harm you! For Christ's sake," he said in an undertone to Mike, "you know the language. Say something."

"¡No tengan miedo! ¡Somos amigos!"

They turned slowly toward each other again, like shy does ready to bolt if the young men came nearer. Mike and Brennan sensed this and stood still, hardly daring to even turn their heads.

"That little one," Brennan said. "Ask her her name. Tell her I'm crazy for her."

"¡No se espanten! ¡No más vamos a nadar!"

"They're not answering. What did you say to them? Ask her again."

"You just don't ask a girl's name so fast. We're enemy soldiers to them. I told them not to be afraid. We're just going for a swim."

"For God's sakes, ask her. Before they run away."

"¡Me llamo Miguel! ¡Mi amigo se llama Juan! ¿Cómo se llaman ustedes?"

The girls turned their heads toward each other slowly and once again exchanged words. Then their soft words became more distinct and bold. "¡Consuela! ¡Panchita! ¡Rosita! ¡María!" came across the water, followed by giggling.

"Is that just the name of one of them?" Brennan asked. "You know how these Mexican names are."

But Mike had watched closely as each girl had shouted the one name only. "The little one is Rosita."

Brennan waved his arms wildly. "¡Rosita!" he shouted. "¡Rosita! Beau-ti-ful! How do you say beautiful in Spanish?" he asked.

"Hermosa."

"¡Rosita! ¡Hermosa!"

Now she lifted her head alertly as if still listening, although the sound of the words had died away. Then, without haste, with a look of surprise on her face, she lifted her arms and folded them shyly across her breasts.

"Oh, God! Mike. Did you see that? Now I know I love her."

Not even removing his clothes, Brennan rushed to the river's edge, threw himself into the water, and thrashed out.

"Come back, you damn fool!" Mike shouted.

Now the girls were laughing at the crazy Americano. The sound of running footsteps grew louder and as Mike turned, a sentry burst through the brush, rifle in hand.

"Halt!" he shouted at the swimming figure. "Halt or I'll shoot!"

The thrashing stopped and Brennan paddled back to the bank of the river. Luckily the sentry was someone they knew. The girls, frightened, had waded from the water and were climbing up the opposite bank.

"¡Rosita!" Brennan shouted. "¡Mañana! How do you say 'here,' Mike?"

"Aquí."

"¡Rosita! ¡Mañana! ¡Aquí!"

"Come on out of there, Brennan," the sentry warned.

"He was just going for a swim," Mike said.

"I should turn you guys in. For all I know you were trying to swim across to join the Mexicans."

"Don't be silly." Brennan had walked out of the water and stood in the sunlight in his dripping uniform. He was ignoring the sentry, watching the girls disappear. Mike had started to walk back toward camp.

"Halt!" the sentry said. "Halt or I'll—"

"Oh, stow it, will you," Brennan said. "You take this all too seriously."

"If the sergeant should—"

"You know what the sergeant can do."

"You don't show the proper respect to a sentry of the United

States Army who caught you consorting with the enemy." His face was red, and he held his rifle stiffly at port arms.

Mike walked back down the trail toward the sentry. "Aw, come on. We were only going for a swim like everybody else, and we saw those girls."

"They could have been decoys for Mexican soldiers waiting in ambush."

Mike looked at the sentry in surprise. He started to say "Don't be crazy," but thought better of it. What if the sentry decided to report them to their sergeant? "Yes," Mike said. "I hadn't thought of that."

"Be careful along the river," the sentry admonished.

Brennan was about to open his mouth, but Mike spoke before he could. "You're right. Thanks."

"Now you best get on back to camp."

They turned and picked their way along the trail, Brennan still dripping from his swim.

The sentry had not needed to report them to their sergeant. They walked past him as they entered camp and Brennan's squishing boots and wet uniform were impossible to ignore. The sergeant took the bottle of Mexican brandy he had been bargaining for with a vendor and called them over. He checked with the sentries on duty along the river and had soon constructed his version of what had happened. Consorting with the Papists. Two days extra duty with restriction to camp and no more swimming. And if that wasn't enough, there would be more. Or hadn't one flogging taught Brennan anything?

Brennan brooded silently at supper. "It's only two days," Mike said.

"I'll kill him," Brennan said. "I'll kill the son-of-a-bitch."

Mike had stared at him. Brennan's complaint did not sound real. There was a tired, resigned quality to his words and tone. As if he had already decided upon something, but it was not to kill their sergeant. Just before taps Mike came upon him sitting alone on the outskirts of a campfire reading. Quickly he had folded the piece of paper and stuck it into his shirt pocket.

That night in their tent, Brennan lay on his back staring. "Tell me," he asked. "What did you dream about when you left Ireland?"

"Meat."

"Meat?"

"On the table. Any kind of meat. Lizard. Snake. Anything but potatoes. And a job. A permanent regular kind of a job that paid you enough that you could buy meat."

Brennan sighed. "You have the imagination of a peasant," he said. "I dreamed about my own place. My own home. With land around it. And trees. And my own little wife to greet me when I came in from the fields. With kids running alongside her shouting, 'Daddy! Daddy!' A family safe and happy in my own castle."

Mike turned on his side and looked at his friend. "You've decided already, haven't you?"

"Decided what?"

"You know."

"I don't know anything," Brennan said. "Except that I'm going to kill that bastard sergeant some day." But Mike could tell from his voice that he didn't mean it. He meant to do something else.

Mike had been asleep for some time when he heard the faint rustlings in the tent. He awoke with a fright, his heart pounding, to see his tentmate fully clothed and crawling out into the open campground.

"Brennan," he whispered. But Brennan had not heard him; he had disappeared. Hastily Mike dressed and stepped out, moving quietly so he would not be heard by the sentries. He ran quickly along the path that Brennan would probably follow to the river. The crazy fool! he thought. I have to bring him back.

At the site where they had seen the girls that previous morning, Mike saw the dark shape paddling strongly but quietly away from the bank. Mike ran even faster, kicking off his boots as he tried to get the swimmer's attention. "Brennan!" he called softly, afraid that a sentry might hear him. "Brennan, you damned fool!"

The swimmer did not seem to hear. Without thinking, Mike tossed his shoestring-tied boots around his neck and waded into the water. He swam strongly, turning so that the current added to the impetus of his efforts. When he caught Brennan he would persuade him to come back. Force him back if necessary. He was in midriver now, drifting south with the current so that he was below Brennan, who was closer to the Mexican side, swimming in an area made clear by moonlight.

"Deserter!" The shout rang clear through the quiet night air, even above the current of the river. A shot rang out, and Mike turned to look back upriver. Then another shot. "I think I got him!" the sentry shouted again. "Over there. He's getting close to the bank now." Then two more shots.

Frantic, Mike struggled even harder to reach the Mexican side, scrambling out of the water and keeping low as he ran toward cover. Christ! he thought. We're done for now. I'll never be able to get him back if he's been shot.

He headed upstream to look for Brennan. Some two hundred feet away he saw the dark shape struggling at the edge of the river, flopping like a fish on the end of a line. When he came up to him, he could see that Brennan was bleeding badly from two wounds. His struggle to get ashore ceased and when Mike pulled him from the water, the body was heavy as if it had settled into death.

From across the Río Grande the voices of the sentries still carried. "Hey! Charlie! I think there's another one." Then two shots in rapid succession.

Mike dragged Brennan away from the bank toward cover as two more shots sought him. Finally, out of breath and shaking with fear, he dropped onto the ground. He peered into Brennan's face, then felt for a pulse. There was none. He started to weep, placing his tired head on his arms as he lay on the ground. Minutes later the sounds of footsteps added to his terror. He looked up and there ahead under a tree was a squad of Mexican soldiers.

"Welcome to México, señores," one said in Spanish.

"My friend was dead, Father," Miguel said to Tercero. "After they buried him they gave me what little he had. His pistol and ammunition which were in a waterproof pouch. His boots so that I had an extra pair. And this notice that, along with the thoughts of Rosita, sent him across the river."

Tercero took the folded and faded piece of paper:

"Soldiers! You have enlisted in time of peace to serve in that army for a specific term; but your obligation never implied that you were bound to violate the laws of God, and the most sacred rights of friends! The United States government, contrary to the wishes of a majority of all honest and honourable Americans, has ordered you to take forcible possession of the territory of a friendly neighbour, who has never given her consent to such occupation. In other words, while the treaty of peace and commerce between Mexico and the United States is in full force, the United States, presuming on her strength and prosperity, and on our supposed imbecility and cowardice, attempts to make you the blind instruments of her unholy and mad ambition, and force you to appear as the hateful robbers of our dear homes, and the unprovoked violators of our dearest feelings as men and patriots. Such villany and outrage, I know, is perfectly repugnant to the noble sentiments of any gentleman, and it is base and foul to rush you on to certain death, in order to aggrandize a few lawless individuals, in defiance of the laws of God and man!

"It is to no purpose if they tell you that the law for the annexation of Texas justifies your occupation of the Rio Bravo del Norte; for by this act they rob us of a great part of Tamaulipas, Coahuila, Chihuahua, and New Mexico; and it is barbarous to send a handful of men on such an errand against a powerful and warlike nation. Besides, the most of you are Europeans, and we are the declared friends of a majority of the nations of Europe. The North Americans are ambitious, overbearing, and insolent as a nation, and they will only make use of you as vile tools to carry out their abominable plans of pillage and rapine.

"I warn you in the name of justice, honour, and your own interests and self-respect, to abandon their desperate and unholy cause, and become peaceful Mexican citizens. I guarantee you in such case, a half section of land, or three hundred and twenty acres, to settle upon, gratis. Be wise, then, and just, and honourable, and take no part in murdering us who have no unkind feelings for you. Lands shall be given to officers, sergeants, and corporals, according to rank, privates receiving three hundred and twenty acres, as stated.

"If, in time of action, you wish to espouse our cause, throw away your arms and run to us, and we will embrace you as true friends and Christians. It is not decent nor prudent to say more. But should any of you render important service to Mexico you shall be accordingly considered and preferred.

M. Arista
Commander-in-chief of the
Mexican Army
Headquarters at Matamoros,
April 20, 1846"

Tercero handed the sheet of paper back to Miguel. "So my friend was dead," Miguel said. "In the eyes of the army of the

United States I was a deserter. In the eyes of the Mexican army I had come to join them. I should have gone to Mexico City to join other deserters who were to form their own battalion to be called San Patricio, Saint Patrick's Battalion. But that was not to be. The war began."

"Then the war has truly started?"

Miguel nodded. "At Matamoros. Just two days after I had swum the Río Grande. There were thirty other Americans there under the commander, Captain Riley. I . . . I acquiesced when they welcomed me. We fought in the battle with the artillery that laid waste to Fort Texas. A few days later, other troops of the Mexican army fought at Palo Alto and Resaca de la Palma."

The battle had lasted some two weeks after the artillery had begun the bombardment of the American fort across the river. At Matamoros they had been expecting a great victory. After all, was not right on their side? Ballrooms had been decorated for the celebration. There would be music and laughter. The women would dress in their finest. Happy day!

But the Battle of Matamoros went poorly. It became the Battle of Matamejicanos. The army retreated through the city in a rout. Halls were left half decorated. Citizens bolted their doors—as much from fear of Mexican troops as from the gringos. Inside the houses women wept and moaned. In some there was only fearful silence.

Outside the city the army panicked. General Arista ordered the troops to march toward Monterrey. Few seemed to hear the orders. In fear for their lives, they ran from the Americans, following blindly those who promised to lead the way to safety. Mike joined the mad stampede.

The Mexican cavalry overran the infantry, trampling their own comrades in their dash for safety. At the edge of the river a Catholic priest, Father Leary, held out his crucifix to hold back the panicked troops. They hesitated only for an instant, then rushed on, trampling him and others into the river, where those who were not already dead were drowned.

Out on the flat on the road from Matamoros, the battlefield was strewn with dead. One young girl—had it been Rosita?—wept piteously beside a fallen young soldier. When Mike looked back she was swishing flies from his bloodied head. Had it been her husband? Lover? Brother?

"I could no longer stand the madness of the war," Miguel said. "The ranks of the fleeing army dwindled each day. There was not enough leadership nor loyalty among the troops to enforce any kind of discipline. Desertions were the rule rather than the exception. Only fools continued on to Monterrey to be slaughtered."

At Camargo he had been assigned to a small party of messengers who were to carry the word to the outposts at Monterrey. He, the gringo who could speak Spanish, could give them the truth about American intentions and strength.

After Monterrey they were sent on to Chihuahua. Just before they had reached there and made their final report, they had been attacked by Apaches. He had been the only survivor. As he rode dazedly toward the town, he realized that he could ride on by. The information he had was old now and probably of little use. He would be just another of those many deserters from the Mexican army who had faded into the landscape. For most of all, he wanted to be out of the miserable war and alive.

Where did one go from Chihuahua? Certainly not toward Texas. Mike had seen enough of the Texas Rangers attached to the American army to know what awaited him there. Where the law was represented by cutthroats and bandits, there really was no law. And as a deserter to the hated Mexican side, he would be dealt with quickly and cruelly. So up the Chihuahua Trail, where with luck, he might take the Santa Fe Trail east toward Missouri, if he dared. Or perhaps he might find a place to settle and forget the past. So he joined a small group of traders on their way to El Paso del Norte.

It was in El Paso that he stole a priest's clothing. He felt badly about that. Guilty. In addition, he was taking the Lord's name in vain by wearing the clothes. It was from here that he set off alone, north along the Río Grande to places unknown. He would know when he found it. A place to stay put. To stop running. To forget his fears of the army—either army—and of the Apaches. He had traveled by night. Gone thirsty and hungry. That was nothing. Then his horse had died after they had crossed the Jornada del Muerto, Dead Man's March, and he had continued on foot until he had collapsed. The next thing he remembered was being in the hamlet of Los Bacas.

"As for my sins, Father. They have been many. Desertion. Twice. Stealing. A priest's clothing and more. Food. Water."

He went on. No longer telling the story of how he came to be here, but of how he had offended God along the way. Tercero half closed his eyes and listened.

9

Today Andrea would help Ana María supervise the laundering of the family's special things. A carreta had been loaded with fine linens, blankets, tablecloths, clothing. If it had been only the coarser, everyday things Mamá would have let the servants launder them unsupervised. Or if they had been only the small things, the laundry could have been done at home. As it was, they would journey to the river with two servant women to do the heavy work and a male servant as guard.

There would be others there from nearby farms, all meeting under a favorite shelter of cottonwood trees where a gentle curve of the river's bank met clusters of large rocks ideal for thrashing dirt from clothes. Back from the rocks a meadow with bushes and high grass waited for the washed clothes to be spread out for drying. Here too on the meadow the women would rest and eat their midday meal of beans wrapped in tortillas, roasted ears of corn, and dried pemmican.

"You'll have to watch that one," Ana María said, nodding toward the younger and larger of the servant women. "She does not care whether things are clean or not. She has no pride; look at her clothes. And her hair is full of lice."

But Andrea was hardly listening. The day was so beautiful. Warm and clear. Her married sisters, Clara and Josefa, would be at the river, as well as her friend from the neighboring ranch, Ynez Griego. There would be all manner of news to exchange, confidences to trade, gossip to laugh about.

The carreta squeaked alongside them as they walked the well-worn road to the river. "Not so fast!" Ana María shrieked at the male servant who led the ox cart. The cart moved forward even slower.

"How old were you when you were married?" Andrea asked.

"You know as well as I."

"Eighteen. The same as my age now. Only I am not even spoken for."

"There is no hurry."

"Yes. You can say that. You're married. But some of the girls are married at fourteen."

"From the poorer classes," Ana María said with disdain. "You are a young lady of family. You cannot marry just anyone."

"Oh pooh! I don't mean to marry just anyone. I mean *the* one."

An ironic smile flashed across Ana María's solemn face. "Whomever God sends will be the one," she said. "And whomever your parents agree to."

"Oh, God," Andrea said, "send me a good one. That way I'll know you've been listening to my prayers. Not one with a long nose like Pedro Sánchez. Nor with crossed eyes like José Romero. Nor one with a puny little mustachio like Enrique Gonzales." Ana María was smiling now, and when she smiled she was pretty. "Nor one with a shriveled up backside whose trousers hang like empty sacks, like Francisco Griego." Ana María laughed. "Be serious, Ana María," Andrea said. "Is it true that men whose trousers hang like empty sacks are mean and stingy?"

"No," she answered. "Narrow thin lips show stinginess."

"But I've seen some who are mean and stingy who do not have narrow thin lips."

"Yes. Full lips can hide a stingy heart so you can never be sure. But thin narrow lips—that is a certainty."

"If you can never be sure, then how do you know? You may think that someone you see has all the qualities, but then as you say, you can never be sure. So how do you know?"

"It is not for us to know. We must trust in God. And honor the choice of our parents. They know better than us. They, in the wisdom of their years, can see through to the reality underneath. That is why it is left to them."

As she said these words Ana María's face stiffened and each succeeding word became more difficult for her to utter. Was that what she had not done. Trusted in God? Was that what had made her barren and therefore undeserving of a husband although she was already married? How could she advise this young girl on whose beaming face shone the joy of anticipation? Will this one be the one? Andrea's expression seemed to say. Will this one be the love of my life? The bitterness in Ana María's heart could only see each eligible young male as a reflection of the dark shadow in her own life.

"There they are," Andrea shouted. "Clara! Josefa!" From the meadow came the wave of arms where the women were unloading their carreta. It is going to be such a happy day, Andrea thought.

Josefa was the oldest, so they deferred to her the way they would have deferred to Señora Rafa had she been present. It was Josefa who had taken charge of the midday meal, dispensing food and ordering the servants about on this task or that. The great bulk of the washing had already been done, and the larger pieces were festooned over large shrubs and across tall grass so that the meadow was a giant crazy-quilt of drying laundry.

"Turn them over when the tops are dry!" Josefa shouted to the servants who had just finished their meal under a distant cottonwood.

"Watch that young large one of ours," Ana María warned. "The one they call Horno because she's the shape of an oven. Did you see how she was washing the clothes?"

Josefa nodded. She had seen Horno, but her mind was on other things. "Tell me," she said. "What talk do you hear about the war?"

"About Indians," one of the women said. "They raided a rancho south of here and massacred the entire family."

Another nodded toward the three male servants who stood lookout around the periphery of the meadow. "What do you think would happen if we were attacked by Indians?"

There was a gasp from some of the women and they looked around in fright. "They would never come to a town as large and strong as this," Josefa said. "No. I meant the war with the Americanos."

"Oh, war!" Andrea protested. "I'm absolutely bored with the talk of war."

"Now, now. When they send all the young men off to fight who will there be left to become husbands?" There was a teasing innocence on Clara's face as she nodded first toward Andrea, then toward Ynez.

"Even little Francisco has joined the militia," Ynez said.

"Little Francisco," Andrea said bitterly. "It was only yesterday he was playing in the mud on the bank of the river."

"He's nineteen!" Ynez protested.

"Well, they're taking the husbands, too," Ana María said. The married women nodded in agreement.

Clara leaned forward to share an urgent intimacy with them. "Father Gallegos has said that the Americanos are barbarians. The few that believe in God are Protestants, but for the most part they are vicious atheists. Worse than the Indians—some of whom, at least, have embraced our Lord Jesus Christ. It would be like the worst imaginable Indian war. Those the Americanos do not kill they will carry away as slaves. Especially the women and children. And the women slaves, you know what they will do with them."

"¡María santísima!"

Clara nodded solemnly. "And if you do not submit—" She made a dramatic gesture with the side of her hand across her throat. "Not only will they defile our bodies, they will also defile our beliefs. Churches will burn. Holy images will be smashed. They will tear the rosary beads from the wrinkled hands of old grandmothers and trample them in the dirt. The priests will be castrated before being put to death. And all who would stay alive must swear allegiance to their false gods."

One of the servant girls who had come to the ladies to ask what to do next stood with open mouth listening. Finally, she let out a soft moan and started to cry.

"And your children," Clara continued. "Those that live will be taken away from you. If you do not let go of their little hands when the Yankees come for them, they will hack that little hand off with their swords. These little one-handed ones will become the slaves who do the most menial of tasks. With lives hardly better than dogs."

The mouths of all the women were open in amazement. They dared not look at each other for the fear in their eyes.

"Father Gallegos told you that?"

Clara nodded solemnly. "And more."

Andrea stamped her foot angrily. "Well, there had better not be any silly war!"

* * *

The last of the laundry had been folded and stacked neatly in the carretas. The shadows of the cottonwoods along the river now pointed east and were lengthening. The women kissed each other goodbye, waved, and went their separate ways toward home and a little rest before supper.

Andrea and Ana María walked in silence, each in her own thoughts. The two servant girls were flirting with the driver of the carreta who watched carefully to be certain the young mistresses were not watching.

"Oh, this hateful, hateful war," Andrea finally complained. "It will either leave me an old maid or the slave of some monstrous Yankee. Or even worse, nursing a wounded veteran like Francisco Griego."

"It will be all right," Ana María said. "Just say your prayers and God will hear them."

"But will He answer them?"

"Only He knows that."

They fell silent once more. If it were not the war, Ana María thought, there would be another reason for Carlos to be away. Sheep. Or cattle. Or Indians. Or crops. Any excuse would do. If we had children it would not matter so much. There would be babies for me to care for, to talk about with other women. As it is, I am like someone's maiden aunt who is tolerated because she helps with the housework, only a step above a servant. Oh, Andrea. If you knew what marriage really meant, you would not be so starry-eyed.

"This war," Andrea said as their adobe home came into view. "This hateful, hateful war."

10

It could not have been robbery, they had said in Santa Fe. The pockets of the dead young Americano had not been touched. His revolver was still in its holster and the clothes were still on his back.

Carlos listened to the gossip in fascinated trepidation. The older Americano, the one who held Carlos' signed and still unpaid notes, had arranged for the burial. They were business agents, someone said, of some large company in los Estados Unidos—the younger man an assistant to the older one. They had been talking to local traders and waiting for the wagon train.

They were also friends of Manuel Alvarez who had connections in high places. So the murder had been protested to the governor himself, who, too busy preparing for the oncoming war, had delegated it to the local authorities. There would be a thorough investigation.

There is no way, Carlos thought, that they can connect me to it. Besides, the man deserved it. His death is of no consequence to me.

He had killed men before—Indians, rather—even taking a few scalps. There had also been the Texas invaders; Carlos had shed his share of blood there too. It was all part of the pattern of frontier life, a logical extension in a land first taken by force, then kept by force. It was a rare death, like this one, that became an issue. Usually one attributed it to the will of God and did not worry about it.

When was it that this attitude toward death had first hardened within Carlos Rafa? He remembered that early in his life the attitude had been in the air, though unspoken. It had surrounded him even in the cradle, for violent death was ever present in the river kingdom. But the first death that he could remember, the first coalescing of this attitude into a palpable act, was when he had been about eight years old.

Carlos and Tercero had been awakened by the early morning clatter of horses' hooves. They heard the gruff orders of their father. As they rushed outside, Don Francisco turned in the saddle and ordered them back to their rooms. Grandfather, whose eyes were not sharp enough to join the riders, took the two boys by their shoulders.

"The dirty Indian thief could not have gone far!" Grandfather shouted at the horsemen as they rode off.

"What dirty Indian thief, Grandfather?" Carlos asked.

The old man's face had set into a hard frown. "Your mother's treasure, her inlaid box from China, has disappeared. This morning one of the servants, old Juan, ran away."

"Old Juan wouldn't do that!" Tercero protested.

"Hush, boy. You do not know the ways of these Pueblo dogs.

They would steal the tortillas from a starving man's mouth."

"No."

Grandfather had tightened his grip on Tercero's shoulder, and the boy grimly closed his mouth and became silent.

"What will they do to him?" Carlos asked.

"Wait and see."

All morning the boys waited. Then, into the afternoon past siesta time. Finally in late afternoon, while wrestling in the dirt, they felt the vibrations on the ground that signaled the approach of horses. They raced out into the field and stood watching the small dots grow larger and larger and turn into horsemen, ahead of whom walked old Juan with hands tied behind his back. The horsemen stopped at a huge cottonwood tree at the edge of the field and the boys, followed by three mangy dogs, ran to join them.

"Carlos! José Antonio!" They ignored their mother's scream, and she hastened after them, followed by Grandfather.

"No," Don Francisco said to her. "They're old enough to learn what happens to a man who steals from me." The señora turned and walked quickly back to the house.

Though sweaty and tired, Juan stood quietly in the shade of the tree. When the señora was beyond hearing distance, he looked up at Don Francisco. "I did not steal the Chinese box, señor. I am not a thief. I went to my brother who was sick. A messenger came to me in the night, so I left without telling anyone. You were asleep. I was coming back when he got better."

"His brother *was* sick," one of the riders said.

Don Francisco stared coldly at Juan as if he had not heard him or the rider. "Where did you hide it? Who did you give it to? Or have you already sold it and spent the money?"

Juan did not answer. He sensed that it was useless. He looked away from Don Francisco toward Grandfather and the two boys, his face searching for someone to believe him. "I think he did it, patrón," a second rider said. "Now he has no choice but to lie."

"Where is the box?" Don Francisco asked. "Or must I beat the answer from you."

Juan shook his head. "You cannot grow corn on a rock."

"Papá!" Tercero said. "I believe him. He wouldn't steal."

Don Francisco turned and struck Tercero in the face. The boy fought back the tears. Juan glanced down at Tercero. "Thank you, little patrón," he said. "Always follow your heart to the truth."

Red-faced with rage, Don Francisco stepped up to the Indian.

90

"No more of your blasphemies!" he shouted. "No more of your lies!" Quickly drawing his knife, he motioned to two of his men to force open Juan's mouth. A brief struggle. A choking. Then triumphant, Don Francisco held up the bloody tongue and threw it to the dogs who quarreled over it. "Put him on a horse!"

While two men lifted the bloody-mouthed Indian, two others strung a rope over a sturdy branch of the tree. "All right, Tercero, put the rope around his neck."

The boy's eyes widened with fear and his voice came out a hoarse whisper. "No, señor." Then Tercero turned and ran toward the house.

For just an instant before any word was uttered by Don Francisco, Grandfather glanced at him and shook his head slightly but firmly, an order from father to son. Don Francisco shrugged and let the boy go. "He's better off in the kitchen with the women," he muttered. Then he turned back to the business at hand.

"Papá," Carlos said. "I will put the rope around his neck."

Don Francisco glanced once again at Grandfather, saw no sign, then lifted the boy up high while one of the men handed him the noose. Carlos dropped it around Juan's neck, not daring to look at the bleeding mouth or anguished eyes. Then Don Francisco lowered him to the ground.

"I am the lord and master here," Don Francisco said to old Juan. "I am the boss, the patrón. My word is law. He who commits a crime against me must answer to the law." He raised his quirt and struck the rump of the horse, who bolted. The Indian dropped and the rope snapped taut. "May God have mercy on your soul."

Carlos watched in fascinated horror, then turned and bolted toward the house, running in a blind fury. He stumbled as he approached the patio, righted himself, then saw his brother bent over beside a tree. Tercero was crying as he vomited onto the ground. Carlos ran from him, too, toward the security of his room.

A week later Carlos sat hidden in the branches of that same tree when his father rode up. His mother was waiting in the patio. Carlos playfully curled himself as small as possible and smiled at this little secret of his. He peeked through the branches, waiting to play a surprise trick on his parents.

"Here," he heard Doña Estela say. There was a strange look on her face. Don Francisco took the object from her hand and turned it over and over. The Chinese box. "It was tangled in the dirty clothes. It must have been there since the last laundry."

Don Francisco handed the box back to her. For what seemed like an interminable time neither of them spoke. "It cannot be undone," he finally said. "If it had not been for this, it would have been for something else. It is of no consequence. He was only an Indian."

Carlos looked away from his mother because he could tell from her face that she was going to cry. He watched instead the stiff, proud man ride away. He was the boss, the patrón. He was the law.

Now, thinking about the man he had recently killed, his father's words came to Carlos as if they were his own. "It is of no consequence. He was only a Yankee."

"I have come only for a moment, Señor Rivera," Carlos said, "to say adiós. The war is no longer a rumor. It has been declared. There has been fighting at the mouth of the Río Grande at Matamoros. Both the regular troops and the militia have been put on alert. I will not be able to visit you and your family again until after we turn back the invaders."

The merchandise slipped through Señor Rivera's hands and his mouth fell open. He turned his anxious gaze intently on Carlos. "War? I did not believe it would come to that. God! What can we do against the Americans? All will be lost."

"Your army is here to defend you," Carlos said.

"Like against the Indians." Señor Rivera looked around at the pitiful selection of merchandise in his tiny store. "I will be ruined. Carlos, we will never be able to go into business. The Yankees will take it all."

"We can handle the Yankees."

"And you. What if you are hurt?"

Carlos did not dignify the question with an answer. He knew what Rivera really meant. How will I get the money to expand my business if you are dead? Well, no matter. Because Carlos had no intention of becoming the partner of a trader. Now or after the war. He watched the older man sort nervously through the items nearest him.

"I never really dreamed there would be a war," Rivera said. "There have been rumors for years. Like rumors of the past.

Cities of gold that turn out to be adobe huts. I cannot really believe there is going to be a war."

Carlos sighed in exasperation. "There is."

"Mamá!" Señora Rivera appeared. "The Yankees are coming. It is to be war." She made the sign of the cross and mumbled some inaudible holy words, then disappeared back into the house. "Celia! Dolores!" A soft patter of feet on the adobe floor, then Celia appeared in the doorway. "Say goodbye to your cousin. He is off to fight the Yankees." Celia mumbled a soft goodbye, a look of worry on her face. "Where's Dolores?"

Celia shook her head. Was her worried look for Carlos or Dolores? "She's— she's still in the back. She won't come."

"Ay, Dios," Señor Rivera said. "Yankees." Celia disappeared into the house. Carlos looked at him questioningly. "Dolores is in mourning. She does not hear when you speak to her. Nor speak anything but prayers. She hardly eats. That's what comes from mixing with Yankees."

"Oh?"

Señor Rivera stepped closer to Carlos and lowered his voice. "You know that young Americano who was stabbed to death over near St. Francis? He had been waiting to see Dolores when she left the church. He wanted to marry her, she said. They had been seeing each other like that for weeks. Then one night he is murdered. Now his friend is looking, trying to find who did it. The murdered man wasn't robbed. So there must have been some personal quarrel. Something. The dead man's friend has been here to see Dolores. It upsets her terribly. She cannot even talk about it. Just more trouble from mixing with foreigners."

"He's been here? Talking to Dolores?"

Señor Rivera nodded. "He must have been rich, that young Americano. A fine catch for a young girl. But now—"

His friend is looking, Carlos thought. A leaden anxiety gnawed at him. But what could the man learn? he thought. That I visit my cousin, Rudolfo, who has a daughter and a niece. That the niece had been seeing the dead Yankee. What does that have to do with me? A coincidence. Yet the heavy feeling did not leave him.

"I would be careful talking to Yankees," Carlos said. "We are at war."

"Yes. Yes. That has already occurred to me. But—"

"But—?"

"What if they win? They will be our masters."

The heavy feeling of anxiety flared into anger. "Señor Rivera," Carlos said coldly, "don't even think such traitorous thoughts. It is unworthy of a citizen of Mexico." Quickly he left the store with a parting, "Adiós."

As Carlos rode along the dirt street he passed the cantina where he had lost at cards that night. There was that debt he still owed. Sometime, somewhere he would have to pay that debt. But for now, he would avoid it.

The New Mexican forces were camped east of Santa Fe on the approach the Yankees would take. It was a motley crew. Militia from the various departments of New Mexico. Regulars from the presidio in Santa Fe. A squadron of troops from Vera Cruz. With inadequate food, weapons, or horses. While racing toward them were two forces—good and evil. The Missouri caravan, which included Governor Armijo's business partner. And the American army under Colonel Kearney, a powerful, well-trained force, well-supplied, well-mounted, with heavy artillery.

There was concern in the New Mexican camp. Was it true that the governor was more interested in the arrival of the Missouri caravan, feathering his own pockets that is, than in repulsing the Americanos? There were many who said so. Then there was that other faction. Those young hotheads like Carlos who were itching for a fight. Ignoring rumors. Ignoring intelligence from the spies sent east to observe the advancing Americans. Wanting only the chance to strike a blow at the arrogant Yankees. Thus, while the governor thought of gold, they thought of glory.

"Carlos!" Carlos turned toward the call. "The captain wants to see you."

He finished currying his horse, then checked to see that it was securely tethered before he walked to the captain's tent.

"I have had a visit," the captain said, "from an emissary of Manuel Alvarez. You know Manuel Alvarez?"

"I have heard of him, Captain."

"There has been a complaint about gambling debts, Lieutenant. Large gambling debts."

"Yes, sir."

"Do you know anything about these debts?"

"I owe no gambling debts to Manuel Alvarez. I have never met the man."

The captain hesitated, quietly studying Carlos. "It is a friend of Alvarez' that he speaks of."

"I know no friend of Alvarez'." Carlos' lips were tight, his face flushed. "What is all this, Captain? An emissary from Alvarez whose friend complained to you about gambling debts that you refer to me? I'm sorry. This is preposterous. If someone wants to talk to me, let him talk."

"The friend is an Americano. William Hammond. Do you know William Hammond?"

"No! Damn it. Besides. We're at war with the Americanos."

"You've never met Hammond?"

"No! How do I know? I meet lots of people. I don't always know their names."

"He is the man whose business partner was stabbed to death just recently."

Carlos felt faint. His clothes clung moistly to his body. Were his hands trembling? He thrust them behind his back so the captain could not see them. Then, through glazed eyes, he peered into the captain's face. Was there more to it than gambling debts? Was he being led into a trap?

"Hammond," Carlos said. "I did not know the name, but I sat in a card game with a man in the cantina."

"He says he holds signed notes from you. He wants to collect them or sell them to Manuel Alvarez who will collect them later. Hammond plans to return to Chicago as soon as he finds who was responsible for his partner's death."

There it was again. The reference to that damned dead Yankee. Again he tried to read the captain's face. "I won't pay! I was cheated!" But Carlos' thoughts were on the dead American. He could almost see the white dead face with open staring eyes accusing him.

"Cheating is a serious charge," the captain said. "These are important people with connections in our government."

"¡A la chingada!" Carlos shouted. "I'm at the end of my patience with this shit! If they want me, have them come see me. Then we'll settle who cheated whom. Otherwise, leave me alone. I don't need third-hand inquiries from some polite Yankee bastard."

The captain's mouth hardened into a polite smile, but his eyes were not smiling. "Let's be calm, Lieutenant. Let's save our fighting for the battlefield like a good soldier. At any rate, Señor Hammond will be here tomorrow. The three of us will talk. Since you are a member of the militia, this is not a matter for the civil authorities but for the military. I am certain we can settle this like gentlemen."

"Tomorrow—?"

"Hasta mañana, Lieutenant."

The captain turned his back as Carlos' fury rose. His temples ached with a pain that shot down to his teeth. He recognized the feeling. It happened when his anger and frustration rose beyond his ability to deal with them. "Until tomorrow, Captain." Carlos turned and strode furiously from the tent.

The next day brought an agony of self-doubt. It could not be called remorse. In the imperious way of the Rafas, Carlos felt that he was above all law but God's and even there there was some question. In the long night he thought briefly of confession but then dismissed it. There were too many other things unconfessed to make an issue of this one. What really agonized him was that his words, and by implication his acts, should be questioned by men whose authority was greater than his own. That was not the way it would have been on the rancho, or, in his grandfather's time, anywhere in New Mexico. The rules had changed and he did not like this new game. It bewildered him and added to his frustration and anger.

Midmorning, Carlos saw the Yankee, Hammond, ride into camp. Shortly one of Carlos' fellow soldiers, the one who had sat in the card game in the cantina, joined Hammond in the captain's tent. As he waited to be called, Carlos felt himself being silently driven into a position from which there was no escape—like a wild horse herded into a box canyon. It was only a matter of time before he would run into the stone canyon wall.

For a moment he eyed his horse, certainly one of the fastest in the camp, and thought of fleeing. But the thought evaporated as he saw the captain's orderly striding toward him. He whipped his lagging spirits and remembered that after all he was a Rafa, a man to be reckoned with, and joined the orderly as he walked to the tent and the waiting men.

The captain and Hammond nodded as Carlos entered. The captain dismissed the orderly and the other soldier, who slapped Carlos on the shoulder as he left. Now there were just the three of them.

"I'm sorry that we have to meet like this, Lieutenant Rafa. Señor Hammond. But as gentlemen, I am certain we can settle the matter."

Carlos watched the Yankee warily. He was a man in his early forties. His temples were graying and his hands looked soft, not the hands of a farmer or a stockman. He was taller than Carlos remembered. Heavier, too, though not fat. A large, solid man with flinty eyes that looked of money.

"I hold these notes of yours." Hammond extended the pieces of paper toward Carlos, then toward the captain, with signatures showing plainly. "I would like to settle them."

Here was the box canyon. Carlos looked from Hammond to the captain and saw the stone canyon wall. Better to settle up and hurry this foreigner back east, Carlos thought. I will admit to the lesser charge so the Yankee will no longer think of me when he thinks of his young dead partner.

"I had some doubt about the card game," Carlos said softly.

Hammond's face turned red but his words were controlled. "You felt that there was cheating during the game. Let me assure you, if there was it was not me. I'm an honest businessman. I pay my debts as well as expect payment from those who owe me."

"We've spoken to other players," the captain said. "It appears to have been an honest game. Unfortunately, you were a heavy loser that night. It is not easy to lose."

"It was an honest game," Hammond repeated.

"Then it appears that I was mistaken."

The faces of the other two men relaxed. "It's not pleasant to lose," Hammond said. "I have been there once or twice myself."

"There is only," Carlos continued, "the problem of payment." The relaxed faces turned troubled again. "I do not have the money."

Hammond's face turned deeper red and he glanced in frustration toward the captain. "When?" was all he said.

"I don't know. Money is hard to come by in New Mexico. Horses. Sheep. Those there are plenty of. But money? No, señor."

"You can always sell horses or sheep."

"I have neither. They are still part of my father's estate."

"In other words," the captain said, "there's no way you can pay your debt?"

Hammond exploded in anger. "I had guarantees! There were men in the game who vouched for you. They said your father was a big landowner near Albuquerque and that you were good for the debt."

Carlos had to restrain a smile. He had acknowledged his debt, but how could they collect? They would not hang him. They could not eat him. And dismiss him from the militia because he owed a Yankee money when it was the Yankees they were at war with? Ridiculous.

"This is very awkward. I admit I lost at cards, even though I have doubts about the honesty of the game. What's difficult for me is that we are at war with your country, Señor Hammond. Even if I had the money to pay you, it would be awkward under the circumstances. What if you are a spy? What if—"

"Señor Hammond is a guest of the Mexican government. Even during war there is protection of the rights of guests."

Hammond nodded to the captain in gratitude. "I have no choice," Hammond said to Carlos. "I can sell these notes to Señor Alvarez who is in no hurry to collect; he knows your family. Or I could go to Albuquerque and talk to your father. Señor Alvarez tells me that he is a man of honor and will give me satisfaction."

It was like a blow that left Carlos breathless. Pale and shaken, he looked from Hammond to the captain and back. "No." The word was a whisper of capitulation.

"What do you suggest then?"

"My father—" Carlos stared blankly trying to gather his thoughts. What could he tell these men? That his father was a man of honor? They knew that. That in this society of New Mexico a father's command was law, perhaps the highest law? Certainly the captain knew that. There were other things he would not tell them. That his father would go into a rage and probably horsewhip him. Or he would disown him. That he, Carlos, was more afraid of his father than of any enemy he had ever faced. That his father's rages were worse than the fiercest elements—demoniacal possessions whose unknown but disastrous outcome Carlos feared above all else. "I do not want my father to know," he finally said.

"You leave me little choice." Hammond's eyes shone with an

aura of triumph, but his face was still set in that controlled, passive expression.

"I don't want him to know!"

"What alternative is there?" the captain asked.

"Sell the notes to Alvarez!"

"Then he will go to see your father."

"¡Chingada!" Carlos said in desperation. "Look. I have a piece of land adjoining the family ranch near Albuquerque. It was a wedding gift. A beautiful piece. Near the river. Rich bottomland for farming. It's worth— I don't know how much. But it's valuable. I could sign it over to you and if I cannot raise the money in a year, you keep it. That way no one would have to know. It would be just between us."

"It would have to be done through legal channels," Hammond said. "Witnesses. Signatures. An official stamp. I would have to have legal protection." What was there to do? Carlos nodded in acquiesence. "I first want to discuss this with Señor Alvarez. It would be awkward for me to go to Albuquerque just now. I want his advice and help with the legalities."

"As long as it is kept quiet."

For the first time Hammond smiled openly. "It is a bargain then."

"A bargain," Carlos said to Hammond, who had extended his hand.

As Carlos shook the fleshy palm, he thought bitterly to himself: This is the Yankee I should have killed.

11

Doña Estela Rafa knelt in the tiny chapel of their rambling adobe house before a small wooden statue of the Virgin that her son Tercero had given her years ago. It had been carved by an old man, a saintmaker, who had briefly worked for them as a shepherd when times were hard and New Mexicans could not afford to buy saints.

In the corner was a crucifix also carved of wood, Christ looking out on his children with agonized eyes. The delicate fingers reached out from the impaling, bloody spikes. The cruel crown pressed over the anguished brow. From His side a livid wound that, in all its grim Spanish reality, made one turn one's eyes in fright as if the gash had been laid into real flesh just at this very moment.

The makeshift altar was covered with fine cloth, sewn and embroidered by the mistress and her daughters. It was here that the small Virgin stood prominently, the protectress and patroness of the family.

The señora prayed that there would not be war, the way she had in the past prayed that the Navajos or Comanches would not attack. That her daughters would marry well. That her grandchildren would be born alive.

Prayer for her, as for many, was praying for favor. From God or from a favorite saint. And when prayers were not answered, like those months and months during which she beseeched the Virgin to bless her daughter-in-law, Ana María, with a child, she would retaliate. Saints were punished for unanswered prayers by being outcast. The way she had turned the face of the wooden statue of the Virgin to the wall for leaving her son's wife barren. But then time would pass and forgiveness would come and occasionally one might even realize that one could not tell God or the saints what to do. Then the outcast piece of wood would be released from exile, would be turned aright and accepted again into the bosom of one's beliefs.

As she knelt, her husband joined her, smelling of dirt and corn and work in the fields. After some moments they crossed themselves and walked into the patio.

"I was praying for Carlos," she said. Her thoughts were heavy as she saw Don Francisco's familiar expression, but she continued. "About the war."

"He has fought before. But I pray for him too. I'm getting old and won't be here much longer. He is my hope." He looked away casually, as if it were of little importance to him. "How is Ana María taking all this?"

"The same as always."

A scowl. A look of exasperation. "¡Demonio! She is a strange one. Do you think she'll ever give us grandchildren?"

"I've given up praying for that. Maybe that's what God wants.

For me to stop wanting that so much. Maybe then He will do something."

"¡Mierda!" he grumbled. "If you want something, you take it. Or you tell somebody to do it and they do it. Or else."

"Do you think he will ever change?"

"Who? God?"

"No, Carlos."

"He had better. He's my heir. Everything will be his when I die. There is no other son to leave it to."

"Ana María has not changed."

"She should have been a nun."

"Why should Carlos change? He has no reason. He knows that no matter what he is your heir. He has followed in the footsteps of his father and grandfather. Since there has been land and sheep and cattle, the men in Carlos' family have done what they had to and done well."

"It's the wildness I'm talking about, not the traditions he has to follow. Damn it! You twist everything I have to say."

"I just wondered why he should change."

"Because I'll thrash him if he doesn't. There is no room for disobedient sons in this family. When he changes, God will send him a son. Another Rafa to be an heir when the time comes."

"Well, I will pray for him."

"A fat lot of good that will do."

"I pray that he won't be killed in the war."

"There will be no war."

Señora Rafa looked at her husband in surprise. No war? She could not in her wildest dreams imagine that. What about the rumors? From wild despair to hope to angry optimism. We would show those Yankees! There were rumors to fit every state of mind and every point of view. But no war? What about the militia? Two companies from Albuquerque. Their son Carlos a lieutenant in one. Why did they call up a militia if there was to be no war? What did Francisco mean—no war? That he was too old to be called so therefore the war could not be real? That the war and the world were passing him by, therefore he had to deny them? That if he was not involved in whatever it was, whatever it was did not exist? Yes, she thought. That supreme ego. The lord and master spoke, therefore it should be so.

"I hope you are right," she said.

"Of course I'm right." But an uneasy look crossed his face,

a look that plainly told her that even he did not believe his own illusions. He is getting old, she thought. It shocked her.

"You are always right, Francisco."

"Now, how about a little something to eat. I have been out in the fields all morning."

"Sí, señor."

The word came first as a formal note. "Most esteemed Don Francisco and Doña Estela," it began. "We humbly request an audience with you on a matter of grave importance to the future of both our families."

When Andrea bustled into the sala, her eyes bright with excitement, her father folded the note and held it tightly captive. His wife, who sat beside him, looked at her daughter as if it were the most natural thing in the world for the two of them to be alone, side by side, in conspiratorial closeness. It did not fool Andrea.

"What are you doing?"

"Please show respect for your father and mother," Señora Rafa said.

"Ooh. You have a letter." Smiling, Andrea playfully skipped toward them. "Who is it from? What does it say?" She reached, but Don Francisco pulled it away. "You're keeping secrets," she said petulantly.

"I don't want to get angry at you," Don Francisco said. "But it is none of your concern."

"Is it from Carlos?" A shake of the head. "From Tercero?" Another shake. "Who then?"

"Please leave us, Andrea." Doña Estela tried to keep the annoyance from showing on her face, but she could see her daughter's bright-eyed insistence, and she thought: How like the rest of these headstrong Rafas. But then, it was business between her husband and herself. It was their decision, whatever Andrea might think.

"Andrea!" Don Francisco's voice was heavy. Threatening. There was no nonsense in it. No indulgence, however much he loved his daughter or how charmingly she cajoled him.

"Sí, señor." Andrea's voice had turned small and grave as she left the room.

They continued to read together. There was no need for long discussion. The letter spelled out the way things were done, had been done for generations. The way the young Francisco, through his parents, had asked for the young Estela's hand those many years past. She smiled and patted him.

Finally Don Francisco broke the thoughtful silence. "What do you think?" She knew she was not expected to answer. "The Griegos are good people. From a fine old Spanish family. Which one is their son, Francisco? There are so many Griegos."

"He is that young, slender one."

"All the Griegos are slender. Skinny is a better word. Like sticks."

"He is in the militia in Santa Fe. That little boy who used to answer the priest in church. Remember? The older brother of Andrea's best friend."

"Well, it doesn't matter. He is of a good family. It will be as we wish. It is time for Andrea to be married. As well him as another. I will write to the Griegos and tell them we would be honored by a visit to discuss the future of these young people."

But it was not as settled as Don Francisco had decreed. Estela Rafa felt the hovering presence of her daughter more insistently than ever. Hints. Questions. Insinuations. Until one day there was an abrupt change in Andrea's behavior. As if she were completely disinterested in what her parents had been discussing those few days past.

"¡Demonio!" Doña Estela thought. "Somehow she has found out." The next day in the kitchen Andrea burst into hysterics over some trivialty.

"I can't do it, Mamá!" The Indian cook turned her passive face toward the mistress and her daughter, then turned back to her work.

"Can't do what, Andrea?" But Doña Estela knew, and she led her daughter from the kitchen to an empty room.

"Not only can't—I won't!"

"Won't what?"

Andrea burst into tears. "Oh, Mamá. You know. You already know. Francisco Griego."

Señora Rafa's grim, tight mouth held back the words she felt inside. What do you mean: Can't? Won't? It has been decided. The way it has always been decided. By your parents. Do you think you have any choice? Does anyone have a choice? I had never seen your father when we were betrothed. I was younger than you and he was already a man of twenty-six years. How old,

I thought. I cried and cried because Mamá and Papá were giving me in marriage to this old man that I had never seen before. Look at us now. It has been almost forty years. It has worked out as well as could be expected.

But her feelings finally gave way before the onslaught of Andrea's unhappiness. "Pobrecita." She took her daughter into her arms. "You don't have to cry. The Griegos are a fine family. One of the finest. In the old tradition. They have good land. You will be well taken care of."

"But—but—his trousers hang loose in back like sacks on a stick!" Andrea's wail distorted her pretty little mouth into a blubbering, noisy gash.

It would not do to smile, the señora thought, but her daughter described that young scarecrow most aptly. "My dear. You do not judge the merit of a potential husband by the cut of his trousers. Trust me. Trust your papá."

"No!" Tearing herself away, she stamped her foot on the floor like an impatient buffalo. "No! No! No! No! No!"

"I've had enough, Andrea. You must respect your parents. We are wiser than you. Now stop this silly nonsense before I call your father."

"Oh, Mamá. I'll die. I'll absolutely die. I'll run away. Give myself to some wild Indian. Mamá. Oh, Mamá. Please."

The señora sat abruptly in one of the hardback chairs. She was torn between parental indignation at the refusal of this spoiled daughter of hers and a touching concern for the girl's wishes. She had raised two other daughters, now grown, married with children of their own. But that had been in a more docile time, when children obeyed their parents without fuss or question. Neither Clara nor Josefa had raised even an eyebrow of doubt when their marriages had been arranged. Both marriages had turned out well. But now this. Her youngest, most independent daughter, Andrea. Trousers hanging like sacks on a stick indeed!

Suddenly Andrea stopped her blubbering. Now perfectly still in the middle of the room, she stared silently at her mother, trying to compose herself.

"You feel that strongly," Doña Estela said.

For a moment Andrea's eyes hovered on the verge of tears and her mouth made a few tentative movements, but she controlled herself. "Yes, Mamá."

"There is no doubt? It is not just another whim?"

"No, Mamá."

Doña Estela sighed. "Then I will talk to your father. I cannot promise anything. You know how he is. But I will talk to him."

A tiny little smile tried but failed to come through the tear-streaked face. "Thank you, Mamá."

As they returned to the kitchen they could hear the cook and the maid jabbering excitedly in the patio. "My God! Look. Look who's coming."

Señora Rafa walked outside to scold the women back to their work. The minute you turn your back, she thought, there they go gossiping.

"Look, señora," the cook screamed in her high-pitched voice. "Look who's coming." The cook and maid turned to each other again, laughing.

"What is it, Mamá?"

They peered through the patio toward the open field beyond which two horsemen were slowly approaching. "It's Tercero," the señora said.

"But who's that with him? It looks like another priest."

Together Señora Rafa and Andrea walked to the periphery of the house to wait for their arrival.

PART II

WAR AND REBELLION

August 1846–February 1847

12

It was August, 1846. Each day the sun rose in the east and travelled west, bringing with it toward Santa Fe what had started as a rumor and was ending up as the American army. New Mexican spies had confirmed it. Twenty-five hundred well-trained, well-equipped, mad dog Americanos ready to rape and plunder their peaceful villages.

Early in August Don Francisco attended yet another meeting with the governor in Santa Fe. There was no doubt what most wanted. Surrender. Their preparations had gone badly. The treasury was bankrupt. There were not enough weapons. What there were were antiquated. Not enough horsemen. Not enough this, that, or anything else. Including not enough commitment to war.

But the majority at the meeting was not to prevail. Democracy had not yet reached full flower in the republic of Mexico. A hard core of belligerents won the day; they wanted to fight. The governor, who sided with the majority, had been asked to resign his military command. He refused. There was still duty, however he appraised the inevitable outcome.

Don Francisco rode back to Los Rafas convinced that it was madness to fight against such overwhelming odds. That the governor had been most prudent in suggesting surrender. Why lose lives and property when it would not affect the outcome? The warmongers, including his own son Carlos, were crazy. Let them fight, he thought. When their blood spills and nothing changes, they will realize how wasteful and stupid it is.

Meanwhile old Don José Antonio II had taken to Miguel Dalton. "A fine young man," he would say to whomever would listen, even if it was only one of the dogs. "A fine young man. He knows about the gringos wanting to steal New Mexico and make slave country of it. He knows that true justice lies with us."

"Hush, Grandfather," Andrea would say. "Can't you see that he is trying to rest."

But Don José could be as deaf as he was blind and he would continue with his ramblings. "A very polite young man. Not like most of this riffraff growing up now. And a Catholic too. The mark of a true gentleman and a man of God."

What Don José really meant was that here at last was a grown man who did not run away from his musings and ramblings. There were no fields for him to cultivate. No sheep to tend. No horses to break. No card games at the cantina. So there was the constant presence of a companion—not an Indian, not a woman, not a child. A companion who slept long hours like Don José, since he was still recuperating from his wounds. Whose physical activities were still slow and limited. Yet whose youth, inexperience, and natural politeness made him an attentive listener. In fact, the ideal companion for an old man.

But others besides Don José had taken to the young stranger. "Pobrecito," Señora Rafa had said. "Poor little thing. Look how skinny he is. How weak. He needs looking after."

Andrea helped look after him with uncertain curiosity. Here was a dreaded Yankee. She had never met one before. Somehow she could not imagine this blue-eyed young man plundering and looting anyone. Not even a hated enemy. But then one was never sure.

As for Tercero, he had his duties to perform. It was seldom that he could return to see how their guest was recuperating. When he did, he would watch with amusement how his grandfather would ramble on, thankful that it was someone other than himself being bored by the endless repetitions of old stories misremembered, misrepresented, misunderstood.

"Grandfather follows him everywhere like a pet dog," Andrea protested.

"So he is seldom alone." Andrea flushed at Tercero's insinuation.

Finally Grandfather would sit, still talking, with the words becoming softer and softer, with his head nodding, until he slipped into sleep, still muttering indistinguishable stories of the old days. It was at times like this that Tercero and Miguel could finally talk.

"I have not gone to the authorities yet," Tercero said. "I have been busy serving the placitas around Albuquerque. And the war is upon us. There will be confrontation in Santa Fe any day now. It would serve no purpose for you to report to the authorities. They might want to take you into custody. You'd recuperate much better here as our guest. On the other hand, after a few bloody battles we might all be Americanos. There would be new authorities who would probably not be concerned about you. So as they say in this country: Mañana. Mañana is plenty of time."

"Yes. But the Americans might want me as a deserter."

"How would they know? My lips are sealed. I cannot repeat what I have heard in confession."

Emotion overwhelmed Miguel and tears streamed from his eyes. "You're so good to me. All of you." He sat, trying to control his feelings, before he continued. "Your grandfather is a fantastic old gentleman. Telling me stories that would curl your hair. Of how the first Rafa in New Mexico was a priest who found the saving of Indian souls so bountiful that he wrote to his brother in Spain who came here as a soldier. 'Here one can be somebody,' the priest wrote. And I can see that. Even now I feel that about this place. I can be somebody too."

Tercero smiled. "You are getting better."

"And as if nature were not enough to tame, there are the wild Indians. It seems incredible to me that people here on the frontier have been warring with the Indians for almost two hundred years. Almost as long as the Irish have been fighting among themselves and against the English. And I never realized that our Irish potato came from the New World."

"You have been listening a great deal."

"One thing puzzles me."

"Yes?"

"The old gentleman talks about the 'right people.' About the purity of the race. About real Spanish. As if there were an aristocracy in this place where—God forgive me—where everyone seems much the same with only a little variation here and there. What is the hierarchy in New Mexico? And how does one know?"

Tercero frowned. "There is no hierarchy but God's." But when Miguel stood silent, waiting, Tercero finally continued. "It is an old story. Told in blood and isolation. Blood spilled and blood passed on from generation to generation. Isolation from our roots and from the rest of the world.

"Very simply, the hierarchy has to do with conquest and

possession. The Spanish came and took the land from the Indians. Their weapons were the sword, the gun, and the horse—driven by a fierce will to possess. Therefore the Spanish were at the peak of the hierarchy—conquerors. While the Indians were at the bottom.

"Then over the years, when people live together, some become more than master and slave. Since they are all God's children, they act like God's children—breeding and intermarrying, if they marry at all, without discrimination. Breeding seems to know no prejudice the way social intercourse does.

"Now the hierarchy becomes confused, more subtle. The 'right people,' los ricos, are those who possess the most: land, sheep, cattle, horses, slaves in the old days. The 'right people' are also those whose Spanish blood remains untainted over the centuries by Indian blood—if that is possible—though they may be small landowners like the Rafas. Thus the right people are Spanish and they own land.

"The others? Mixed blood. Civilized Indians. Wild Indians. Peons. Field hands. Servants. All the children of God whose natural position seems to be on their knees, whether to God or to man.

"But in truth, I do not believe in man's hierarchy. There is only one hierarchy. God's."

"Your grandfather told me stories."

"He is an old man. He does not always remember clearly."

"There are people who rule this land. There is a hierarchy."

"All is vanity. It too shall pass. Only God will remain."

Tercero's attitude puzzled Miguel. It was almost as if the young priest were angry at the mention of aristocracy when Miguel had expected him to be pleased and proud. After all, weren't the Rafas part of the "right people"?

Even though Tercero would disclaim their wealth, there was much that a poor young Irishman would consider wealth. True, it would not look like wealth to a rich Philadelphia merchant. The large house was made of earth, the furniture spare and crude. But there was land, even for smaller landowners like the Rafas. More land than it seemed any one family should possess. More land than many lords in Ireland might claim.

There is only God's hierarchy, Tercero had said. That might

be all right for heaven, but not here on earth. Man had to survive and prayer is a poor substitute for tortillas and beans.

How strange, Miguel thought, that in Ireland he had been a peasant's son working on the rented land of some great lord and eking out a life that was a constant race with starvation. While here he was a guest, an equal with landowners who need not doff their hats or tug their forelocks to any lord. All because of land.

"It was a long, long time ago," Grandfather Rafa had told him. "Perhaps two hundred years ago. Almost as if God had foreordained what happened. For the Rafas it seems to come in twos. Two hundred years ago. Two Rafas in New Mexico. First the priest who had come to the New World to convert Indians. From the hard, poor country of Estremadura. Country so hard, so barren that the deserts of New Mexico looked like home, maybe even a little better.

'Here one can be somebody,' he had written to his brother in Spain. 'Here there is land and opportunity.' So the brother came as a soldier, another man from Estremadura. Married the daughter of another settler and had a son. That was how it all started. Here, in the Río Grande Valley. They called it Río Abajo, Lower River, which means 'below Santa Fe.' "

"Was that what you meant—happening by twos? The first two Rafas, a priest and a soldier?" Miguel asked.

The old man smiled. "That was only the beginning, those two. The soldier had a son, Francisco, who in turn had twin sons. These twins were the first José Antonio and his twin, José Blas. But the law of twos worked in another way: skipping a generation so that every second generation the Rafas produced a set of male twins. Another José Antonio and his twin.

"I am the second José Antonio and my brother was José María, God rest his soul. My grandsons are the third such pair. Always one has been a priest and one has been a soldier. Like a magic pattern. We will go on for as long as it pleases God. Perhaps forever."

"Then the Rafas are descendants of soldiers. Fighters."

The old man looked puzzled. "No. We are priests too. And ranchers. And farmers."

"But priests do not have offspring."

The old man's face cleared. "Oh. Yes. The line is carried on through the soldiers. But the magic of twos is still there. It is this magic that carries on the generations."

"And they have been here ever since? Through all that time?"

"Francisco, the first Rafa born in New Mexico, was killed in the Great Rebellion of 1680 when the pueblos rose under the infamous Popé and drove the Spanish from the valley. His widow and their twin sons were among those who escaped and lived in exile at El Paso del Norte until the Reconquest. Then they came back and settled in Río Abajo. It was my grandfather, José Antonio I, who first settled in Los Rafas. That was in 1706. When Albuquerque was founded."

What could one say about the old days? Memories were lost in the haze of time. What endured was the thin thread of life nurtured by tradition and protected by the grace of God. A thread constantly threatened by a sudden outbreak of hostilities by Navajo or Apache or Comanche. By a drought that left the fields parched, the corn burned. By a flood when the river took possession of the land. Or a plague like smallpox, sweeping the sparse settlements with deadly rapidity. Any one of a number of nature's whims, and the thin thread broke. A family line came to an end. Old historic names disappeared. Faded into memories. Remaining only on crude anonymous wooden crosses in old graveyards.

Life was hard. And repetitious. And dangerous. Like his first buffalo hunt when José Antonio II was a boy. He remembered it clearly all these years. The hunt was a community outing. A gathering of as many as two hundred in the party. Hunters. Skinners. Cooks. Carreta drivers. Sometimes an entire family would join the expedition, taking their provisions with them as they trekked east to the staked plains. To buffalo country.

Even then, as in still earlier days, the grass grew high as a horse's belly. It sprang up as they passed, leaving barely a trace of where their hunting caravan had been. José Antonio II had been almost uncontrollably excited; this was the first time he had been allowed to go. His twin, José María, had stayed on the rancho. His father promised, if the right situation presented itself, he would be allowed to use the old bell-barreled musket to try to add to the family meat stores.

They had traveled east beyond the mountains, moving in slow caravan, when the scouts came riding hard into camp late one afternoon, conferring with the leaders of the hunt.

"The buffalo are closer to the mountains than ever before," his father said later.

"Do you think I will really be able to shoot one?"

"Undoubtedly. But first things first. We will make our hunting camp here. Then tomorrow early we will see about buffalo meat."

The whole caravan was alive with excitement while they set up camp. That night José Antonio II could barely sleep. It seemed that he had hardly closed his eyes when his Uncle Carlos shook him by the shoulder. Then, as he tried to blink open his heavy lids, he felt the ground move in a mysterious and powerful rumble, like the sound of distant drums.

He looked up in alarm at his uncle who was smiling. "Get control of your feet, boy. Otherwise their footsteps may knock you down."

Then he heard his father laugh. "It's a big herd. Not more than a mile or two from here."

The boy dressed quickly in the early morning coolness, then stood staring east trying to imagine those shaggy monsters whose footsteps shook the earth.

"You should be here in the months when they are mating," his uncle said. "These little footsteps are nothing compared to the sound of their roaring voices. Like thunder. I remember when I first heard that sound I looked up into the sky for clouds, but it was clear as far as one could see. That was enough to fill my bladder—the sound of thunder when there were no thunderclouds. You can hear their bellowing for a league or more—three miles."

Although they let José Antonio II ride out with them, he was allowed to do nothing but watch that first morning. Later, two hunters dragged a small calf in on a reata. It would be a pet for their children. But they did not reckon with the stubborn tenacity of the little buffalo and finally tied it among three trees clustered at the edge of the camp.

"Pobrecito," some of the women commiserated. "Let the little thing go."

"I promised my Juanito a pet," one of the hunters said. "This is it."

But José Antonio II saw that the calf would not calm down. As he watched, it bumped and jumped and pulled and bellowed at the rawhide reatas that held it tight. Every so often it would shudder and shiver, crying out like a baby, as its sides heaved while it tried to get its breath. Then back to its bucking and kicking and twisting. Until finally, exhausted, it fell to the ground. It tried to rise. Gave a few feeble kicks. Then collapsed once more. Only this time there was something final in its collapse.

The boy turned away as two men ran toward the calf. "¡Demonio!" one of them shouted.

"You can't tame a wild thing," Uncle Carlos said. "You cannot capture a free spirit and make it into something it does not want to be." But all José Antonio II could think of was that little buffalo that had bucked itself to death.

The next morning all was forgotten in the excitement of the hunt. The herd was moving south, still a mile or so east of their camp. There had been good hunting that first day. After the herd had passed the carretas followed the hunters to butcher and haul the meat back to camp where it would be dried. Now the hunters would move among the rear members of the herd, killing quickly with musket or lance so the buffalo would drop in their tracks, neither alarming nor impeding the tail end of the herd.

José Antonio II had never seen anything like it. As they moved along, the entire prairie was a solid mass of thick, shaggy fur as far as he could see. The ground shook with a terrifying rumble that his little buffalo-hunting pony took as a matter of course.

"See," his Uncle Carlos shouted. "Even though this is a tremendously large herd, when they are grazing peacefully you can see that it is made up of many small herds. Most of the year they graze in clusters. Females and young buffalo at the center with the older males off to the side. But when they migrate, these small clusters come together, and you can see buffalo for miles. This is the largest herd I've ever seen."

They stayed at a respectful distance, watching through the cloud of dust, kerchiefs pulled over their faces.

José Antonio II's father rode over from the lead group of hunters. "Look," he shouted. "We're not sure how it will go. But I will try to separate one from the edge of the herd and use my lance to drive it this way. Be ready with the musket, José Antonio. Remember all I told you about where to shoot." His father nodded to Uncle Carlos who patted his own musket as he stayed beside the boy on a knoll overlooking the herd.

His father had ridden off with the other hunters amid the noise and dust and confusion. He could see how the more expert

114

hunters would ride up beside a buffalo and aim their muskets. There were those expert with the lance who could bring one down almost as easily. They followed the hunters and the herd from a distance, watching for his father to come riding out of the pack in pursuit of what would be José Antonio II's first buffalo.

At that point, his uncle Carlos shouted and pointed toward the mass of brown-furred animals to their left and just ahead. He could see his father's familiar figure through the dust, the red kerchief across his mouth, his sombrero down firm on his head, his lance singling out one young bull that he was trying to cut out from the thinning herd.

Then it happened. Almost before José Antonio II could open his mouth to shout. One moment the rider and lance were driving the young bull toward the outermost edge of the herd. The next moment the buffalo turned and as his father tried to disengage the lance, the buffalo's sharp change of direction tore it from his hand. Off balance, the hunter reached for the lance as his horse swiftly changed direction to avoid the oncoming bull. One instant his father was turning in the saddle reaching for the toppling lance. The next instant the saddle was empty and a mass of shaggy beasts closed the open gap in a rush. Then, as if sensing that something was wrong, the herd picked up speed, rushing from that fatal place.

There was nothing to do but wait for the herd to clear. One of the hunters led the terrified and crying José Antonio II back to camp while his Uncle Carlos joined the others to recover what was left of the body. They brought back the remains wrapped in a blanket. There was no question that they would bury it here, even though there was no priest to conduct the burial rites. It was almost a week's journey across the edge of the prairie and back through the mountains to Los Rafas. The next morning they gathered at the edge of camp, said their few prayers, and commended his mortal remains to God and to the prairie.

The buffalo herd had passed on but the heart had gone out of the hunt. They broke camp that same day and headed back toward home.

"It was like that in the old days," Grandfather Rafa said to Miguel. "One day life went on as usual, the next day—" He waggled his hand back and forth. "It was all in the hands of God."

13

"In his grandfather's time," Miguel said, "Grandfather Rafa told me you were counted among the ricos, the rich ones of New Mexico. All of Los Rafas belonged to the family. But with each succeeding generation there were more and more Rafas so the land was divided again and again. Today, there are people living in Los Rafas whose names are not even Rafa. That just shows what time can do. But in the old days—"

"Did he tell you about his Navajo grandmother?" Tercero asked. The young Irishman looked at his companion in surprise. Tercero smiled. "Ah, yes," Tercero said. "One can always talk about the right people. Los ricos. Those who received land grants. Caballeros. So," he continued, "he did not tell you about his Navajo grandmother. My great-great-grandmother. Well, let me tell you, because somehow this is as much the story of the Río Grande as conquistadores, land grants, and ricos."

Grandfather's grandfather was the first José Antonio. José Antonio I. He had received a grant of land, part of which was now Los Rafas. But then, in the old days, it went west across the river to the hills between the Río Grande and the Río Puerco. And it went east into the Sandía Mountains. A strip of land perhaps two miles wide and thirty miles long, divided in the old Spanish way to include desert, river, bottomland for farming, sparse hills for grazing. A cut of land that gave the grantee a little of everything in the neighboring terrain, like nuts and raisins in a cake.

But that was not all. From his maternal grandfather he received another grant lower down the river. This one, even larger, he saw as the source of growth and riches among his holdings. The first, part of which was to become Los Rafas, was ideal farmland on the outskirts of a settled royal villa with neighbors who would band together for mutual protection when threatened by marauding Indian bands. The second tract, more remote and therefore more dangerous, could be a place one could turn loose rams and ewes to breed themselves to infinity with ample water and open grazing land that seemed endless.

For the first few years this woolly breeding ground prospered. Rams and ewes did what they always do. Lambs gamboled among their prodigious seniors. All grew fat and thick-coated under the watchful eyes of José Antonio I's shepherds, with the flocks numbering into the thousands, even after the annual caravan to Chihuahua where a goodly number were sold.

But this false summer did not last long. It was almost as if alien eyes had been patiently watching, waiting until the size of the flock and the confidence of the shepherds had reached that critical point where they were committed to remain no matter what adverse circumstances might arise.

Then it began. Like the seasonal ebb and flood of the river. Or the inevitable summer winds in the desert or winter snowfall in the foothills. A thing of nature. A band of Navajos would swoop down out of the hills, herd together a generous portion of the flock, and run them west to their own land.

The first year Don José attributed the loss of sheep to fate and offered a novena as penance for whatever evil he had done to incur the wrath of God. Prior to the second year he offered up even more prayers, but with a certain hesitancy, as if he were trying to decide if God were about to play a trick on him. The third year, when the season for sheep rustling drew near, he only made a sign of the cross in the air, gathered his band armed with a few old muskets and bows and arrows, and rode south to intercede for God, since his messages did not seem to get through to the great beyond.

"It's Ojo Torcido. Twisted Eye," the shepherds told him. "It was him both times and by God, it will be him again."

"It will be his scalp," Don Jose threatened, brandishing his musket. "No heathen Navajo son-of-a-bitch is going to steal my sheep."

The shepherds looked at each other slyly, not quite smiling, with that peasant knowledge of where the power lay and that caution, even when the patrón's back was turned, in case he should suddenly wheel about and see smiles on their faces.

"It seems to me," one of the shepherds said, "that I heard similar words from Ojo Torcido last year."

"Ojo Torcido could have killed us," the other said. "But he chose not to. 'You are good shepherds,' he said. 'You take good care of these sheep and for that I spare your lives. When I come back next year, I want them fat and woolly. Or else—!' "

"I had expected to see my maker that day. Now, patrón, you are here to send that cross-eyed Indian to his maker and here we are—the ones in the middle who always seem to get the stick up our tails."

"More than that if you let him steal," Don José threatened.

The armed men scouted the most likely approaches and set out sentries. Don José had heard of the Navajo warrior not only from his own shepherds but also from others along this southern part of the river valley. Ojo Torcido could speak Spanish. There were rumors that his mother had been a Spanish settler who had been kidnapped in one of those many raids in which the Navajos captured slaves and wives. Whatever truth to the rumor, Ojo Torcido spared many a life that another might not have. His captives were sheep rather than settlers. His tribe was said to have the largest flocks in New Mexico. Larger by far than the richest don in the Río Grande Valley.

This year will be his undoing, Don José thought as he sat in a dark, sheltered vista chewing on dried buffalo meat and wishing for the warmth of a small campfire. That thieving Indian bastard.

He sat like that for three weeks, taking turns with the other armed men at the various approaches to the flock. Don José thought about all the tasks undone back in Los Rafas. About this year's crops and the ditches that needed to be cleared. Then he would hear the tinkle of a bell and the "baa-baas" and turn his gaze on his plump, fleecy flocks.

Hurry up, you thieving Navajo, he thought. Or I'm liable not to be here when you come.

Then he realized what he had just thought to himself. Frustration began to nibble at him, then gnaw, then devour what was left of his self-control. His anger at the loss of sheep was compounded by the frustration of waiting for the thief's return.

When Don José's frustration was at its deepest, Ojo Torcido struck swiftly and quietly. It was not where expected. Nor at the time of day expected. As if, while they had been waiting, he had been studying them. The first Don José knew was when one of his sentries came riding pell-mell toward his outpost.

"Navajos!" he shouted. "They're already fording the river with the sheep!"

Don José was on his feet and onto his horse immediately. "For Christ's sake! Why didn't you fire the alarm?"

"They captured Pedro and took away his musket. I don't have a firearm."

"¡Chingada!" Don José pointed his musket in the air and fired a shot, then waited impatiently for the other guards to rally. "How many were there?"

"I don't know, patrón. I was riding outpost. I hadn't seen Pedro for some time when I came across old Juan, the shepherd, cowering in a gully. 'They took Pedro,' he said. 'They're probably across the river already.' And I hadn't heard a thing."

Now that they were all together, they rode toward the ford where the sheep rustlers had crossed. They would not be moving fast, held back by the sheep they had stolen. Hopefully they would not expect to be followed; perhaps they thought that Pedro was the only armed guard. But then the signs showed that this was not so. Exhausted sheep dotted the trail, most of them dead. Don José's fury rose as he saw the bodies of his sheep, driven to their deaths by fast-riding Navajos.

Finally, by the time they reached the Río Puerco, the trail turned north toward the land of the Navajos. The trail they now followed was of horse's hooves; all the sheep had either dropped by the wayside or had had their throats slit. There were six Navajos, moving as best they could on tired horses toward sanctuary in their own country.

The pursuers stopped to rest their horses while Don José paced nervously, staring northwest where the thieving, sheep-murdering enemy had gone. It was no use pursuing much further. Soon they would be well into Navajo country and the six Navajos would become sixty, then six hundred. Inside he raged, with an anger that burned like pure fire and a resolve that only death would deter. He would have his revenge on Ojo Torcido. Next year it would be different.

Only it came earlier than expected. At Taos that fall, under a tenuous treaty, there was an informal gathering of settlers and various Indian tribes—Comanches, Utes, Navajos, Pueblos. All rode for miles to trade and barter. It was not a gathering that Don José would normally attend, but this year he had an excess of sheepskins, mostly from the victims of the raid. He had already sent more than he wanted of sheep and hides to Chihuahua, where a recently increased government tax bit more deeply into the already low price that he received for his hard labor and risks. Perhaps at Taos he could recoup some of his losses.

He and his men camped at the edge of the meeting ground with other Spaniards from up and down river. There were all manner of goods offered. Horses, sheep, hides, various crops from along the fertile Río Grande Valley, knives, beads, other trinkets. The Indians brought woolen blankets (Where did they get the wool? Don José asked himself in anger), dried buffalo meat, horses of their own (Before the white man there was no horse, Don José thought, again in anger), corn from the pueblos, turquoise.

One of the biggest traffics was in human flesh. Captives. Slaves. From other tribes, to be sold back if the price was right. From raids, not only on Indian pueblos but on Spanish settlements too. Grim, worried faces looking for someone they knew to redeem them. Or, failing that, someone to take them as slaves to be worked in another place, hopefully under better circumstances. Even the Spanish bought slaves here, Indians to help with work in field or house.

"Don José!" One of the men came rapidly to him. Quietly. As if he would be overheard. "Don José. I saw him." There was a questioning look on the patrón's face. "Ojo Torcido," the man said. "Camped across the valley with a group of his Navajos."

Don José's face turned scarlet, and for a moment it looked as if he might burst into flame. He rose to his feet and was already moving when he spat out the word: "Where?"

Frightened, the man led his patrón quickly and without question toward a vista and pointed out the Navajo camp. Don José dismounted and watched long and patiently. To hell with the sheepskins and the paltry return from them. Here was opportunity worth savoring. A sweet retribution that was food for the soul as well as for the body. Revenge.

The comings and goings in the Navajo camp were slow and mysterious. There appeared to be a dozen of them. Ojo Torcido was obviously their chief. There were no preparations for trade and barter as in other camps. A few blankets were piled in view, but surely not enough to warrant a dozen traders. There were no extra horses being groomed for the best possible presentation. All in all the atmosphere was austere. Guarded. As if they were buyers rather than sellers. Looking for something very special that they wished to keep secret from others.

A recognition flashed through Don José's mind as a Navajo rode quickly into the camp and rushed to Ojo Torcido, just as his peon had rushed to him but a short time ago. He could see the furtive nodding of heads, the eyes turning in a certain direction, the rigid stoicism of their postures with only the turning of their eyes betraying what must have been an emotional exchange. They are looking for something, Don José thought. And they have found it.

Don José's curiosity was piqued. His rage subsided in the light of this mystery that brought Ojo Torcido into human perspective. This was not just the thieving bastard who took his sheep with impunity and treated his shepherds with disdain as if they were Ojo Torcido's servants and not Don José's. This was a man who wanted something badly enough to risk coming into a neutral trading ground to barter for it, for surely no man in his right mind would attempt to steal anything from this place. He would get no farther than a few feet when the entire camp would turn on him and kill him.

It must be a woman, Don José thought. What else would drive a man to such action? Unless it was God, he thought. Then: No. Not these heathen Indians. Only a Catholic would feel that strongly about God. Maybe it's a horse, he thought. Indians are crazy about horses.

He sent his men through the camp to discover the object of Ojo Torcido's search. The Navajos did not know Don José or his men by sight; neither the shepherds nor Pedro were in Taos. So with caution, they could learn much. Just listening. Looking. Not even having to ask questions. It did not take long. The next day one of the men led Don José toward an area across the periphery of the valley.

"There," the man said, only his voice betraying his alertness. Don José turned casually as they rode past. His eyes narrowed, and his pulse skipped a beat, then beat several times in rapid succession. His companion smiled, his eyes bright with a pleasurable glow. She was beautiful as only a Navajo woman could be. With long black hair and golden brown skin. She was young, still almost a child, yet she stood with a proud bearing as befit one of The People, even though it was obvious that she was a captive. She turned as they rode past. Casually. As if by accident. Yet Don José knew that she was aware of them and curious not so much in the way of a frightened captive as of one who knows her fate, accepts it, yet wants to comprehend it.

"See?" the man said to Don José. Her glance turned straight

toward them. There was the haughty look, becoming in a beautiful girl. The same twisted eye, not so pronounced here, but noticeable and shocking—a counterpoint to her beauty. "They say she is Ojo Torcido's daughter."

Don José moved quickly, with the kind of heedlessness that had enabled the Spanish to conquer Mexico and push northward to settle the Southwest. There was still enough vitality in the blood to act out old assertiveness on those rare occasions when one thought of pleasures more immediate than "mañana."

She would make a fine addition to the household, this daughter of Ojo Torcido. A personal maid for Don José's wife as well as nurse to the youngest of their five daughters. Don José thought of his family with some misgivings. He loved them dearly, yet he had no son to carry on the family name. Two males had been stillborn and another died when but a few months old. It was a curse he bore in the same way that he suffered sheep stealing by the Navajo chief. Having the daughter of his tormenter as a slave somewhat avenged the loss of sheep, but there was no remedy for his lack of a son. His wife was getting older and tired after bearing nine children of which only the girls survived.

The purchase of the slave girl was quick. Within limits, price was of no concern, for revenge was an indulgence worth paying for. Ojo Torcido had not yet made his move toward negotiation. The general bargaining had not yet begun. There were many participants still on their way to Taos from distant places.

Don José and his men took leave of Taos in the dead of night, poorer by one good horse and one not so good, the cursed sheepskins, and a generous pouch of Spanish reales. The sellers, who were told that these ricos were from Santa Fe, were pleased. There was much to see and buy in Taos, especially with Spanish silver that was rare in an outpost like New Mexico. Don José was ecstatic. They would be halfway to Los Rafas before Ojo Torcido would even know that his captive daughter was no longer there.

But eluding Ojo Torcido was the simplest part of bringing this Indian slave into the household. Doña María Rafa eyed her with suspicion from the very first. Here was a beauty who made her plain daughters appear even plainer. A girl in the full bloom of fertility while she, a mature woman, had left behind her childbearing years. There, smiling with what she supposed was an old lecher's anticipation—she did not recognize her husband's smile of revenge—was Don José still without a male heir.

The señora had a grim sense of humor, for she named the slave girl Concepción. Then she watched her like a hawk. Not the usual mistress prodding a lazy slave, but a jealous wife oppressing a potential rival.

It was to no avail. In fact, Señora Rafa's watching, her treating Concepción as a potential rival, was a seed that finally bore fruit. If she had not watched so closely, the girl might have made good one of her several attempts to run away. And if Señora Rafa had ignored the girl's beauty, Don José might have ignored it too. As it was, his wife's concern constantly reminded him until he could have sworn that the idea was his wife's and not his own.

The conception was anything but immaculate. Don José had his way with Concepción as was his pleasure. Partly it was for revenge. There was no question that it was for lust. Perhaps too Don José hoped for that son that he did not have. And—at some level even he did not understand—he might have intuited that any son of his who was a grandson of Ojo Torcido would be a force to be reckoned with.

It was only after she recognized the thickening of the slender girl's body that the señora realized she had been a fool. She should have let the girl run away. But now it was too late. For one day there suddenly appeared a guard, a trusted servant, who was always with them. Don José, she realized, had seen that thickening body too. Bewildered, the Indian girl did not even try to escape. Now that she was with child she gave up. Like an animal that is hurt.

"I will have my revenge," Señora Rafa said to whomever would listen. When no one would listen she would hiss the words out at the adobe walls.

A few months later Doña María Rafa was pregnant once again. The rivalry was not for Don José's bed, but for who would bear him a son. A one-sided rivalry that only Doña María engaged in.

"Something is wrong," Don José said to his wife in suspicion, placing his hand on her thickening abdomen. "How can it be?" For he scarcely remembered the last time he had made love to her.

"It must be the will of God," Doña María answered. "That same will that did in our unmarried servant."

Don José swallowed his anger and suspicion. The will of God? he thought. Cuckolded by God? Then he went out into the fields and struck the first hapless peon who was unfortunate enough to be in his way.

Concepción's day of delivery came quickly. Don José's joy was boundless. "A son!" he announced to whomever he met. But when he thought to add "At last an heir!" he would see his wife's living admonition, as if, in revenge, she would bear twins at least.

There were whispers on the rancho and among members of the family. "Concepción," they would say to each other, smiling. Then one might mention Doña María and—smiling even more broadly—they would whisper, "But whose?"

Don José was guarding his sheep when, not many months later, an exhausted mustang labored into camp. "It is time, Don José!" the rider shouted. "The señora's time has come!"

With my luck, he thought, that thieving Indian bastard will wait until I leave to take what's left of my flocks. Where once he thought that Ojo Torcido's daughter might be the means to a treaty to put an end to this annual thievery, now he knew that was impossible.

What if it is another son? he thought as he rode feverishly to Los Rafas. My God, why should life be so complicated? As his half-dead horse neared the house, he saw a grim committee waiting for him.

"I did all I could, Don José," the midwife cried, whereupon she fell on her knees in tears. "It was not my fault," she whimpered. "I did all I could."

Then the wailing started and all he could hear as he pushed his way through the group into the house was, "The señora—"

His sister-in-law sat beside the bed, weeping. The fool! he thought. Why did she get pregnant again at her age? Then aloud, "The child?"

A servant woman came running from the other room, a tiny bundle crying lustily in her hands. She held the bundle out, afraid to open it. His rough, sweaty fingers pulled aside the shawl to see the red face topped by a shock of reddish hair that belonged to no Rafa nor to anyone on his wife's side of the family.

"A male?" his anguished whisper croaked. The servants were afraid to answer, but he knew it was yes anyway. "Send for the priest," he said. "We must bury the señora and baptize her son." *Her son!*

Don José retired to a room with a bottle. Cuckolded by God, he thought. He drank the liquor as if it were water. Two sons, he thought. A man should be happy. He opened another bottle.

Dawn found him still seated alone, the empty bottles on the table before him. There can be only one heir, he thought. Better that it be the half-Indian bastard that I sired than that red-haired bastard that God sired.

Then he began to weep. For finally, with that problem resolved, he thought once more of the wife who had given him so many years, so many children, and—with one exception—so much loyalty.

Thus absorbed, he barely heard the scufflings and arguing voices outside his door. Then a loud knock startled him and before he could shout "Enter!" one of his brothers-in-law burst in.

"José! Your favorite horse has been stolen." Another bolt of lightning. As he rose to hurry to the corral, his brother-in-law continued, "It is too late. She has already been gone for hours."

She? His favorite horse, his best horse, was a magnificent stallion.

"The Indian," his brother-in-law went on. "She ran away on your best horse."

"The baby!" Don José said in shock. He turned and headed for the nursery of his first-born son, Félix Blas.

"My luck!" he agonized. The servants in the hall parted to make way for him, their grim faces unable to hide what Don José saw in their accusing silence. The wages of sin, they seemed to say. When one breaks God's law, one pays.

"What about your horse, José?" his brother-in-law shouted after him.

"To hell with the goddamned horse! What about my son?"

He burst into the nursery where the Indian wet nurse gave a scream and gathered a tiny bundle tighter into her arms. Now his tears were tears of relief. "He's all right," Don José said. "She didn't take him."

Bewildered, the nurse could only nod her head. "I still have an heir," Don José said. "I still have an heir."

Miguel sat quietly listening with open mouth. Then Tercero began again. "Concepción had not been interested in the baby, being only a child herself and no doubt hating anything to do with anything Spanish. So she had abandoned little Félix Blas, preferring to return to her own people.

"Even the raid on his sheep just a few weeks later no longer upset Don José. It was retribution that he now accepted. And in succeeding years, the sheep raids became more frequent and more vicious. Shepherds were killed and dismembered, where before none had been so much as struck. Finally, he abandoned the grant. The family cursed the day he had ever seen Concepción. 'Retribution!' they said. 'We would have been ricos if it had not been for that Indian!'

"But for Don José it was enough that he had his son. Two sons. The dark-skinned one with the twisted eye and the other. The redhead whom he accepted only because of his wife's death."

As Tercero turned so that he looked off in the distance, the young Irishman saw the slightly twisted eye, the ojo torcido, and felt a chill pulse through him.

"So you see," Tercero said. "Ultimately all things are reconciled in the blood. Since we are all God's children, it is inevitable. Especially here on the Río Grande."

After hearing this story, Miguel listened to Grandfather Rafa as politely as ever. Yet now there was always a nagging doubt in his mind. How good was the old gentleman's memory? Where did memory end and exaggeration begin? At any rate, he thought, the old man's stories were never dull—even after he had told them several times—because they were always changing.

14

The days of August marched on as relentlessly as the approaching American army. The forthcoming battle crowded from Carlos' mind any thoughts of unrequited love, murder, or unpaid gambling debts. American businessmen in Santa Fe had been given permits to leave the town, including the dogged Señor Hammond. Reports announced the progress of the Yankees. They were at Bent's Fort, Carlos heard. Then a contingent rode into Santa Fe: an officer; the American trader, Magoffin, who was well known in Santa Fe; and a dozen dragoons.

The Palace of the Governors swallowed up the officer and an

interpreter; Governor Armijo awaited them. Magoffin quietly disappeared and reappeared at the houses of prominent citizens. Some said that he brought a personal message from the President of the United States. Others that he was crossing palms with gold as an expression of American good will.

In the meantime, contingents of the militia and regular troops marched east to Apache Canyon to prepare for the Americans. "A good place," Carlos said to one of his men. He surveyed the narrow pass that commanded the road from Pecos, the road on which the enemy would be advancing toward Santa Fe. "A handful with cannon and guns could hold this forever. The Americanos have no chance."

With joy he directed his troops in setting up barriers of sharpened tree trunks shoulder high, with points slanted toward the advancing enemy. But there were others Carlos knew who were not overjoyed at the prospect of battle. There had been a few, indeed, who had disappeared from the ranks of the militia. They had made their contribution to the war in cash, to the governor, and departed, back to protect their ranchos. The Navajos, ever watchful, had seen the exodus of able-bodied men to Santa Fe and attacked with impunity those unprotected ranchos in the outlying areas.

"Don't work us so hard, Lieutenant Rafa," one of the men complained. Man? A sniveling cadet who should have been in the kitchen with his mamá.

Carlos impaled him with a look. "We are here to fight a war," he hissed. "In the tradition of our brave ancestors who settled this country. Now get back to work! If erecting barricades is too hard for you, then go help take care of the horses and mules."

The boy, on the verge of tears, returned to his place in the work party. Carlos turned his back in disgust. He pretended not to hear the mutterings among the militia. Cowards! he thought. No wonder nothing ever gets done in this country. Everyone from the governor on down worries about his own hide and feathering his own nest.

"Over here!" He waved toward the distant horseman riding toward the work party.

"The governor!" the horseman shouted. "He's coming from Santa Fe. With the legislative assembly." With that he rode on to another group.

Carlos tingled with excitement. This must mean that the

127

gringos are almost here, he thought. The governor has come to lead us to victory. "¡Andale muchachos!" he shouted to his work crew. "Here comes the governor! And the war!" He laughed in anticipation, not hearing the continued muttering of the troops.

The governor and the assembly rode through the camp to a hillside at the perimeter of the work area. One of Carlos' fellow officers nudged him with an elbow. "I hear that the Americanos are but five leagues away. They've already captured Las Vegas. They are now as near to us as we are to Santa Fe. Tomorrow we shall see them."

"Tomorrow," Carlos said in anticipation.

The governor's party stopped and dismounted. Carlos turned his attention to the group, straining to hear what would be said. He could see the tall governor towering above the others, the epaulets of his uniform shining in the sun, the picture of a man of force and decision.

"Members of the Legislative Assembly of the Department of New Mexico," his voice boomed. "As you can see, all is in readiness as ordered by your Governor and Commanding General." His huge arm swept grandly toward the barricades, toward the work parties finishing their preparations, to the artillery out in the open some distance from the mouth of the narrow pass.

"The gringos will get through," Carlos said, looking at the artillery. "Those cannon will never reach them while they're still in the pass." His companion shrugged and turned his attention to the governor.

"—what I want from you now, for the last time, is your decision. Gentlemen! What would you have me do? Shall we fight? Or shall we sue for peace with the powerful American forces?"

Even from this distance Carlos heard the consternation in the grumbling voices of the assembly. Men turned briefly toward one another, then away lest Governor Armijo feel left out of their concern. Yet they could not look the governor in the face, lest their secret thoughts be read. Finally, one of them, a short, skinny man unheroic in appearance in contrast to the tall, stout Governor Armijo, spoke up. The little man's face was red, whether from the heat of the day or from anger Carlos could not tell.

"Your Excellency," the man said. "With all due respect, Your

Excellency. But your question is an improper question!" The grumbling in the group became louder. The governor turned his huge head abruptly and riveted his eyes on this upstart. "We are here as soldiers, not as legislators. Our duty as soldiers is to fight as necessary and above all to obey the orders of our commander."

A shout of agreement came from the rest of the men gathered around the governor, whose eyes narrowed and whose immobile face betrayed nothing. "Then as soldiers," he bellowed, "you are dismissed!"

As the meeting broke up, Governor Armijo gathered briefly with a few of his subordinates, who then sent off dragoons in various directions.

"What the hell is he up to?" Carlos asked.

"Officers of the militia!" one of the dragoons shouted. "We are to gather with Governor Armijo!"

Carlos and his companion moved across the camp to where the governor stood waiting. "I don't like this," Carlos said.

"How would you like to be the one to give the order to fight the Yankees?" his companion asked.

Carlos turned to him angrily. "I would move the cannon closer to the mouth of the canyon. Where it narrows. With a handful of men in the hills I would destroy the American army. There is no doubt in my mind. They will never get through here."

The officers of the militia gathered from all directions. They formed a semicircle around Governor Armijo who stood on the slope of a hill, slightly elevated above the group, his guard of dragoons around him.

"Officers and gallant volunteers of the militia," the governor began. Then Carlos listened impatiently as the governor built up to that same question he had asked before. "Gentlemen! What would you have me do? Shall we fight? Or shall we—"

The question died on the charged air. "Fight!" Carlos shouted, more to his fellows in the militia than to the governor. "We have assembled in camp to fight. That is what we should do. That is the wish of our gallant men of New Mexico."

Others took up the cry. "Fight!"

"Protect our homeland!"

"Yes! Fight!"

The governor listened with inscrutable eyes until the shouting had died. He appeared to be waiting so that he could speak again, but before he could address the militia, there came another voice from the ranks—nervous, almost apologetic, yet with an insistence on being heard.

"Your Excellency, honorable sir. As you know, the Yankees have occupied Las Vegas. There, in the plaza, the Yankee commander spoke to the people, making this proclamation. 'We come as friends,' he said. 'Not as enemies. We come to protect you, not to conquer you.' He said that he was now the governor of New Mexico. And that those who stay peacefully at home with their crops and their herds shall be protected. Not just their property or themselves, but their religion too. He said not a chili, not an onion will they take without our consent and without paying.

"The Yankee commander said he would protect us from the Apaches and the Navajos. No more will they steal our sheep and our women.

"And he said he would protect our religion. That contrary to what some of our priests have told us, they would not ill-treat our women nor brand them on the cheek the way we brand mules. These are all lies, he said. The American government respects Catholics as much as Protestants and allows each man to worship as his heart tells him. Their laws protect Catholic and Protestant alike. The weak as well as the strong. The poor as well as the rich. And though the Yankee commander is not a Catholic, one of every three Yankee soldiers is.

"Finally he pointed to his army. That was just one small part of it, he said. There were more coming. To resist is useless."

An angry undertone swept through the militia. "Who cares what the Yankee general said!" Carlos shouted. "We're here to defend our country. We're here to fight."

But it was as if Governor Armijo had not heard this angry outburst. Instead he had fixed his gaze on the militiaman who now stood nervously in the empty circle where his fellows had backed off, leaving him alone and exposed. The governor's face had clouded with a look of great disgust.

"Cowards!" the governor shouted. "We are here to defend New Mexico and what I hear is a report on the enemy. Cowards!" he repeated. "I will not compromise myself by going into battle with men who have no military discipline. This militia is not worthy of being led into battle. Return to your homes. The regular army will handle this. A few brave men under my leadership will do what ten thousand cowards could never do. Go! Leave the battle to the brave. You are dismissed!"

The men turned to each other in confusion. At the perimeter of the gathering what little military bearing was left dissolved and militia volunteers mounted their horses and rode from camp, scattering in all directions. Carlos stood bewildered, watching the fighting force dissolve around him.

"This is madness!" he shouted to no one.

"Grab a horse, you fool," someone shouted at him. "No sense staying here to be fodder for the Yankees."

For a moment Carlos thought of rushing up to the governor to offer his services along with the regular army. He was close enough to see the strange self-satisfaction on Governor Armijo's face. Something was wrong, Carlos sensed. Somehow he knew it would do no good to talk to Armijo. There was a finality to the man's bearing that would brook no disagreement. Yet to turn and run was against Carlos' every instinct and passion. He was here to fight. To defeat the arrogant, invading gringos.

"Carlos!" He turned, searching for whomever it was that sought him. "Here's your horse, hombre. ¡Andale!" With a final exasperated shout, Carlos mounted his own fine horse. "I almost had to shoot two peons who were eying this beauty of yours."

"Gracias, amigo."

They turned and slowly picked their way through the confusion. At the edge of the camp Carlos stopped for a last look at the barricade on which he had worked his men so hard, at the cannon too far from the narrow pass to do the necessary good. There, he thought, went his last chance for glory. His last chance for revenge against the hated Yankees. Abruptly he turned and headed west toward Santa Fe.

At first Carlos considered staying with his cousin Rudolfo, but then he quickly dismissed the thought. The beautiful Dolores in mourning would only remind him of his unrequited passion, undiscovered revenge, and unfulfilled hatred of anything American. He found a room in town where, for a day or two, he could think about what to do next. Others were riding south, back to their ranchos, but Carlos was not yet ready to leave Santa Fe.

The comings and goings these few days showed a people in confusion. The disbanded militia had scattered, disappearing into the general populace. Then the regular army swooped into

Santa Fe like marauding Navajos and disappeared almost as quickly, leaving in their wake a flood of rumors.

"Armijo has fled," one of Carlos' friends rushed to tell him. "That was him with his dragoons who looted his own capital before racing toward Chihuahua."

"That cowardly Mexican bastard! To desert us when he was responsible for defending New Mexico is the worst sort of treason." Carlos felt a rage that made him dizzy, not knowing whom to hate most, the advancing Americans or the fleeing governor.

"That's not all. There are rumors that the Yankees bought him off. That along with New Mexican money and supplies, there is Yankee gold on his pack mules."

"If he were here, I would kill him!"

"And his business partner, that Prussian Jew, Speyer, must already be in Chihuahua with a wagon train of supplies that came from Missouri. He has tricked us all, that Armijo. He has retired to the south a rich man."

"Rich in gold, poor in honor." Then another realization came to Carlos. "If the regular army has run with Armijo, who is there to stop the Yankees?" His companion did not need to answer. Carlos moved quickly to grab his own weapons as he headed for the door.

"Don't be a fool," his friend said. "The gringos must already be approaching Santa Fe. Those New Mexicans who have not fled south to save their own hides will probably rush out to greet the Americans—to save their own hides. What few there are that would fight would be massacred in minutes."

"I neither want to meet them nor to run away," said Carlos, handling his pistol thoughtfully.

"Then let us bide our time. There will be other patriots who do not like what has happened. The Americans think that their gold and their armies entitle them to whatever they want. There are others of us, with God's help, who will show them differently. But first patience."

Carlos nodded grudgingly, then placed his musket back in the corner of the room and tucked his pistol back in his waistband. "Let's celebrate," he said ironically, "down in the cantina. We'll lift a few to commemorate the sellout of our country by a coward."

* * *

The next day was drizzly and rainy and Santa Fe was quiet. Many prominent citizens had fled the advancing American army, moving to distant retreats that offered sanctuary from their conquerors. They were used to the ways of conquerors. Hadn't they been conquerors themselves? The best thing was to take one's property of value and hide.

The advancing Yankees had been seen moving into the edge of town. By late afternoon they came through the rain with sabers and bayonets drawn, marching to the plaza. From his room Carlos and his friends watched the Americans take over, drinking sullenly. From the adobe houses—almost all of the conquered were indoors—came the wailing of the women.

"Did you see the letter from the American general that was posted?" Carlos asked of no one in particular.

"Yes. Lies. All lies. We'll see how the gringos keep their word."

"There goes the artillery. Up to the hills overlooking the town."

A few drinks later the sun broke through as the American flag was raised over the plaza. Then from the hill came the tribute of the American cannons.

"Well, Carlos, what are you going to do?"

Carlos sighed, finally taking himself from the window where he had peered into the plaza watching every move of the enemy. "I'll stay a few more days to see what happens. Then I ride south. Back to Los Rafas. There are rumors that Armijo is raising an army in Albuquerque."

One of the men laughed. "Yes. The same way he fought so gallantly at Apache Canyon."

"At any rate," Carlos continued. "I will go home to see how things are. Then I will come back. It is here in the North where things will happen."

One of the men raised a glass. "To the war," he said bitterly. "To our mother, Mexico. To freedom."

They drank solemnly as the Stars and Stripes flew over their plaza in Santa Fe.

15

Down river near Los Rafas, the concern seemed less acute than in Santa Fe. Carlos passed through the fields where nature's bounty was flowering. Past the dark, almost black, delicious grapes, the succulent melons, the golden-skinned peaches. It was as if there were no war until, in a quiet aside, some sunburned ranchero would tell him: Yes. The governor, rather the ex-governor, had been through. Commandeering horses and cattle from those unlucky enough to be in his path. Commandeering was the military word, one ranchero said, but the real word was stealing. Yet the people down river seemed to accept things with grace. The war. The Americans. Their fleeing ex-governor. As God wills it, one would say. Then turn quietly to his fields.

As Carlos rode through Alameda he veered closer to the river, following its shallow, muddy path the way he had when he was a boy. He rode past fields, past paisanos who waved greetings. Then onto the rise which was the northern boundary of Los Rafas, where he paused.

It was here that the family women brought their servants to do the laundry. To picnic in the shade of the cottonwoods, watching the river flow south. It was here that he could remember playing with his brother and sisters. Deep in the tall grass like a sheep-stealing Navajo, waiting for the right time to strike. Like a disciplined soldier, waiting for the enemy to advance. It had been easier then, he thought. But then who said life had to be easy? Carlos turned and spurred his horse cruelly, heading in a fast gallop toward the rancho.

"Oh, my God! Look who's here." As Carlos walked toward the house his mother came running and threw her arms around him. She felt his arms and ribs. "Qué delgadito. You haven't been eating enough."

Then the scream of joy from the patio. His sister, Andrea. "Carlito!" She dropped a basket, ran toward him, and kissed him.

Finally a familiar head protruded from the kitchen and looked around. He had almost forgotten her. His wife, Ana María. He walked toward her, listening to the jabber of his mother and sister, feeling a lift of spirits from their welcome. Ana María stepped from the kitchen into the patio and waited. She did not rush to meet him as the others had, but let him come to her.

"Well," he said, "aren't you happy to see your husband?"

Her face crinkled into what might have been a smile, but looked more to Carlos as if she were on the verge of tears.

"I prayed for you," she said. Then they embraced stiffly, formally, perhaps more for the spectators than for each other since at that moment the servants burst from the kitchen and added to the noisy welcome.

"Let's not stand outside like a herd of cattle," Señora Rafa scolded. "Inside. So you can tell us the news, Carlito. About the war. About the Americanos."

Dinner had long been over and the women had left the room. Grandfather, who had dozed off, had been awakened and led off by Señora Rafa. Only the three of them sat over their cigarillos and wine, solemnly blowing smoke into the air in silence. Finally the young Irishman rose.

"If you will excuse me, Don Francisco. Don Carlos. I think it is time I should retire."

Carlos' eyes met those of his father as Miguel left, the soft closing of the door a punctuation between silence and the stirring up of words. He spoke quickly, in irritation. "Who is that?" he demanded. "I come back from an aborted war with the Americans to find one in my home."

"Gaélico," Don Francisco answered simply.

"¿Gaélico? He didn't fly across the ocean and drop from the sky into the middle of the New Mexico desert. Is Irish any better than American? Put them together and you get the most dangerous kind of foreign dog. Like the Irish-American Magoffin. Rumors are that it was he who bribed Armijo to turn us over to the Americans."

"Señor Dalton is our guest. Under our protection. Tercero found him wounded and lost when he was making his rounds of the outlying churches."

"Let the church take care of him."

"He is a most pleasant young man. Your grandfather finds him great company."

"And so does Andrea."

At last Carlos had ruffled his father's composure. Señor Rafa threw his cigarillo to the floor and ground it viciously with the sole of his boot. "She is promised to Francisco Griego." Carlos' smile was insolent and Don Francisco continued coldly. "I am still master in this house. There is no danger." Carlos' smile faded and he set on his face an expression more appropriately respectful. "But you," Don Francisco continued. "What are your plans now? When are you going to present us with an heir?"

Anger flared through Carlos. Not only anger at his father for that damnable question—his father had an uncanny sense of a person's vulnerability. But also at his wife, Ana María. Perhaps more at her, since it was she who should be the vessel for the perpetuation of the Rafas. Barren, she would bring an end to this branch of the family. His brother Tercero was a priest and not a candidate for the perpetuation of Rafas. Not that some of these priests weren't above that. But not his brother. Definitely not his brother.

"It is in the hands of God," Carlos finally said in a trembling, angry voice that he could just barely control.

They both welcomed silence now. Welcomed the empty time so their anger could dissipate. Tit for tat. Their provocations had been equal, so they were not at war with each other, but not at peace either.

Don Francisco filled their glasses and sat quietly staring into space. Carlos lifted his glass. Salud. And downed it quickly.

"You are my heir," Don Francisco finally said. "When I go— and it won't be long— you will become the patrón of Los Rafas. Being an heir is very important in our way of life. There are responsibilities." Here Don Francisco sighed. "Not just family. Nor the land. Nor animals—the horses, cattle, sheep. But the peons who work for you. The servants. All of them the patrón has to worry about." Carlos nodded; he knew his father waited for some kind of acknowledgment. "We are all links in a chain that flows from the beginning of time, when God made the world, to the future. That is what an heir is. He receives the past as a gift, preserves it during his lifetime, then passes it on to the future."

"Yes. You have told me that before, Father."

"So you are the future," Don Francisco continued. "You must always remember that."

"Sí, señor."

"Before I die I want to see Andrea properly married. Then

136

all my children will be properly taken care of. I can die in peace."

Carlos did not know what to say. He had always thought of inheritance as possessing physical things. Of the pleasure and power such possession would give. He never thought of responsibilities. That was old men's talk.

Don Francisco continued, "The war in New Mexico is over. I'm thankful you're alive. Now that you are back you can help me oversee the rancho."

It had come. What Carlos had been expecting and had thought about on the long ride home. "I am going back to Santa Fe. And I need money."

A great roar burst from Don Francisco that must have been heard in other parts of the house, even through the three-foot-thick adobe walls. Whether it was anger or pain Carlos could not tell, but it terrified him.

"What do you mean, back to Santa Fe? Your place is here!"

"No, señor. The war is not over. That coward, Armijo, sold us out, but there are still many ready to resist the gringos. I'm going back to join them."

"The war is over. Our capital is in the hands of the enemy. His army is powerful. This talk about resistance is madness."

"There are many who hate the Americans. Many from the leading families. Many who see the real danger from the Americanos."

"What is this talk about money?"

"To raise and supply an army."

"There is no money." Now it was Carlos' turn to be shocked. "There are debts," Don Francisco continued. "These have been difficult times with the Navajos and the war. What fool would try to herd sheep south to Chihuahua? There is no market now. I need you here to help work this out."

"What about my inheritance? Can't I borrow from that?"

"Right now your inheritance is debts. But with a good season or two it should be as much as ever."

"You mean there is no money?"

"Yes, damn it! Haven't you been listening? There is no money. I need you here to help get the rancho out of debt. I'm not getting any younger. Now, what else is there to say?"

Carlos felt a burning anger in his chest. He was bewildered. He could have struck his father. But the hell with it! He didn't need the money as long as he had his two hands to fight with.

When your cause is right, he thought, God will look after you.

"So stay here," Don Francisco said. "As head of this house I command you to stay. There is work to be done and it is yours as well as mine."

Somehow Carlos kept his temper. He sat, trembling in anger and confusion, but he sat quiet.

The days in Los Rafas dragged. Carlos met with old friends, old acquaintances who might be sympathetic to the cause he espoused, but there were few ready to take up arms. One day, early in September, he heard the thunderous roar of cannon as he rode home from yet another unsuccessful liaison. From high ground west of the river he saw the white burst of smoke from the cannon and farther away, barely in view, an advancing column. The American army.

He rode quickly back to the rancho. Don Francisco was off with a contingent of local citizens who had gone to greet the American general. As Carlos rushed to his room to pack a few things, he found Ana María kneeling before a niche and praying to a statue of the Virgin. Without a word, he sorted through those few things he would take with him. She continued to pray as if she had not heard him, then finally she crossed herself and stood.

"I knew it," she said. "I've been waiting in dread for this day."

"I have business," he said curtly. "I have been here too long."

"Where are you going? To some other woman no doubt."

Carlos looked at her in surprise. Her words did not coincide with his image of her. She was the silent, long-suffering type who prayed before wooden statues in dark corners of rooms. There were thoughts she would never think. Words she would never utter. A dark, moody, silent woman.

"You're going to another woman," she repeated.

"Shut up! It's none of your business."

"Like on our wedding night," she said. "You thought I never knew. You thought I never knew anything."

"Shut up! The rest of the house will hear you."

"Let them. I'll shout loud enough that even your father will hear us in the fields."

"I'm going," he said, "and I may never be back." He couldn't waste his time being angry at this woman. She was nothing to him now; that time had passed. But a flickering thought of what might be ahead passed over him like a cloud, along with the thought that if she had borne him children things would have been different. "The war is not over," he said. "In spite of what you hear. I am going to fight the Americans and I may never be back." The words' implicit meaning hung unspoken in the air: I may be dead.

Ana María's dark, serious face stared deeply at him like a thirsty soul seeking water. Then her expression turned angry. "It's another woman," she spat. "There have always been others. Like there have always been lies."

"Yes!" he roared. "That's it! Women. Women. Women. Everyone but you." Then he rushed from the house trembling in anger. He could have killed her.

In a matter of minutes he was mounted and on his way, crossing the Río Grande and circling wide to bypass the American army. He knew where he must go now. Away from here with its acquiescent peons who fired cannon to welcome their conquerors rather than to kill them. To find others who thought as he thought. Colonel Don Diego Archuleta. Other patriots who were not yet ready to become gringos. As for his home, his parents, his wife—that was all behind him now. There was first the unfinished business of the war. There would be time later to think about Los Rafas.

16

It had been almost six months since Father José Antonio had returned from the seminary at Durango. Since then, it seemed that he had been constantly traveling, spending more time on his seat on a horse than on his knees praying. He had visited every little placita, chapel, village, and pueblo within the jurisdiction of Albuquerque. Birth, marriage, death. Birth, marriage, death. It seemed an endless cycle of repetition. He was a farmer of the soul, he realized. No different from his father or grandfather. No different from the uneducated peons who hung on his every word. Till the soil. Plant the seeds. Water. Weed. Drive away the destroyers of crops. Nurture. Only his crops were souls rather than beans or corn.

Yet, instead of satisfaction a heaviness had settled onto him. A heaviness, he knew, that had to do with his brother, Carlos, whom he had not seen since those first weeks after returning. But, as José Antonio made his rounds and lay at night quietly under open skies and meditated, the heaviness separated in two. There was the foreboding about Carlos. But there was also something else. Something that he had not dared recognize heretofore. A serious doubt—more than that even—an almost physically painful dissatisfaction with his work.

Render unto Caesar, he thought. And unto God— But the temporal world did not separate cleanly into Caesar and God. No more easily than his own heaviness had separated into concern for Carlos and for himself. It was the Caesar in his superior, Father Gallegos, that he warred with. While the God incarnate in Father Gallegos' position merged and emerged so that the two, God and Caesar, became confused.

What does it profit a man to gain the whole world and lose his soul? José Antonio pondered that. Meditated on that. Until the simple illumination came. It was Caesar who was wrong and God who was right. He would rebel if necessary against the Caesar in Father Gallegos. Against the man's card playing, drinking, dancing, fee collecting, God-knows-what-else. He would carry on God's work as his conscience saw it.

It was in this state that José Antonio returned to the villa of Albuquerque, determined to seek out his brother on the one hand and to carry out God's work on the other. But first he had to report to his superior who, as always, was away on some errand that José Antonio hoped was befitting a priest. So instead he went to his room after asking the housekeeper to prepare a hot bath.

He sat half-dreaming while the water, heated over a wood fire in the yard, drained away the tiredness in his muscles and dissolved the dirt from his body. In the distance he could hear the housekeeper scolding the young ladies of the household. It was almost as if he were home. As if it were his mother and sisters teasing and laughing as they went about their work.

A knock on the door woke him from his daydream. "Father!" It was the housekeeper. "There's someone here to see the priest."

He sighed. The tub was so satisfying. "In a moment," he shouted back. "Let them wait in the office."

With regret he lifted himself from his bath, dried, and dressed. As he walked into the office, the visitor's back was to him. A woman. As she turned, he stared at her in surprise.

"Ana María."

Herself surprised, she started to move toward the door. "I—I can't stay. I thought . . . Father Gallegos would be here."

"Please sit down. He should be back soon. I have just now returned to Albuquerque. You're the first of the family that I've seen."

Reluctantly, it seemed to José Antonio, she took a chair. She was nervous, her hands twisting and turning, clasping and unclasping, working the fringe of her expensive rebozo. When she looked at him, it was as if there were tears dammed up behind her eyes that would start at any moment.

"You startled me," she said. "I had been expecting Father Gallegos. Then when I turned and saw you, my mind did not understand. For a moment I thought you were Carlos. I didn't understand what you were doing in those clothes with your moustache shaved. Oh—" But the tears started and she could not go on.

Tercero sat there uncomfortably and let her cry. What was it about women's tears that rendered him powerless? There was nothing he could do, he realized. No way he could console her. It was Carlos, he thought. She would not speak to him of that. She had come to see Father Gallegos.

After a while the tears exhausted themselves and Ana María daubed at her red, swollen eyes with her rebozo. "I'm so unhappy," she said. Then she remained silent, perhaps deciding how much she should say. "Carlos has gone to Santa Fe to fight the Americanos."

"But he has been in Santa Fe for months. The war is over."

"He came back. Then he left again three days ago."

"But the war is over!"

"Not for him."

"¡Demonio! He's crazy. The same old foolishness." Then he realized to whom he was speaking and he cut off the flow of words while his thoughts raced on. But Ana María was not shocked nor had she returned to tears. Her face glowed almost triumphantly and her eyes sought his in a way that made him uncomfortable.

"You know!" she said emphatically. "You understand exactly how it is."

Now it was he who was reluctant to go on. There was a look in her eyes, an almost crazed look, that disturbed him. He did not want to understand exactly how it was. He did not want to enter a conspiracy of understanding with her.

"You're his brother," Ana María continued feverishly. "You've lived with him all your life, so you know exactly how it is. I can't talk to anyone else."

"I think you should wait for Father Gallegos."

But she did not seem to hear him. "You can't imagine how unhappy a marriage can be. Even my parents—with my angry father striking my mother when something did not please him. Some little thing like the chili not being to his taste. Even that was not as unhappy as ours. There were other times with my parents. Happy times. The talking and the laughing. Of course, one could not laugh too loud. That would offend God and the saints. But nevertheless we could laugh. But my own marriage that I dreamed of as a girl. It is what a young girl with dreams would consider hell. Complete indifference. Disloyalty. Other women—"

"Please," Tercero protested.

"Whores. The lowest types."

"No more!" Tercero rose angrily from his chair. "My God, woman. I can't listen to this. No matter what the truth, he's still my brother."

The glazed look on Ana María's face softened, as if she realized now where she was and whom she was talking to. The tears started again. "No one listens to me," she whimpered. "You Rafas are all the same."

"You came here for a priest. Not a Rafa. It is not proper for me to hear you out. I'm only another human with his weaknesses and faults. Priesthood does not bestow sainthood on a man. It just gives him different duties from others."

"You do not even listen as a friend."

Tercero shook his head. "I can either speak to you as a priest or as a brother-in-law, but not as both at the same time." She sat quietly in her tears now, savoring them, giving in to them, and somehow rebuking him with them. When she did not reply, Tercero continued. "I'm going to leave," he said. "As soon as Father Gallegos returns, he will see you. Would you like someone to come sit with you?" She shook her head slowly and he left the room.

Although she remained physically in the office, Ana María pursued him in his thoughts. Tercero had never really thought a great deal about her marriage to his brother or about any marriage for that matter. He had performed the ceremony countless times for rich and poor, old and young, for some who had lived together for years in sin. In the confessional he had consoled many who had come with woes of an unhappy union or had come guilt-burdened with offenses committed against their spouses. But somehow these had existed as abstractions. He felt disconnected from the people whose only reality was the sound of whispered voices behind a dark cloth in the confessional.

But his brother Carlos! Was this the premonition, the foreboding that had weighed on him these past months? No, he thought. Marriage was not that important. To him or to Carlos. These problems were just a symptom of something bigger gone wrong with Carlos' life. A ripple far removed from the center, where the stone had splashed large on the water's surface and sunk.

Tercero would have liked to drop back in the tub of warm water and turn off his mind. Instead he made his way to the private chapel, draped in black silk, where the flickering candles barely illumined the life-size crucifix. He knelt and prayed.

Time passed. He could feel his fingers on the beads of his rosary, feel the tautness in his throat, and the motion of his tongue and lips as he prayed. He remembered nothing. It seemed like a minute yet he knew that he must have been here for at least an hour. He had not been asleep. He had slipped into some peaceful state where time had become inconsequential, where it had slipped its moorings and drifted with its own set of rules. How could an hour pass like a minute? Yet he felt refreshed, as from a night's sleep. And he knew he could bear anything. Ana María's gossip. The worst possible depredation that Carlos could commit. The wrath of Father Gallegos.

As he walked back to his room, the old housekeeper rushed to him.

143

"Father has been looking for you everywhere. He's in the office." Then she rushed off as if fearing to be near when the two met.

"Ah, there you are." Father Gallegos sat behind a table that he used as his desk. "I have been going over some of the records from your travels." He folded his hands across his stomach and looked thoughtfully into the air. "There are—some irregularities." Father Gallegos sat as if waiting for something from Tercero. A denial. An outburst. But Tercero stood quietly, thinking to himself: At last! "What have you to say?" Father Gallegos finally asked.

"Render unto Caesar the things that are Caesar's. And render unto God the things that are God's."

Father Gallegos' fleshy face turned crimson and his voice trembled, though he kept control. "You talk in riddles, young man. I don't want riddles." He tapped a long forefinger on the book of records.

"You want to know about the fees," Tercero said. The answer was a nod of the huge head. "There are no fees."

For a moment Tercero thought that the older man would have a stroke. He sat wheezing, his face turning almost purple. "You have given away the money to the poor?" Tercero shook his head in denial. "You lost it?" Again the head shake. "You stole it!" Father Gallegos roared, pounding the table.

"There was nothing to steal. There are no fees. I could not collect from people who had no money. What fees there were I accounted for. But very few people can pay fees in this poor country."

"There have to be fees! For baptisms. Marriages. Funerals. How can these sinners learn charity if they are not made to give to their church?"

Tercero found it difficult to control his irritation. How could he make this stupid man understand? "These poor people have no money! You cannot collect what people do not have."

"Then collect corn. Or beans or chili. A goat. A cow. Whatever. If they truly have nothing, then you should not baptize or marry or bury them. They are giving to God. If they cannot give to God, they cannot receive the Church's sacraments."

"What you are saying is let New Mexico go to the devil."

"Of course not! What do you mean go to the devil?"

"You complain about poor, ignorant sinners. Living together

as man and wife while unmarried. Having children who have not been baptized. Dying in their adobe hovels without receiving the last rites. Sin! Sin! Sin! Yet you do nothing about it but complain. They cannot pay so we cannot help them on the true path. That's blasphemy! That is the worst sin of all. We are God's priests. It is our sacred duty to save these people."

"Do not preach to me about sacred duty. It is your sacred duty to obey your superiors. To do your duty as you are told. Whether it is to your personal liking or not. I think we have had enough of this caterwauling. Your accounts are in arrears. If these poor parishioners cannot pay, perhaps your family can."

"No. This has nothing to do with my family. Whether or not I collect fees is between me and God."

"And your superiors."

"No. Not my earthly superiors. Only God."

"We will see about that. You realize that I am being forced to report you to the bishop."

Tercero repressed a smile. "The Bishop of Durango? This is no longer part of Mexico. New Mexico now belongs to the United States. Even if you could have a letter delivered through what is now a battlefield, I'm not certain that the bishop would consider this part of his jurisdiction anymore. We are without a bishop."

A gleam flashed briefly in Father Gallegos' eyes. So, Tercero thought, he can see himself as Bishop of Albuquerque. But then the gleam turned into a look of authority pushed beyond its patience.

"Your parents are good friends of mine. I have known you a long time, young man, and felt concern and affection for you. Let us not leave things at this impasse. Some day you too will have your own parish and assistants. Then you will understand better. There are superiors and there are assistants who do their bidding. It has always been so. Anything less is chaos.

"We will arrange something to take care of these fees. I sympathize with your good heart, but once these peons are given blessings for nothing they are worth nothing to them. It is an old law of human nature. The more one pays for something, the more it is worth. So let us not part angry. I need you to be off again. There have been reports of trouble in Los Bacas. You remember Los Bacas? They need you and I want you to go with less anger in your heart."

Tercero did not know what to say. This sudden cooling of Father Gallegos' anger left him tilting against the wind. The man's words were reasonable. Yes. One was taught to obey his superiors. Not just within the Church but within the whole fabric of family and social life. Perhaps, Tercero thought, this is why nothing ever changes. But then again there was the reasonableness of the older priest's words. Without obedience there is no order. Without order there is chaos and the devil takes charge.

"There is much to be done," Father Gallegos continued. "As you say, we are probably no longer under the jurisdiction of the Bishop of Durango, our Mexican bishop. There are opportunities now, thrust upon us by events outside of our sacred work. Opportunities for young priests who do their duty."

Tercero stiffened. There was no need for this enticement. God and Caesar, he thought. God and Caesar. "I will do my duty as God wills it," he said. "I will go to Los Bacas as soon as I can get ready."

"Good." Father Gallegos was smiling.

Because of the need to gather a few supplies and attend to a few urgent duties, it was three days before Tercero was able to leave. He rode south on El Camino Real, which paralleled the Río Grande, and was barely out of the villa when a local ranchero waved and joined him. Then, almost as if they had been waiting, others joined, until Tercero could see that several of the more prominent families in the area were represented.

"Gentlemen," he said, "where do you all ride so early in the morning? The church of San Felipe is the other direction, so you cannot be on your way to pray."

"Oh. We are just out for a little ride."

The rancheros nodded to each other in agreement, then rode along in silence for some time before another ranchero spoke. "It is interesting, young Father Rafa, that you should mention the church."

"Yes. Yes," came the current of undertones.

"What do you think will happen to our church now that the Americanos have come?"

"I have heard," another said, "all kinds of rumors about the Protestant atheist gringos."

"There are Yankee Catholics much like us," Tercero answered. "Many. They have given their pledge to respect our religion and property and leave us in peace. I think nothing will happen to our church."

"That is good," several echoed.

"We hear that since we are no longer part of Mexico, the Bishop of Durango is no longer our bishop."

Tercero's body suddenly pulsed with alertness and he surveyed his companions with more concern. Yes, he observed. Many of the richer landowners were represented in the group. Old settlers who were the backbone of the community. Friends and supporters of Father Gallegos.

"We are now part of the United States," Tercero answered with restraint. "Durango is part of Mexico. It seems to me that there will have to be some adjustment."

"But until then?"

"Until then Father Gallegos is the head of the church in Albuquerque."

There was an almost audible sigh of relief. Though Tercero did not dare look at his companions, he could sense the smiles on their faces.

"Father Gallegos is our friend," the oldest of the riders said as if speaking for them all. "He has married some of us. Baptized our children and grandchildren. Buried our parents and grandparents. We owe much to him and we are loyal to him. It is fortunate that he has a young, strong helper like you, Father Rafa. One who comes from one of our important families and knows how it is."

"Yes," others echoed.

Tercero nodded in acknowledgement to the old gentleman.

"We understand," another said, "that you are on a mission to Los Bacas." Again Tercero nodded. "The Apaches have been riding again. You must take care, young Father Rafa."

They had reached a point where the trail crossed the river and the rancheros slowed their horses to a halt and let Tercero proceed alone.

"Watch for the Indian devils," one said. "We would not want anything to happen to our young priest."

"Your concern touches my heart," Tercero said warily.

"Go with God, Father."

"Adiós."

As he left them behind, Tercero resisted the urge to spur his horse faster, instead reining in the beast so that he moved across the shallow ford with deliberation. He did not know whether he was more angry or afraid, but whichever, a prayer came to his lips. Not of thanks or for protection, but for the courage to do and think what was right.

Now, in autumn, the ride was more benign than it had been those few months past. No longer did the sun weigh heavy on the traveler. The days were shorter. Crisp in the early mornings that were clutched by night to hold them back. Lingering in the evenings as if the golden hours of twilight would last forever. A time to rest. When even the earth started to yawn and stretch and settle down for the winter.

There was time to think on the ride. Of Ana María, with a prayer that she might find peace. Of his brother, Carlos, with hope that matched the beautiful autumn days. Of Father Gallegos. Of the Americanos and the changes that would surely come.

Things changed slowly in this land of tradition, but change they would. Already the American army had been welcomed wherever it had appeared. Fears and apprehensions had been alleviated for now. Yet things had stayed much the same. Even the peons—the poorest and least educated—saw the coming of the Yankee as a welcome change. The Americanos would bring money. There would be more trade. Perhaps they would even conquer the Apaches and Navajos and Comanches, something that the Mexican government could never do.

The familiar trail went quickly and easily along the river, then east into the mountains. There was the place where he had met the woodcutter who mistook him for a witch. The hamlet of Los Bacas was but a short ride away. He stopped to rest, to water his horse, and to pray. Refreshed, he remounted and set out again on the trail. He would be there before dusk.

The last part of the trail, winding through the trees, seemed strangely silent. There was no sound of barking dogs. No faint bray or whinny from burro or horse. Only the sound of the wind crying in the ominous silence.

He slowed his horse and rode uneasily along the final turn that widened into the small valley of Los Bacas. He stopped in the shelter of trees and carefully surveyed the hamlet. There was no sign of life. It was empty even of a rooting pig or a pecking chicken; the dust settled as if untouched for a long time. The little adobe houses sat back from the trail, their few windows like blind eyes on impassive faces staring into nothing. The sky was clear and smokeless—no fires to warm the empty houses. The fields were abandoned. The only sign of life was the disinterested circling of a buzzard high overhead who glided off onto a current of air toward another valley where there might be better pickings.

"¡María santísima!" Tercero crossed himself and descended slowly down the trail looking for signs. Of what he did not know. He headed toward the little chapel. That would be the first place to look.

Surveying the valley cautiously, he dismounted and walked up the dirt path to the tiny adobe building. The unpainted door, dry and weatherbeaten, hung half off its leather hinges as if it had been battered open. A dry rasping creak welcomed Tercero as he pushed his way in. A powerful stench overcame him and he stood for a moment, letting his eyes adjust to the dim light.

The chapel was a disaster. The altar had been pushed over and smashed, then set fire to. In the middle of the chapel a heap of cold ashes was all that was left of altar, crucifix, and santos. As he sorted through the rubble with the toe of his boot, a huge ash in the shape of a cross crumbled into dust. He followed his nose toward the dimmer corners of the chapel. He thought he recognized the mummified body that sat propped against the wall, cruel arrows protruding from its chest like a cluster of porcupine quills.

"Don Ignacio?" he said aloud, trying to see through the remains to the mortal man who had once occupied that shell. He crossed himself and surveyed the rest of the chapel. Finding nothing, he escaped the foul air and the desecration by bolting through the door and vomiting into the dirt.

It was a long time before Tercero could bring himself to survey the rest of the buildings. In many the door had been smashed. Most were empty, though in or around a few were skeletons picked clean of flesh—skeltons of various sizes, including one tiny set of delicate bones with a bashed-in skull. But the remains did not account for all of the inhabitants of Los Bacas. There had to be more, many more. Survivors hopefully, who had escaped. Prisoners, if not so lucky.

Finally a dozen persons were accounted for. Dead for God knows how many weeks. But there must have been another two dozen unaccounted for.

It was dusk now and in the eerie silence the ghostly hamlet unnerved him. There was nothing he could do tonight. Tomorrow he would say a mass for these poor dead souls, unrecognized except for Don Ignacio. Then he would see about digging a grave for those bones that would soon enough return to dust. Sleep came fitfully during the night. The cry of a coyote would bring wakefulness, then, with a prayer on his lips, Tercero would drift back into a restless dream. One cry crashed through his sleep with a peculiarly plaintive wail that was almost human and he stared into the dark listening. It came again. Softer. He was certain that there was someone out there. He could not sleep after that, hearing the same sound at long intervals throughout the night.

At daylight he rolled onto his stomach and stared down the slope from his sheltered camp into the valley. There, flickering across the hamlet in the soft daylight, a shadow wandered from house to house. Was it his imagination? He watched. Only the chapel was exempt from this ghostly visitation. Then finally, at the last house along the trail, the shadow stepped into the sunlight and let out a cry that was more animal than human. His clothes were in rags and his hair wild and unkempt.

"¡¡Diablo-o-o!!" The cry was a distinct word now. Then Tercero squinted at the bearded features and saw through them a familiar face. The woodcutter.

Tercero rose, folded his serape, and repacked his horse. He did not shout toward Los Bacas. No doubt it would frighten the woodcutter who might bolt. He mounted and made his way slowly through the trees, keeping hidden as long as he could. When he broke into the clear, he could see that a short distance away the woodcutter was standing and watching. By then his horse had sped into a canter and the woodcutter waved exuberantly.

"¡Amigo!" the greeting came. "¡Gracias a Dios! Thanks be to God!"

As the horse reined to a stop, the old woodcutter rushed to Tercero and feebly grasped his hand. "Food," he croaked. "For the love of God, do you have anything to eat? Those Apache devils took everything that they did not kill or burn. A stale tortilla. A chili. Yes. A fat, delicious chili. Food. Anything, señor."

150

They entered an empty cabin and shared a breakfast from Tercero's supplies. He watched the old woodcutter eat until he thought the man would burst. Only then did the woodcutter sigh and sit back in a semi-stupor, satisfied and able to consider more than just his empty belly.

"It has been so long," he said. "I don't know how long now. I lost track." Tears started to stream down his face. "My little Juanito," he cried. "My poor little Juanito." Then he broke down and sobbed so hard that his words were unintelligible. Tercero placed a hand on his shoulder to comfort him. "My burro," the woodcutter finally said. "I had to eat him. May God forgive me."

Then the woodcutter's story gushed forth, at times loud and angry, at times quiet and hushed as if he whispered to secret listeners only he could see.

"It was—I don't know. Three, four weeks ago. Maybe longer. I don't remember. I was off in the mountains at my work. Just me and Juanito. Juanito had been lame. He was getting old. We had gone farther than usual. No reason. It's just that I was tired of finding wood close to the valley and I wanted to see some new trees for a change. So we stopped to sleep under the stars and rose early the next morning to return to Los Bacas.

"We were coming down over there." He pointed back up the mountains where a narrow trail wound its way into one end of the valley. " 'Juanito,' I said. 'we'll be home soon. Then you can rest your tired old bones. I'll get something from the weed woman for your poor leg.' Oh, God. If I had only known that we would never see the weed woman again.

"We saw them as we were halfway down the trail. Just where it turns at that ridge from where you can see clearly into the valley. 'Stop!' I said to Juanito. We looked together, seeing the riders racing among the houses. Even that far up we could hear their shouts. Diablos! Indian devils! The people of Los Bacas were no match for them. Some of the Indians had guns and at best the people from the hamlet had bows and arrows. It did not last long.

"They herded all of the survivors out of the houses. Then they ransacked everything. The houses. The corrals. Even the chapel. Don Ignacio tried to stop them. He had been hiding, but when he saw them enter the chapel, he rushed at them with all the fury left in his old body. He did not last long against the young braves. Afterwards I could see them gathered outside the chapel door motioning to each other and laughing. They took their bows and shot arrows into the chapel, each shooting once and then letting the next take his turn.

"Juanito and I stood terrified on the trail. They led the captives away and we watched until the last of our friends had disappeared into the mountains. I did not have the heart to go down into Los Bacas. What if they come back? I kept thinking. I knew that there was no one alive down there.

" 'Juanito,' I said. 'we had better head for someplace friendly. To the big rancho by the river.' So we set off through the trees, avoiding Los Bacas and the main trail. It was slow going. Juanito's leg got worse. Finally he stopped—you know how stubborn burros can be—and began to bray. 'I can't go on,' he was telling me. 'Hush, Juanito,' I said. 'What if the Indians are near?'

"We stayed like that a long time. Me trying to calm and quiet him. We slept huddled together that first night. But even the rest did not help Juanito. He would not budge the next morning.

" 'What am I going to do?' I asked him. 'We can't stay here like this. We'll starve. Or the Indians will come back and kill us.' But he would not budge that entire next day. I foraged for him, bringing him choice little morsels. I dug roots for myself. But he would not move.

"Finally, the third day I left. There was nothing else I could do. It starts to get cold in the mountains this time of year. I headed in what I thought was the direction of the Río Grande. But somehow I got lost. I went farther into the wilds than I normally go. The trees were so thick I could not see the stars at night to find my direction. I must have wandered for days, living on roots and the bark of trees. One night I heard this faint braying while I slept. 'It's a dream,' I thought. 'A dream of my little Juanito.' But then my eyes were open and I was staring into the dark toward the sound.

"I had wandered in a circle and come back to where I had left him. Those little cries I heard in the night must have been his last. Pobrecito. Poor little thing. He had gotten to his feet and tried to find his way, but he was not strong enough. He had fallen into a gully and died there. Trapped. I meant to bury him, but I was too hungry. Eating him gave me the strength to find my way back to Los Bacas." Now the tears came back and the old man became incoherent again.

"There," Tercero said. "It is because of your burro that you are alive." The woodcutter's mouth moved soundlessly. "You're safe now," Tercero said. "You rest while I bury Don Ignacio and the bones of the others."

The woodcutter finally calmed down enough so he could speak. "It is only by the grace of God that I am here."

"Then thank Him."

The old man crossed himself and moved his lips in prayer while Tercero went out to bury the dead. He dug the shallow hole and filled it with Don Ignacio's remains, surrounded by the bones of the unknown others. After he covered them and outlined the communal grave with rocks, he knelt and prayed. For the repose of the souls of the dear departed. For mercy for all who have gone before. For Juanito in whatever burro heaven God had taken him. Last of all for a safe trip back to Albuquerque. The land was still wild and dangerous. Dangerous most of all in what man did to man. For with New Mexicans fighting Americanos, and Apaches, Navajos, and Utes fighting both, the day when one would love his neighbor as himself seemed as far away as the beginning of the world. Back to the heritage of Cain and Abel.

17

It was Sunday and siesta time. The Rafa family had ridden to mass at San Felipe church and after brief visits with friends and relatives had ridden back to the rancho. There had been American soldiers in the plaza. There was talk that a contingent would be stationed across from the church. It would be a large contingent to protect the villa and its surrounding farms where over a thousand people lived—maybe even two thousand.

Perhaps it was uneasiness at seeing American troops in their plaza that caused Don Francisco to curtail what was usually a social occasion. Although he had been bitterly disappointed—nay angry—at Carlos and still hoped that the young fool was more talk and bluster than action, he felt more comfortable at the rancho than in this public place.

Now the rancho was quiet. Don Francisco and Doña Estela rested in their rooms. The servants had ceased their jabbering and had settled down in the work quarters. The cook dozed in a warm corner of the kitchen, lulled by the boiling of a pot of frijoles. Ana María prayed solemnly in her room, while Andrea peered restlessly from a window, pouting.

There would be no more postponing of the meeting with Señor y Señora Griego. The game of delay was over and the matter would have to be settled. Mamá had done her best. First persuading Papá that with the war and young Francisco away, they should postpone the decision. The family was too upset. All manner of things happen during a war. There would be time enough afterwards. Then, with the greatest delicacy, the greatest diplomacy, Mamá and Papá had talked to the Griegos.

The right note had been struck. Señor Juan Griego was a high-strung, nervous man from whom energy sputtered even as he sat still. No wonder the Griegos were so thin. Everything they ate was consumed in agitation so there was never anything extra to add fat to their bones. And the war— Ah, the war. Nightly the entire Griego family would go into the candlelit chapel, really the corner of the main room in their farmhouse. There they would pray their rosary for the safe return of their youngest son. So the suggestion that any decision wait until the war was over met with agitated agreement.

"We will talk again," Señor Griego said. "When Francisco returns."

Now Francisco had been home for several weeks. He appeared one Sunday, as if by magic, dressed in his finest clothes with silver buttons along the seams of his tight trousers that flared over his shiny boots. The Griegos had been conspicuously early for mass and had lingered long afterwards.

"Oh, Lord," Andrea had thought. "Oh, unhappy day." She almost burst into tears when her parents greeted the Griegos like long-lost relatives even though they saw them most Sundays after church.

"We must get together," Señor Griego had said politely, not daring to breach his sense of propriety by more overt and aggressive words.

"Yes. Of course," Don Francisco had answered. "Soon."

Soon had come, Andrea now realized. Even today her father had grumbled on the way home that it looked as if they were avoiding the Griegos when in truth it was the presence of American troops that cut short their stay in the plaza.

It was still in the patio. Even the dogs slept, stirring only to swish a fly with their tails or nip quickly and briefly at a flea with their eyes still shut. A sound of quiet footsteps. She turned and felt a warm glow of pleasure as she saw Miguel sit down on the ground in the sunlight and sigh.

"Psst," she whispered. He looked around, uncertain where the sound came from. Not certain if he truly heard a sound. "Psst." Andrea bit her fist to keep from laughing. He looked so funny turning his head here and there, his blue eyes wide in surprise. Then he turned toward her window, their eyes met, and she beckoned to him.

"Help me through," Andrea whispered, ignoring that prim and proper look of his. "Come on."

"Why not the door?"

"It squeaks. It will wake half the household."

Miguel blushed and again she had to suppress a giggle. What a strange young man. So shy on the one hand, yet so friendly. Treating her as an equal rather than with the heavy-handedness of New Mexican men who seemed to want docility in their women.

She stepped through the large window, holding his hand, and tiptoed to where he had been sitting. Quietly, he carried a rough, unpainted wooden bench and placed it in the sunlight where they sat together.

"What were you doing?" she whispered.

Miguel looked at her, then looked away into the distance. "Thinking." His voice was soft and wistful. "Thinking about home. About Ireland."

A soft hand touched him. "Don't you like it here?"

His eyes, when he turned toward her, were moist. He tried to blink them dry and smile. "It's been like a second home."

"There. It's settled. Papá says he could not get on without you. Especially now with Carlos off on his craziness." His face brightened as if the sun had come out from behind a cloud. Andrea caught her breath. Suddenly she felt shy and self-conscious. Realizing it, she became angry at herself and turned to Miguel. "Don't look at me like that! I am the daughter of the patrón and you should do what I tell you. It's time for my lesson in English."

But his smile did not dim, though he nodded and shifted from his slow Spanish into the American language. "Girl," he said, pointing to Andrea. "Muchacha."

"Stop that! You are being silly. Now what is that?"

"Alamo," he said in Spanish. "Cottonwood. Arbol. Tree."

"Cot-ton-wooo-d tree." Repeating the words again, Andrea nodded in satisfaction, then pointed to the window through which she had come.

"Ventana," Miguel said, "Window."

"Ween-dough."

"Win-dow."

"Ween-dough."

"No. Win— Win—"

"Ween— Ween—"

Miguel laughed, then squeezed her hand and placed it against his chest. "Corazón," he said. "Heart."

Her hand felt tiny and helpless in his large, rough paw. She could feel the pounding in his chest—not the slow, steady thud she expected from a large, strong man, but a fleet racing as if inside there lived another creature who felt with quick emotion.

"Oh, you mustn't." She grasped his hand as she pulled her own from his chest and let them both settle on the bench between them. She looked down from his gaze and saw his gentle hand, its rude, field-hardened fingers cupping her brown hand that felt disembodied and strange. Her own fingers slender and bony, with little nodules of fat between each joint and deep, deep lines running across her palm.

"Will you have to marry him?" At first Andrea was not certain if she heard the words right. "Will you?" Miguel repeated.

"No!" she answered angrily, grasping his hand tight. "I will run away."

His voice sounded shocked. "But—your mother and your father—"

"It's my life!"

Miguel's other hand joined its twin, stroking Andrea's captive one. "I will run away with you," he said solemnly.

Then she started to cry. She could not help it. And he was kissing her eyes, kissing her tears, to make them go away. "You mustn't," she said when her tears began to slow.

An alien sound, a low rumble intruded. Drawn out, then abruptly ending only to begin again. "My God! What's that?" Miguel let go of her and slid to the opposite end of the bench.

Puzzled for a moment, Andrea looked around, then started to giggle. "Grandfather," she whispered, pointing across the patio toward one of the rooms. "He's snoring."

Relieved, Miguel took her hands and smiled. "I will," he insisted. "I will run away with you. I—I love you." There. He said it. What had been building all these weeks as Andrea had helped nurse him back to health. He had dared declare himself to the daughter of the patrón, his benefactor.

Again the tears, only different this time. Gentler, as if in relief. Grandfather's snores became especially loud and they looked at each other and started to laugh again.

"He will wake everyone up," Andrea said. "We will have to talk another time." She leaned over and kissed him quickly on the lips. "Tonight," she said in English. "I go through ween-dough to cot-ton-woood tree, my heart."

His answering smile was more than she could bear. She kissed him again, then ran to her room without looking back. This time she went through the door, its dry squeak punctuating the rumble of Grandfather's snores. She threw herself on her fluffed-up pallet and wept tears of joy.

"He loves me," she said to herself. "Oh, my heart, he loves me."

The house bustled with activity. The Griegos were calling this afternoon. Everything must be just so for their visit. The servants had sprinkled water over the earthen floors so they could be packed hard and gleaming. The furniture had been rearranged. New candles had been placed throughout the sala, not only in the holders placed in strategic locations for light, but also in the votives for the wooden saints resting in their niches in the walls. In the kitchen, hectic preparations were made for serving the finest, frothiest chocolate and newly baked biscochitos, little cookies flavored with anise or cinnamon.

Don Francisco had escaped to the bedroom. The frantic gabblings of the women at work annoyed him. They talked incessantly. Moving hither and thither in quick, light movements that never settled on any one task but scattered over a dozen things at once, with a push here, a wipe there, a removal somewhere else. Leaving things half done. Eventually everything would be finished. How he was not certain. But of one thing he was sure, he could not tolerate being in the presence of this haphazard way of work. Give him the fields or the pastures. There was order there. Quiet. Even solitude. A man could be at peace.

Don Francisco sat stiffly on the edge of the bed, one of the few beds in the villa of Albuquerque. Like other treasures throughout the house, it had been brought overland by carreta from the interior of Mexico. It had survived the elements, the Indians, to bring a touch of civilization to this country far, far away from the land of his ancestors across the ocean sea. There were other treasures in other houses in the villa. Newer treasures bought with newer riches. Imported from England or France. Brought across the Santa Fe Trail from los Estados Unidos. And while he cast a longing eye on some of these treasures in the homes of the richer dons, los ricos, that did not demean the value of his own older symbols of a richer past.

He lit a cigarillo and smoked distractedly. He felt tight, harried. Pushed by events rather than controlling them. Harassed by change and newness. There was no stability any more. No order. Somehow all of the things that worried and angered him seemed to ally themselves and assault him all at once like an army of Navajos.

There was the war with the Americanos. It was over here in New Mexico, but still raging south in Mexico proper. He was an Americano now, a fact that stung him with its absurdity. How could a man live his entire life in the same place, the place his father and grandfather had lived, the place of his ancestors for generations—and suddenly become something different? It was preposterous. He was no more an Americano than he was an Indian. Yet he could not deny his eyes. Already there were troops from the American army in the plaza. There would be more. Then other Americanos would follow. It had not yet begun, but in the years ahead there would undoubtedly be others. The invasion was not over just because their army had won.

Then there was his financial problem. That cursed Mexican government! He had loaned the government money in years past. Sold a little land—a piece here, a meadow there. Then he had to borrow himself when things got bad and the government defaulted on its debts. Having to borrow when the farm did not produce well. When there was a bad year for sheep. When the markets in Chihuahua were poor and it cost more to journey down the Chihuahua Trail than his goods were worth. It had been a slow erosion during his adult life and now here he was—sixty-six years old, facing bankruptcy. Bad! he thought. ¡Muy malo! With one more daughter to marry off. A dowry to raise. One more demand on his dwindling resources.

Don Francisco walked to the door and flicked the remnant of cigarillo into the patio. He could hear the commotion across the way—his wife's angry scream at one of the servants. It would quiet down soon. Their guests would arrive. And this reminded him of the biggest problem of all. His children. He sighed and dropped back onto the bed.

Yes. There would be the immediate matter of Andrea and her proposal from young Griego. It was a good match in Don Francisco's eyes. His daughter was not getting any younger. Eighteen already. By eighteen his other two daughters had had the first of his several grandchildren. But this one— He shook his head in concern about his youngest, spoiled daughter. But it was not just her. It was the other young ones too. His sons. Why couldn't they have been like their older sisters? Yes, he thought. This was the biggest problem of all. His younger children. They were as unpredictable and changeable as the war and his finances.

He lit another cigarillo. A daughter, he thought. She made a nice marriage and that was the end of that. She became her husband's problem. A dowry? Well, yes. A little something. A piece of land like with his Josefa and Clara. Or maybe a few sheep or cows or horses. But sons! ¡Demonio! It was not so simple. Sons were the lifeline by which the family survived from generation to generation. But that could only be true for Carlos. José Antonio belonged to God.

Don Francisco shook his head in despair. A priest. True, his uncle had been a priest, following a family tradition. That was fine for an uncle. But for a son? His wife had been delighted. She would be. But for Don Francisco, a priest would never carry on the family. Never sire heirs. Never keep the generations going in an unbroken line.

Then the other one. Carlos. Again Don Francisco shook his head in despair. Young hothead. One thing after another. As if he would never grow up. Brave? Well, yes. If you called such foolishness bravery. He had fought the Navajos and Apaches. He had fought the Texans. He had prepared to fight the Americanos and when that had not come to pass, he had run off to God knows what. He had not told his father. But to leave a wife like that. A home like that. It could only be to plot and fight again. There were rumors about trouble in the north. In Santa Fe. Taos. That's where Carlos would be.

Yes, Don Francisco thought, there was a strain of hotheadedness in the Rafas. One of his own brothers had been killed in a duel. An uncle—not the priest—had spent his life fighting Indians, and when he wasn't fighting Indians, he would fight whomever was near. His wife. His children. His neighbors. Until he had been murdered out in his field one day; they never found out by whom. So his son's behavior did not surprise Don Francisco. It was as if Carlos were a reincarnation of those hotheaded Rafas. As if, over the decades, people did not change but were reborn to live out their destiny.

What did infuriate him was the lack of grandchildren through his son. His daughters gave him grandchildren in profusion, but there had never been even a false pregnancy through his son. Maybe, just maybe, Carlos and José Antonio would be the last of the Rafa clan through this branch. True. There were other Rafas in abundance. Uncles. Cousins. Nephews. But not *my* Rafas, Don Francisco thought angrily. Me! Mine! *My* grandsons!

¡Demonio! he thought. It must be his daughter-in-law, Ana María. God almighty, why had his son ever chosen her. Maybe that was it, he thought. Maybe that was where all the anger and hotheadedness ended. With no children. When we do not learn and change our ways, God finally gives up and puts an end to it. Then eventually there will be less anger in the world.

That would be the worst thing of all. No Rafa grandsons to inherit whatever he could hang on to. The land going to non-Rafas. To disappear into the possession of those families whose names survived. As if all he had worked for his entire life, all his father had worked for, and all the fathers before that—as if all that had been in vain. No! he thought angrily. That could not be!

There was a polite knock on the door and his wife entered. "It is finished. We can wait in the sala now if you want. Everything looks beautiful."

With a grunt, Don Francisco rose from the bed and strode across the patio to the living room, his wife pattering softly behind him.

They were sitting in the sala, waiting. One of the servants had come running from the field to tell them breathlessly that the Griegos were approaching, dressed in their Sunday best, riding in a carriage. A carriage? Where the devil did the Griegos get a carriage? Only the richest of the ricos could afford a carriage.

160

Then, in the next breath, the servant described the luxurious vehicle. Don Francisco nodded. Yes. Don Manuel's carriage. They had either borrowed or rented it on this auspicious occasion, and he began to feel even more uneasy.

"So Andrea still says no?" he asked his wife.

"She is dead set against it. Stubborn as only a Rafa can be."

"What do you think?"

"Whatever you think, Francisco."

"That's no answer. Goddamned children! We should never have had children. They're the curse of the world."

Doña Estela looked at her husband warily. "You don't really mean that." Her voice was soft so that he would realize that she was not contradicting him.

"Renting a carriage," he said in disgust. "They probably paraded through Albuquerque just to show everyone before they drove out here."

"We should be flattered, Francisco."

Don Francisco sighed. Actually it was more of a groan than a sigh. "Pretentious. What the hell difference does it make whether they come in a carriage or on a mule? Everyone knows what they have. There are few secrets in a place like this. The important thing is: What do we want for Andrea?"

"What does Andrea want for herself?"

"No! What do we want for Andrea!"

A knock at the front door echoed through the hall and into the sala. A murmur of voices. Then the maid peeked through the door as Don Francisco and Doña Estela rose to greet their visitors.

"Señor y Señora Griego. Welcome. Our house is your house."

The tall, skinny Señor Griego and his short, dumpy wife settled onto the guest chairs in all their Sunday splendor. Even his boots were free of manure, Don Francisco noticed. And the señora's hair was pulled back and held firmly in place with large combs, rather than hanging over her face.

"You are most gracious to receive us," Señor Griego began. "May the blessings of the Lord be on you and your house." Quietly, furtively, his wife glanced around the room. "We are here," Señor Griego continued, "about a matter of urgent importance." Polite nods all around. "About the future of our families." More nods. Smiles.

The maid entered and stood silent a short distance from Doña Estela, waiting to be acknowledged. Señora Griego put a hand on her husband's arm and he looked up, surprised to see the maid, and ceased talking.

"Would you like a cup of chocolate?" Doña Estela asked. "Our son brought us a delicious new kind from Durango."

Yes, the Griegos nodded politely, although the pucker on Señor Griego's mouth seemed to say "vino" rather than chocolate. The maid left the room quickly, returning with the steaming cups and a dish of biscochitos.

"Tell me," Señora Griego said, biting daintily into a corner of a cookie. "We have not seen much of Father José Antonio since he returned from Durango, although like good Catholics we are at church every Sunday. Where does Father Gallegos keep him?"

Where indeed? Don Francisco thought, but it was Doña Estela who responded. "Father Gallegos is getting older. Now he has a young priest who can ride out to the placitas and the little villages that have not seen a priest for years. No criticism intended, but old men need the help of young men to do their work." Don Francisco stared uncomfortably as his wife continued. "Not all the faithful can be here neatly in a villa with the priest just a few miles distant and available every day."

"What a blessing for a mother to have a priest for a son. A blessing." Señora Griego crossed herself solemnly.

Señor Griego nodded, his farmer-rough hands clinging to the cup with awkward unfamiliarity. "Tell me. How did Father José Antonio find Mexico?"

"My son seldom volunteers information. A priest's life is one of prayer and contemplation. One of service. But when badgered by our Andrea—" Ah, yes, Andrea. There were smiles all around. "—he will tell us stories. Of things to do, people to see in the great cities to the south. It makes us feel so isolated here. So far away from everything. The ships come into Vera Cruz from Europe. Other ships come into Mazatlán or Acapulco from the Far East. The treasures of the world find their way into Mexico of which we see but precious little."

"Has he been to Mexico City?"

"¡Cómo no! Of course. To the cathedral. Also to the very church founded for the Virgin herself, our Virgin of Guadalupe."

Señor Griego balanced his cup on his knee. "There is no city in the western hemisphere like our Mexico City. Not even in los Estados Unidos. New York. Philadelphia. St. Louis. They are nothing compared to Mexico City. Squalid little towns full of arrogant, pushy gringos."

"Now, Papá," Señora Griego said. "You'll spoil our surprise."

Don Francisco came alert. Surprise? What surprise? Weren't they here to ask for the hand of his daughter Andrea in marriage to their son Francisco? He straightened in his chair and glanced from his wife to Señora Griego who sat chagrined, realizing that she had been the fox who had chased the hen from the coop. Doña Estela stirred uncomfortably, too polite to ask the obvious question, while Señor Griego gulped the last of his chocolate and looked up to see all eyes on him.

"I'll tell them now," he said to his wife. He paused dramatically for a moment, then looked Don Francisco in the eye. "We are going to Mexico," he said. "We are selling out to Don Manuel and moving south to our home country."

The consternation! The oohs and ahs! The effect was as dramatic as Señor Griego could have wished in his wildest dreams. To Mexico, Don Francisco thought. My little baby. My little Andrea to Mexico. You're crazy, he thought, looking at Señor Griego, but his mouth kept still.

"What a shock." Doña Estela fanned herself with her hand.

"We are not the only ones." Señor Griego nodded firmly, as if he knew great secrets. "There are other families up and down the Río Grande. We did not come here to fight Indians and fight nature so that we could turn it all over to the gringos. We do not need gringuismo in this land of ours. So for us the best thing is to sell what we have and move south. I'm negotiating for property in Chihuahua."

"But there is a war raging down there," Don Francisco said. "Here the war is over."

"Yes. Here we lost. But down south the glorious Mexican army will repel the Yankee dogs."

Don Francisco did not say what he thought. If the Mexican forces had lost so easily here in New Mexico, what was to change them into victorious defenders of the homeland south of here?

"Does that mean your entire family will go with you?" Doña Estela asked. Even Francisco? she thought. And any bride he might take?

Señora Griego deferred to her husband who nodded solemnly.

"Of course. In my family my word is still law. All of them will go. Even grown sons and daughters with their wives, husbands, and children."

"Now, Papá." Señora Griego touched his arm as if to soften his words.

"All of them!" he answered with a trace of pique.

"That is indeed a surprise," Don Francisco said. "You say there are other families moving south?"

"More than you realize. There are many who think Yankee ways are not for them." Señor Griego paused a moment and looked at his wife as if for some secret signal. Then he continued. "We wanted you to know this before we spoke to you about the real reason, the important reason we are here."

Yes, yes, Don Francisco thought impatiently. Let us get on with it. While the women smiled to each other confidentially.

Señor Griego continued. "It is a matter of the gravest importance to the future of our families. We have come to ask for the hand of your beautiful daughter Andrea to be given in marriage to our son Francisco. It would please Francisco beyond measure to be welcomed into your family as a son-in-law, Don Francisco, Doña Estela."

There would have been a time only yesterday when Don Francisco would have said yes immediately. But now he asked, "When do you move south to Mexico?"

"In the spring."

"You do us great honor, Señor y Señora Griego. We have long been aware of your handsome son. He is a brave, God-fearing young man who would do honor to any father. But there is much to consider. Marriage is not only a sacrament of God, it is a bond, a commitment for life. Too serious an undertaking, as you well know, to be left to young people alone. You and your son do this house great honor. I am only sorry that we cannot answer now. There is much to consider. The future lives of two young people. A new life for Andrea in Mexico. Andrea, who has been the comfort of my old age. We hope you understand when we ask for a short time to consider. It is, as you say, a most important matter."

"There is no hurry, Don Francisco. As you say, these young people have their whole lives before them. We are here but to seek, in the humblest way, a word from you when it is appropriate. When one does not speak his intentions, others may mistakenly seek the same prize."

Don Francisco grunted. What the hell did he mean by that? Others may mistakenly seek the same prize. "When the word comes, it will be as sacred as God's honor."

"We but await your pleasure."

Doña Estela clapped her hands and the maid appeared in the doorway, carrying a heavy pitcher from which she refilled the empty cups.

The talk drifted now to lesser things. Although Don Francisco would comment on the merits of a certain horse or the succulence of so-and-so's melons, a nagging concern worked at him. The words, "others may mistakenly seek," whispered themselves to him and he stared intently at Señor Griego thinking that if he only watched closely enough, he might see the meaning in his guest's eyes.

Then Don Francisco thought: Renting a carriage indeed! And now leaving their home to move south. They want their skinny little son to marry our beautiful Andrea and take her away. Ridiculous. Then again the words: "others may mistakenly seek." ¡Demonio! Why was life so difficult?

18

The brisk autumn air chilled into winter. It was December already and the anticipation of Christmas softened the shock that had come with the invasion just a few months past. There would be snow in the mountains and ice in the river. With the harvest long over, it was time to be indoors beside a warm fire, roasting piñon nuts or dozing in dreams of glory and history.

Few cared where ex-Governor Armijo was now, and as for what he had taken with him—it was too late to worry about that. Most of his followers had fled New Mexico or had melted inconspicuously into the general populace.

There was a new government in Santa Fe. The Yankee trader, Charles Bent, was governor—a man who knew New Mexico and its people. Hadn't he married into a prominent New Mexican family? The native New Mexicans were represented by one of their own. Don Donaciano Vigil, who had been lieutenant governor under Armijo, was now secretary under the Yankees.

The first burst of enthusiasm for the Yankees had dissipated. Life returned to its old patterns. In the mountains in the north quiet rumors began to circulate. Rumors that the war was not truly over. Rumors that rebellion was brewing.

Yet, even with the coming of Christmas, Don Francisco's anxieties did not lessen. First there was the matter of his daughter. Although he had not yet responded to the Griegos' offer of marriage, he knew that the matter was settled. No! Andrea would not marry in order to leave New Mexico with the Griegos. The fact that Andrea did not want to marry young Griego was incidental. It had nothing to do with Don Francisco's decision.

However, that visit had opened his eyes where they had been closed before. Suddenly he became aware of Miguel Dalton in a new way. Heretofore the young man had been a wanderer, infirm, someone his son, José Antonio, had brought home as an act of Christian charity. Then, as the young man grew in strength and health, he began to help on the rancho. It was the act of a man repaying kindnesses of the past.

There had been talk, Don Francisco remembered. Not about this young man and Andrea. There had never been a breath of comment about them. But about the man himself.

How was it, someone had asked, that there was an Anglo staying with the Rafas when we were enemies of the Yankees? Where did he come from? Was he a spy?

Then the curious would come by in the hope of seeing this stranger with dark hair and sunburnt skin and, it was rumored, piercing eyes. Azul. The color of the sky. Or a mountain lake.

But with the excitement of the Yankee invasion and its aftermath, curiosity about the young Miguel receded. Oh, the Anglo over at the Rafas? A trader. Lost. Robbed by Apaches. Found wandering in the desert. Lucky to be alive. Carlos Rafa has gone north so the Anglo helps with the work now. The Rafas are fortunate to have a strong young patrón.

And there would be the young girls, Don Francisco remembered. Suddenly there seemed to be numerous reasons why Andrea should be visited. He would see them hidden from sight, staring into the patio from one of the windows, their whispered giggles giving them away. He learned to expect them when Miguel worked at the house.

166

Yet through it all, he never thought of Andrea in connection with Miguel until now. When he looked at them he could not help but come to the inescapable conclusion that they were in love. They did not even have to look at each other or to speak. It was in the air. Like the pull of sun and moon.

A pauper, Don Francisco thought. A foreigner. What kind of a prospective husband was that? And where did he come from? From what kind of a family? As if dropped from the sky into the desert, claiming Ireland as his homeland.

They will be the death of me, Don Francisco thought. Children nowadays give their parents no rest.

"Yes. It's definite. I have to leave." Miguel sat uncomfortably in Father José Antonio's room at San Felipe church.

"You don't feel welcome at the rancho? Have we not been hospitable to you?"

"If anything I have felt too welcome. Almost as if I belong there."

"Then what is the problem?"

Miguel looked earnestly at Tercero. Could he tell him? And if so, in what way? As a parishioner asking advice of his priest? As friend to friend? As an outsider talking to a member of the family? As a sinner to his confessor?

"I have been with your family six months now. I owe you a debt I can never repay. I owe you my life." Tercero sat impassively and his solemn stare made Miguel uncomfortable. His voice rose angrily. "I'm well now! I don't have to be looked after any more!"

"Yes. Of course."

"So I have to go! Don't you see that? I really have to go!"

"No one will stop you."

"Damn it! You don't understand." The words collapsed into stark silence. Self-consciously Miguel looked away from Tercero. "I'm sorry," he said. "I didn't mean to get angry. It's just that you don't understand."

"Then tell me."

"I—I can't."

Tercero shrugged. "Then don't tell me."

"I can't!"

"Then I'll have to find one of those village brujas to mix up a magic potion so I can read your mind."

167

He is smiling, damn it! Miguel thought. He is making fun of what is a very serious matter. A matter of life or death. "It is very awkward," Miguel said.

"About Andrea?" Miguel's mouth fell open. "She spoke to me," Tercero said.

Miguel could feel his face flush a deep red. "Then you know why I have to leave. It's impossible."

"You mean my father?"

"Yes. No. There is Francisco Griego, too. I—I don't know what to do."

"Andrea has not been promised to Francisco."

"How do you know? Andrea herself does not know that."

"Because I know my father. If he had agreed, he would have done so immediately. He does not want his daughter to marry and leave this country forever."

"Are you sure?"

"Ah." Tercero's arms went out, then dropped resignedly to his sides. "Who can be sure of anything? Only God. But I am as sure as I can be."

"Then there is still hope?"

"There is always hope."

"Oh, don't talk in your priestly philosophical riddles. You sound like my older brother. What I want to know is would your father accept me as a son-in-law?"

"What if he didn't?"

"Damn! There you go again. I ask a simple question and instead of yes or no I get another question. Would your father accept me?"

"There is an old Spanish law. Going back—oh, I don't know—probably to the Middle Ages. Since parents do not always agree with their children about marriage, the Church in its wisdom provided a way out. The prospective groom makes formal complaint to the highest authority of the church in the presence of witnesses. Then the future bride can take sanctuary in a neutral home until she is certain she wants to go against her parents' wishes. If she insists, the marriage has to take place. It is rash and dangerous to go against family wishes and the law is rarely invoked since it has on occasion led to bloodshed. But it has the sanction of the Church when all else has failed."

"You mean marry against Don Francisco's wishes?" Tercero

168

did not answer. Miguel shook his head solemnly. "I could not do that. Your father has been my benefactor. I could not betray him like that."

"There is also the story in the Bible about Jacob. He worked for Laban for seven years so that he could marry Laban's daughter, Rachel."

"Yes," Miguel said. "But Laban did not give permission after those seven years. Jacob had to work another seven."

"Because Rachel's older sister was still unmarried. Andrea's older sisters *are* married."

"But Laban had already made an agreement with Jacob."

"So you should ask Don Francisco."

Miguel shivered. He did not know what would frighten him more: asking Don Francisco for Andrea's hand in marriage or running away with her. He had fought in the war and faced the enemy—both sides. But there was something about the imperious Don Francisco that frightened him even more than battle. Was it that this man and his offspring were truly superior to him, a son of Irish peasant farmers? In a way it was as if he courted the daughter of the lord of the manor.

Tercero continued. "What good would it do you to leave? You have no horse or burro. You could not go far on foot. Soon you would be no better off than when you were found wandering in the desert."

"I could work. I could be a trader. Be a go-between for the local people and the Americans who will undoubtedly be coming. I could earn enough to set up shop. Earn enough that I could go to Don Francisco and ask for Andrea as a proper suitor, not as a beggar."

"What does Andrea say?"

Could he tell him? Should he? Run away, Andrea had said. Now. Hurry. How can we wait for your fortune? What if it never comes? I can't wait ten years for you to become rich.

"You know Andrea better than I." But it pained Miguel to admit that. How could anyone know his love better than he? No. It was not true. The heart could know in an instant what might otherwise take years.

"She would say: 'Ask Papá. If he says no, we'll run away.' "

Miguel flushed. The unerring truth made him squirm in discomfort. As if the young priest could look deep inside him and see everything. "I must speak to you as a friend," Tercero went on. "Not as a priest or a potential brother-in-law. Follow your heart and you will find the way. Whatever you do, I am with you."

Tears came to Miguel's eyes. It was as if his own brother had spoken to him. Once again, as during the past six months, he felt as if he were an intimate part of the family. As if destiny had intended him to be a Rafa.

"I could ask no more." He clasped Tercero's shoulders and returned his smile.

Doña Estela sat quietly in her little chapel. She had prayed to the Virgin and all that she could do now was wait for the prayers to be answered.

Don Francisco knows, she thought. I have seen it on his face and in his eyes. He had barely noticed Miguel before and now he watches the young man like a wary hunter studying a dangerous beast. And he watches Andrea as if guarding some mythical treasure.

Ah, these men, Doña Estela thought, glancing from the little wooden statue of the Virgin to the wooden crucifix in all its painful, gory realism. They think love can be kept away by close watching, like a high wall built to barricade against marauding Indians. But love is not flesh. It is spirit that no wall can keep out.

She heard the swift swirl of skirts, the soft patter of bare feet, then felt a weight ease onto the bench beside her. Andrea crossed herself and waited quietly to be recognized.

What now? Doña Estela thought. She began another Ave to keep her mind from agitation over why her daughter was here in what she considered her one sanctuary in the house. She ignored the soft cough and clearing of throat.

"Mother."

Doña Estela ignored the whisper too. "Hail Mary, full of grace," her silent lips mouthed. "The Lord is with thee. Blessed art thou amongst women and blessed is the fruit of thy womb, Jesus. Holy Mary—"

"Mother!"

She turned. A dark scowl on her face. "Shhh!"

"Mother. I have to talk to you. It's a matter of life or death."

"I will be finished in a moment. Now shush."

170

Holy Mary, Doña Estela thought. Holy Mary and all the saints in heaven. What now?

She finished her Ave. Added one more for good measure. Then crossed herself and rose. Andrea followed her out into the patio.

"He's going to leave," Andrea said. "You have to stop him or I'll die."

"Oh. So serious is it?"

"Mother. Do not make fun of me. It is serious. Deadly serious. Miguel wants to go out and seek his fortune. He wants to leave the rancho."

"It's up to him. He is free to do as he pleases."

"You don't understand. I—I love him. He loves me. I want to marry him."

Then most certainly he'll need a fortune, Doña Estela thought to herself.

For a moment she did not know what to say to her daughter. This admission was something she had dreaded but expected. But what to do about it? "So serious is it?" she finally said.

"You'll have to help me, Mother, or I'll die."

"You know the way things are done. The customs."

"Customs al demonio! I don't care about customs! Silly, stupid old rules that no one knows the reason for. It's just habit, like scratching fleas."

"Andrea!" Doña Estela was shocked, her voice angry and threatening. "I won't have any of that ugly talk. Wisdom is passed on down through the generations. If we do not see the value of it, that is our own blindness, not the fault of wise words. To a fool, all wisdom is stupidity. There are ways things are done because those who have come before us have learned best. Now, I'll have no more of your blasphemies."

Andrea's face had turned pale, then her mouth had twisted out of shape, fighting back the tears. "Nobody cares," she wailed. "It doesn't matter whether I live or die. Whether I'm miserable or happy. Oh, Mamá. What am I going to do?"

Doña Estela's anger died as quickly as it had flared up. Tears were more in her domain and her heart went out to her daughter. She took Andrea in her arms. "Pobrecita. So bad is it?"

"Oh, Mamá. I really love him."

"Yes. I can see. What do you think we should do?"

Tears still streaked Andrea's face, although her crying stopped, and youthful hope, ever present, had come quickly out of hiding. "Talk to him," she said. "Tell him he does not have to go."

"I could talk to your father on behalf of you and your young man. It would have to be in the right way at the right time. You know how your father is."

A smile burst free from Andrea's despair. Doña Estela smiled back and kissed the tear-stained cheek.

"Oh, Mamá. I knew you would help. Now everything will be all right."

Andrea squeezed her mother tight, kissed her on the cheek, and rushed through the patio into the house. Doña Estela stood, watching her skip away as if the world had now been set aright. Ay, Dios, she thought, giving a quick glance up at the sky. If only life were really that easy.

A head peered around the edge of the kitchen door. Had one of the servants been listening all the time? "You! Over there! Back into the kitchen! Your business is preparing the food, not what is happening in the patio."

Doña Estela stalked angrily toward the kitchen, a fist already closed ready to cuff that nosy, lazy Indian girl.

19

"Patrón!" One of the workers came running from the field toward the house. He stood outside waiting while one of the servants went for Don Francisco.

"There were two men looking for you, Don Francisco. One of them was a Yankee. I sent them the other way. Toward Los Griegos." Pedro smiled expecting that the patrón would be pleased.

"What did they want?"

"I do not know, Patrón. But I did not like the looks of it."

"Is that all?"

"The Yankee's name was Señor Hammond. The other man I did not know. I think he said something about Santa Fe."

"Gracias, Pedro."

Don Francisco watched him hurry from the house back toward the field. Two strangers, he thought. Well. It means nothing to me.

He returned to his office. The rude wooden table was covered with papers that he shuffled and sorted into stacks. Yes, he thought, going through one of the piles. Here is what is owed me.

After looking at the top slip, he removed it from the pile and placed it face down on the table, jotting down a note on a clean sheet of paper.

"Tomás Rivera. Two fanegas of corn."

"Manuel García. Two ristras of chile."

"Widow Roybal. One goat."

After a while all of the slips were face down and he looked over the entries and placed the summary sheet on the same pile.

"Now," he said to himself. "What do I owe to others?"

This second pile was not so high, but the entries were for greater amounts. He looked at one and shook his head in agitation.

"San Felipe Church. Funds owed by Father José Antonio Rafa. Two hundred pesos."

"¡Chingada!" Don Francisco muttered. It wasn't enough that he had his own debts to worry about. There were the debts of his children. A grown son. A priest at that. Who was in debt to his church.

"Don't pay!" Tercero had said angrily when Don Francisco had confronted him with the note from Father Gallegos. "It's an outright fraud!"

Don Francisco had been furious. However, there was no focus to his anger. If it had been Carlos, he would have felt that his son was lying. But not Tercero. He could believe Tercero, so his anger was not at him. Yet his anger was not directed at Father Gallegos either. He was an old friend. But then there was that note: *"San Felipe Church. Funds owed by Father José Antonio Rafa. Two hundred pesos."*

Don Francisco had shaken the note in his son's face. Angrier now because he did not know whom he should be angry at. "What about this?" he shouted at Tercero. "What the hell is this?" Over his son's shoulder he could see a face peer anxiously through the open crack in the doorway, then the door closed shut.

"That old moneygrabber," Tercero spat.

"It is your debt. You are a grown man. Old enough to take care of your own debts."

"I know that." Tercero grabbed the note and quickly read it. Then he crumbled it and threw it into the unlit fireplace. He stood quietly, trying to calm his breathing, and after a moment the anger drained from his eyes. "It is my problem, Father," he finally said. "I'm sorry that Father Gallegos sent you that note. It is no debt of yours."

"What is it? Do you need money?"

"No, señor. You know that when I took holy orders I renounced material things. I even gave up my inheritance and I know what an important thing that is to you and the family. To our tradition. So, no. I do not need money. It is something else. A disagreement between Father Gallegos and me about fees from the poor."

"But he is your superior." What was this madness? Don Francisco thought. Where sons talk back to fathers. Where some sons talk rebellion against their government. While other sons rebel against their priests and their church. The world was going mad. Where was tradition? Obedience?

Tercero sighed and shook his head. "I will tell you, Father. I do not mean to trouble you nor to bring shame to you and the family. It is as I said—a disagreement between Father Gallegos and me. A matter, in my opinion, of serving God instead of man."

So Tercero told him about the disagreement. Don Francisco listened. Yes, he thought, hearing Tercero's impassioned words. There are the poor peons, the half-breeds, the genízaros, the Indians in their pueblos—throughout New Mexico. But then there is the Church. What if everyone who wanted the sacrament of marriage, or a baby christened, or a loved one buried—what if they all wanted these things done for free? Where would religion be? There would be no money for a church, much less the schools that the good padres ran. There would be no vineyards with the succulent grapes that made such wonderful wine. What about the missions? How could they afford the missions that brought the word of God to the heathen Indians? It all cost money. Nothing was for free, damn it! The Church needed those fees.

It was as if Tercero had read his mind. "So what do we do about the poor, Father? We can let them live and die in sin, or we can give."

"For the most part they are lazy liars and thieves," Don Francisco said. "If their God is important enough to them, they will find the money somewhere. Give up something else so they can pay their priest."

"Like food?"

"Damn it! No! Why do you vex me so?"

"Throughout New Mexico there are many who live in sin because they are too poor to pay the marriage fees. So I marry them for no fee. Their children live unbaptized, ready to plunge into limbo the instant that they die. I baptize them for no fee. If they're dying, I give them the last rites. For no fee. Now Father Gallegos sends you a bill for the fees that were never collected. He acts as if I were a thief, while in truth it is he who is stealing food from the mouths of the poor or taking the burro that they need to earn a living. There are enough New Mexicans who can afford to give to the Church without the Church taking from the poor."

Not quite enough, Don Francisco had thought. But all he could say was, "He is your superior. It is for him to decide what is best."

"It is not your problem, Father. I will settle it with Father Gallegos." Tercero fished the crumpled paper from the fireplace and straightened it. "I don't want you to worry about my problem."

That had been the end of the discussion. Now, working over the bills, Don Francisco looked at the second note from San Felipe Church. The matter had not been settled. Tercero had said it was his problem. But his sons' problems were also his own. There was no way to separate them. Blood was the strongest tie of all. With a sigh, he placed the note on the table and looked at the next bill.

"Don Francisco." The whispered, subservient tone annoyed him more than a shout would have.

He looked up from the last of his pile of bills in irritation. "Yes. What is it?"

The servant girl's voice dropped even lower. "There are two strangers to see you, Don Francisco. Señor García and Señor Hammond." Then her face broke into a wide-eyed look of curiosity. "One of them is a Yankee."

Two strangers. Were these the men that Pedro had sent off

this morning? What did they want with him? And one a Yankee.

"Show them into the sala," he said. "I will join them in a moment."

He finished his work, making a mental note to speak to Father Gallegos. Then he looked at the bills owed to him, selecting two in particular. Overdue notes from the Mexican government for loans made by Don Francisco to the general treasury of New Mexico. Worthless paper, even when Mexico had owned this country. Even more worthless now that they had been conquered by the United States. But his frustration and anger were spent and he merely placed them back on the pile and sighed.

Before he left the room, Don Francisco stepped thoughtfully to the one tall window that looked out onto the orchard where the barren trees showed no promise of what spring would bring. He felt like those trees. Leafless. Fruitless. With a long winter ahead before hope for something better. What will become of us all? he thought. Silently he crossed himself before he went into the sala.

The two men stood close together with their backs to the door, speaking in undertones, when Don Francisco entered.

"Gentlemen," Don Francisco said. "What can I do for you?"

"Don Francisco Rafa?" The Yankee spoke Spanish slowly and with a flat, harsh accent. "My name is William Hammond. This is Señor Tomás García." Don Francisco bowed stiffly to each. "I hope we are not intruding, Don Francisco."

But you are, Don Francisco thought. And you really do not care. "Not at all," he said politely.

Hammond smiled. "Are you related, Don Francisco, to one Carlos Rafa, recently of the New Mexico militia?"

Don Francisco's eyes narrowed and his heart skipped a beat. Quietly he looked from one visitor to the other. Señor García smiled. Were these men from the law?

"He is my son," Don Francisco answered.

"Then I have some possibly unpleasant news," Hammond said. He reached into his jacket pocket and extracted a paper.

The scrawled words meant nothing to Don Francisco. Only the familiar signature at the bottom: Carlos Rafa. He handed the paper back to Hammond. "I do not read English, señor."

"It is a debt," García said in his mellifluous Spanish. "A gambling debt that your son owes to Señor Hammond."

176

"Do you know where he is?" Hammond asked.

"Up north. Santa Fe."

The two strangers looked at each other. "We have just come from there. I think that if he had been in Santa Fe, we would have found him."

"Then I don't know, señores. He is not here."

"He lives here?"

"Sí, señor. This is his home. But he is not here now."

Tomás García took the paper from Hammond and moved alongside Don Francisco. "I am here with Señor Hammond," he said, "to represent him in any legal matters involved. We want to be certain that there is no misunderstanding about what could be a difficult matter. This paper, Don Francisco, turns over to Señor Hammond in payment for a gambling debt certain lands in Albuquerque belonging to Carlos Rafa. It is all legal and properly drawn."

For an instant Don Francisco could not see. His eyes were open but nothing came through. He felt dizzy, almost as if he were going to topple over. Certain lands? His lands! That one piece that was in Carlos' name, that piece that had been a wedding gift, was still part of the family's property. It was not to be sold, given away, or lost in a game of cards. Where was that desgraciado? That insufferable son of his?

"All I have is the word of two men I have never seen before," he said angrily. "With a paper in a language that I cannot read. My son is up north, not here where he can speak for himself."

"Your son owes me a considerable amount of money," Hammond said stiffly. "I don't want his land. I prefer cash."

Cash! Always cash. Always a hand out for a loan or for payment of a debt. It was as if some devouring monster was gobbling everything he had. What he had worked a lifetime for. What his father had left him. And his father's father before.

"Señores. What can I say? I am not responsible for my son's debts. I am not aware of any debts. As I said before, you come to me strangers with a paper in a language I cannot read. I do not see how I can be of help to you."

The two men spoke in the Yankee tongue, but Don Francisco caught only a few familiar words here and there. Words he had heard from that lovesick swain, Miguel.

"Gentlemen." The two stopped speaking. "I will just be a

moment." Then quickly he left the sala and sent a servant to bring Miguel Dalton. "Señor Hammond. Señor García. This is our honored guest, Señor Dalton."

There was an uneasy shift in the atmosphere. An invisible shift to a certain wariness by the strangers. "I understand," Miguel said in English, "that you have some sort of legal document."

Don Francisco reached toward the paper and Hammond gave it to him. Miguel took it and read it aloud slowly in Spanish.

"Dated June 7, 1846. I, Carlos Rafa, acknowledge a debt to William Hammond, citizen of the United States of America, in the total of 1,000 pesos. If by one year, on June 7, 1847, said debt has not been paid, I promise to turn over to William Hammond a parcel of land bordering the Río Grande River just north of the villa of Albuquerque. Said land is duly registered in my name with the Mexican government. Signed: Carlos Rafa."

"This is December," Don Francisco said. "There are six more months until June."

"I don't want land. I want cash. I am thinking of going into business here in Albuquerque."

"One thousand pesos. That is one thousand sheep. A lot of money in a land that has little. Besides—Carlos is not here."

"I have heard, Don Francisco, that you are a man of honor." The red-faced Yankee nodded at his host. "I too am an honorable man and only want what is due me."

"Then you must find Carlos for I know nothing about this debt."

"Find Carlos," Hammond echoed.

"Sí, señor."

Hammond and García nodded to each other and said their goodbyes. As he watched them leave the rancho, Don Francisco felt drained. The signature at the bottom of that Yankee note was certainly that of his son. In six months, he thought. In six months that piece of land will go because Carlos cannot raise one thousand pesos. In six months the rancho will start to go. First one piece. Then, who knows—

"Can I be of further help, Don Francisco?"

In surprise, he realized that Miguel was still in the room. "Have José Antonio come see me," he said in a tired voice. "He must find Carlos."

20

In just those few days before Christmas a great change had come over Don Francisco. Tercero could see it. It was as if the fire had gone out of him, leaving a tired, listless façade with cold, dead ashes inside. "Find Carlos," he had said. It had been more a plea than the imperious command of old.

Now Tercero brought his horse to a halt and turned for a last look south toward Los Rafas. It was windy and a light snow obscured the view. The snow had let up in the short time since they had left the rancho and he felt certain that soon it would stop altogether. But the wind was still bone-piercing.

"What's the matter? Are you all right?"

Tercero turned in his saddle. Miguel was riding toward him leading the pack horse. "I'm just taking a last look," he said.

"Do you think we should go on?"

"Of course. If it keeps up we can stop at any of the ranchos along the way."

"The river is frozen."

"We will be too if we don't move on."

Pulling their hats down over their eyes, they hunched over the horses and turned north toward Santa Fe.

"I will have to ask permission of Father Gallegos," Tercero had said to his father when the subject of Carlos came up. "I have my churches to take care of. My flock to help. I do not know what my superior would say if I asked for time to hunt for my brother."

Instead of growing angry and shouting red-faced that he had to do what his father commanded, Don Francisco had sat silent and looked off in the distance through the window.

"I have promised to pay your debt," Don Francisco finally said, as if that settled the matter.

Tercero turned away so his father could not see his angry face. He tried to control his voice. "There was no need to do that. That is for me to settle with Father Gallegos."

"I do not want to be estranged from my church." For a moment Tercero swore that his father was ready to pull out a rosary and pray his beads like the little old ladies who spent more time in church than in the kitchen.

"I will ask my superior," Tercero said. "There may be business he would have me do in Santa Fe. Then I could serve you both."

Don Francisco had nodded solemnly. Tercero left him sitting and staring and went to say good-bye to his mother.

"He is not well," Tercero said to Doña Estela.

She glanced cautiously about to make certain none of the servants was listening. "I have heard them whispering," she said, "that someone has put a spell on him. That an evil witch flies over this house to keep the sun from warming it."

"Oh, Mother. That's nonsense. Just more of the silly superstitions of the poor, ignorant peons around here. There are no such things as witches."

"I know that. I was just telling you what they are saying." But she cautiously crossed herself as she spoke. Tercero shook his head, thinking how easy it was to shift from a belief in the Virgin Mary to a belief in witches and the evil eye.

"He is getting old," Tercero said. "Sometimes it happens like that. One day a person wakes up and all of a sudden he is old. He shows his age."

"He worries too much. About his children. About the rancho. About debts."

It's sad to see him grow old, Tercero thought. But he did not want to say it aloud. He knew what would happen. His mother would go to one of the many mirrors hanging on the walls and study herself with tears in her eyes.

"He shouldn't worry," Tercero said instead. "Except for Andrea, all of his children are old enough to take care of themselves. And she will be on her way soon enough." Doña Estela smiled sadly and kissed him on the cheek. "He is a nice young man," he said, referring to Miguel. Then he left.

Up ahead the snow was dissipating and the air was clear. A shout from Miguel woke him from his reverie. "Ireland was never like this!"

"Neither was hell!"

They both laughed and continued on their way. The trail from Albuquerque to Santa Fe was an old and well-traveled one. It paralleled the Río Grande until north of Bernalillo, then turned gently east and north away from the river. It climbed from the desert altitudes to a height of seven thousand feet.

Along the river, like beads on a rosary, were strung the successive cities of the Pueblo Indians—Sandía, San Felipe, Santo

Domingo, Cochiti—with their adobe houses, earth-insulated and no doubt cozy and warm in the winter's blast. It was among these pueblos and others like them that Tercero's Franciscan predecessors had brought God's word to the heathen Indians. It was among these pueblos that priests still labored to keep the word of God alive and hold back the persistent and pernicious tenacity of paganism.

Small villages and occasional ranchos also dotted the sixty-mile trail to Santa Fe. There too the adobe houses were warmed by fires whose smoke sent greetings to distant travelers, letting them know that there was warmth and hospitality long before they arrived.

"Hurry," a traveler would say. "There's a place up ahead where there'll be a plate of frijoles and a hot tortilla. Maybe a spicy chili or two. Or even a cup of hot atole. And someone to give us the news."

He had traveled the way often enough, Tercero thought. In all seasons. In all kinds of weather. In the summer with the hot desert wind blowing like a thousand devils and dust so thick one could hardly see, much less breathe. In the lovely spring or early fall, when the sharp edge of summer heat had broken and the cold knife of winter had not yet come. When, it seemed, God walked the earth on clear and sunny days with just the right crisp edge to the air to make one feel exuberantly alive. Where one could see for miles in any direction and feel a small but significant part of God's earth. These would be days that made one's soul cry out with joy at the beauty of the earth and all its creatures.

Meanwhile, the cold wind continued unabated. Miguel's horse slowed and Tercero looked back. "My boots are frozen to my stirrups," Miguel said. "I'm going to walk for awhile if I can get off this horse."

"There should be a little settlement not too far ahead. I think we should stop to rest the horses and warm ourselves."

Tercero dismounted and joined Miguel. Yes, he remembered as he walked along. Perhaps just a mile or two ahead. A cluster of houses. What had once been a large rancho that had gone into decline. Only the descendants of those who had herded the sheep and worked the fields still lived there. The ricos had disappeared—only their name remained as the name of the place and of a few illegitimate descendants of the coupling of the old aristocracy with Indian servants or poor laboring girls.

"I see smoke!" Miguel shouted. Eagerly they mounted and hurried toward the village.

21

Carlos Rafa sat alone in the little room built onto the corral some distance from the main rancho. He was alone by choice. Tired of the endless talk—what had been whispered talk in Santa Fe and had degenerated to drunken talk here.

"Fight!" he whispered to himself. There had been talk enough. The time for that had passed. It was time to fight.

He rose and opened the door a crack. It was snowing. Large, fluffy flakes drifted slowly downward. Soon the ground would be white, the trees bearded, sound muffled so that the earth would be suspended in a white silence.

Christmas had come and gone almost three weeks ago. It had not been much of a Christmas. He closed the door pensively, thinking of all the Christmases at Los Rafas, and a sadness came over him. He felt very alone. Now with the snow falling and the silence descending it was as if he were the only person in the world. No one to hold him. No one to keep him warm. No one to kiss his pains.

They would have gone to mass in Los Rafas. No doubt his brother would have helped at services. Carlos could see the rapture on his mother's face. Oh, holy night. The birth of our Lord and Savior. It was almost as if he were at mass himself. The candles lit, flickering, throwing shadows along the church walls. When he was a boy, he remembered that most of all. Christmas mass at midnight. The blazing candles projecting a moving panorama on the wall, and his boyish fears and wonder at the changing shapes. There a buffalo head. Or angel wings. A dark, sinister figure leering straight at him. At him!

"Turn to the front, Carlito. Say your prayers."

His mother's whispered voice was insistent, while his fearful eyes turned sideways to see what ghosts were gathering in the shadows to come for him.

Then the singers would enter. Cold. Stamping their feet and rubbing their hands. Some—most—had made their trek in the cold, singing as they walked from house to house, asking in their song for a room for the night. A room for the mother with child and her carpenter husband.

Well, Carlos thought. He had his room. Not a stable but a corral. The same thing. Although he could go to the rancho with the others. Some were off on missions, spreading the word to the villages and pueblos that would join them. Making ready, once and for all, to drive the gringos from their New Mexico.

Those that stayed behind took their courage from a bottle. Well. Some did not need aguardiente to move them to action. The presence of the enemy was enough. Their patriotism was enough. He would not call the drinkers cowards. After all, they were his friends and comrades-in-arms. But he would trade a dozen of them for one more like Don Tomás Ortiz.

Yes. Who but Don Tomás would have saved them in Santa Fe like that? And that traitress who had tried to give them away to the Yankees. That goddamned traitress. He had turned and taken in the features of her face. He would know that face in hell. Some-day— When the time came. That woman. Others. Out to a grove of trees. They would be strung out, one per limb, like dried strings of chili hung on the vigas outside adobe walls.

Once again he opened the door and watched the snow fall. His whole body shivered, even after he closed the door and drew nearer to the fire. Then his teeth began to chatter and he felt that even if he stepped into the flames he would not be warm enough. Maybe a little aguardiente would help, he thought. Not enough to get drunk. Just a nip.

Yes, he thought. Santa Fe. They had lost there. The strong-hold of the gringo army and government. But that was only one villa. There were others. Many others. Here in Río Arriba, here in the mountains, they were all united. Ready to take up weapons at a moment's notice.

But Santa Fe. Carlos still did not understand what had hap-pened in Santa Fe. Traitors. There was no doubt about that. But who? It would have to be one of their own. A New Mexican. But who? One of the conspirators? Certainly not, he thought. There was not one—not one of the inner council whom he would not trust with his life. They were patriots all.

Then someone from their families. A wife. Or a servant. He

thought quietly of the ones he knew. Their faces conjured up from memory as he slowly searched each one for signs of treason. There were some—more than a few—whose images looked away uneasily. They were capable of informing. Wives who no longer loved their husbands. Servants who secretly envied their masters and would gladly see them ruined.

An image, an outsider, intruded into this line of suspects that he scrutinized. Ana María. His own wife. Now it was his turn to look away uneasily. What was she doing here? She had nothing to do with this. She knew nothing of what transpired in Santa Fe. She would be in Los Rafas, wringing her hands, running nervous fingers over rosary beads, cursing him for the husband he was not.

Wives who no longer loved their husbands. The words repeated themselves to him and he nodded in agreement. Husbands who no longer loved their wives.

Or friends, he thought. Trying to cleanse his vision of that woman he had known so well for so long yet hardly knew at all. Friends! he insisted. And the vision slowly dissolved to be replaced by a crowd. So many friends, one could never scrutinize them all.

Had it been only a few weeks? What Carlos remembered most had been the election. He had looked around the crowded room. They were men he recognized and knew to one degree or another. Ricos all. Men of property. Men who had voted—those months just prior to the invasion—to fight the Americanos. They were still ready to fight, even after that initial defeat. A loyal group with more than the common interests of property and patriotism. For, in addition, there was the strongest tie of all. Blood. Fathers, sons, cousins, in-laws. All, in one way or another, of one family. One nation. One outlook.

They would found a state, they agreed. Their own. Free of any trace of gringuismo. They had elected their first governor, Don Tomás Ortiz, who had been a general in the Mexican army. The brother of Juan Ortiz, Vicar General and head of the church in New Mexico.

The inner council, though mostly owners of large ranchos, had other representatives too. From the clergy there was Padre Martínez, the virtual lord of Taos, whose influence spread far beyond the pulpit. At meetings he sat quietly with great self-assurance, seemingly satisfied with the way things progressed.

Next to newly elected Governor Ortiz sat Colonel Diego Archuleta, who had been elected commanding general. A man after Carlos' own heart. A fighter who had been sorely used by the Americanos and who swore vengeance with all the passion of his being. "Fight!" he had often heard the Colonel say. A word that soothed Carlos' troubled soul.

"We have other important business," Governor Ortiz said. The group fell silent. "How to make Santa Fe ours."

"I think," someone said, "we should talk of Taos instead."

There was a murmur in the group before another spoke up. "We might do better in Taos; it is a stronghold for us. But the heart of the American operation has to be our first target. Take Santa Fe and we have taken their military and government head-quarters. It's obvious. Our first task is to retake Santa Fe."

Carlos had been watching Padre Martínez, who nodded sage-ly as other eyes turned to him at the mention of Taos.

"Are we together on Santa Fe?" Governor Ortiz asked. A murmur of agreement and again Carlos saw Padre Martínez nod, this time to Ortiz. "Good. Don Diego and I have a plan that we want to propose." Archuleta unrolled a manuscript as Ortiz be-gan to explain.

The attack was to be Christmas Eve. The townspeople would be in their homes awaiting the coming of the holy birthday. The American forces would no doubt be celebrating. With many—hopefully most—drunk and unable to fight.

There would be two groups to carry out the plan. One, under Ortiz, would gather at the church, while the other, under Archu-leta, would await the signal. Then, as with the martyred Mexican hero, Father Hidalgo, the tolling of the church bell would ring out the revolt.

Ortiz' forces would rush to the Palace of the Governors and seize the Americans at their headquarters. Then, with the cap-tured artillery strategically placed about the square and in the streets, they could hold off any counterattack, which would like-ly be feeble.

Meanwhile Archuleta's group would rouse the populace and this fervent army of patriots, soldiers, and citizens would storm into the center of Santa Fe to join Ortiz. Together they would rid their homeland of Yankees and traitorous New Mexicans. So be it. As there was a God above, their cause was just and on this holy eve of His son's birth, He could do no less than bless their efforts at justice and freedom.

Carlos looked out again at the snow and smiled ruefully; he should have been angry. He would have been in times past. Perhaps he was too grateful to still be alive. Or perhaps it was the memory of the ridiculous end to their plan. At any rate, he stood at the open door smiling, watching the snowfall start to slow.

"Carlos!" He heard the call from the distance. Someone was looking for him. He closed the door, still smiling.

They had gathered together the day before Christmas. Carlos had been one of the small group selected to go with Tomás Ortiz. He had been hidden with Ortiz and another, waiting for the day to pass. Hoping for the blackest of nights with no star in the east to light the way for the hated Yankees who had come from the east.

"Don't pace so," Ortiz had said to Carlos. "Walking does not help. Time walks at its own speed." Then, just as calmly, Ortiz turned to their other companion and replaced the cork in the half-full bottle. "We must be clear when the time comes."

Carlos had sat and closed his eyes, hoping to doze off. He could hear the popping of the fire and the heavy breathing of the man who could no longer drink. After awhile he could stand it no longer and he stood abruptly. "I need to take a walk, Don Tomás. With your permission."

Don Tomás nodded. "I wonder," the other man said, "how the others are doing?"

Don Tomás shook his head. "Stay close. We will meet them in the church soon enough."

Carlos had not needed the admonition. It was unwise to be seen together. It was better to be in smaller groups that would meet at the appointed place at the appointed time. He walked slowly down the narrow streets of Santa Fe, toward the main plaza. Everything seemed normal.

Then he turned back, sensing that he had been gone long enough. He was almost back to their hideout when he sensed a stirring, a commotion. A hand pressed on his back.

"Compadre," the whispered voice said. "It is all over. Our plot has been discovered."

Carlos did not even turn his head, but continued at the same pace. Every nerve in his body screamed for him to run. But he knew that anything—anything at all—would attract attention. He walked silently beside his companion.

"I was watching the gambling halls," the low voice continued. "Watching for anything unusual. Helping a few Yankees drink themselves blind. I don't know how or from where, but I caught the whispered word just a short while ago. The authorities know and have already dispatched troops to arrest our people."

"You're certain?"

"Even if it were not true, if the Yankees heard what I heard, they would be on their way."

"¡Chingada! Do they know where to look?"

"I don't know, Carlos."

"I must warn Don Tomás. You go to the others. Hurry!"

Carlos crossed the dirt street while his companion turned toward the plaza. As Carlos cast a last glance, he saw a pair of uniformed Yankees approaching his fellow conspirator.

God damn it! he thought. This is going too fast. Perhaps he can bluff his way through.

He loitered for a moment, waiting to see. The soldiers stopped, blocking the man's way, but when one of the Yankees laid a hand on the New Mexican's arm, Carlos knew that it was over.

He walked briskly down the street, cut through a back alley, resisting the urge to run and shout. "They're coming!" he said as he burst into the house. "The Yankees have discovered our plot. They've arrested Cipriano. There are soldiers searching the streets."

It took but a moment to gather their things. "This way," Carlos said, leading Don Tomás through an alley. "I have a cousin who owns a small store near here. He can help us."

But the third man had turned in the opposite direction, mounted his horse, and galloped off.

"Crazy fool," Don Tomás said. "The streets will be watched. There is nothing as conspicuous as a fool racing a horse through the streets."

Still on foot, they hurried through another side street and up an alley. Carlos stopped at the back door to Señor Rivera's house and listened a moment before entering. His cousin sat on the floor, dozing by the fire with his mouth open.

Carlos shook Rivera's shoulder, stifling a groan with a hand over his cousin's mouth. "Where are the women?" he whispered. Rivera blinked his eyes wide in terror.

"In church. All three of them."

Don Tomás turned and looked at Carlos. That was where

their rebellion was to start. Don Tomás walked to the front of the little building and rummaged through the goods.

"What do you want?" Señor Rivera asked. "Isn't that General Ortiz?"

"We need your help," Ortiz said. "Do you have a woman's dress that will fit me? Carlos. Put on some worker's clothes."

"I'm a poor man," Rivera protested. "I don't have clothes to give away. What have you done? I don't want any trouble with the authorities."

Carlos slipped out of his own clothes and into worker's cottons. "A trade," he said to Rivera. "You get the better of the bargain." Then to Don Tomás. "Over there. His wife's chest. One of her dresses should fit you. With room to spare."

Meanwhile, Rivera had slipped to his knees and crossed himself. His lips were moving in a buzz-buzz of prayer.

"I'm supposed to be your wife," Ortiz said to Carlos. "I'm sick and you're taking me to the doctor. Rivera. Do you have a burro?"

A moan of fear burst from Rivera as he shook his head.

"Liar!" Carlos hissed. He tightened a cord around the waist of his trousers and knelt in front of Rivera, looking him hard in the face. "We are leaving, Cousin. When we do, you say nothing to anyone or they will accuse you of being with us. Loyal Mexicans who would rather die than live under Yankee domination. Say nothing. Burn my clothes. And when New Mexico is free again, we will remember you."

Don Tomás closed the door. "There is no burro outside. We will have to go on foot. Hurry."

"Adiós, Cousin Rivera."

They went out the front of the shop, heading toward the outskirts of town. It was not long before a patrol came toward them, stopping at houses along the way. Don Tomás pulled the rebozo tighter over his face and leaned into Carlos. They stopped while the soldiers were still some distance away. After a few moments one of the Yankees looked at them and Carlos picked up the figure in woman's dress and walked ahead.

"Hey! Over there! You!" Carlos stopped and placed his burden down. The soldiers turned while the one who had shouted approached them. A brown-faced woman stood beside the open door of a house watching.

"Hey! You! Where are you going?" When Carlos answered

in Spanish, the soldier turned his bewildered face toward the others, one of whom shrugged. Then the soldier turned back to Carlos. "No hablo. Can you speak American?"

"My wife. Seeck. Going to doctor."

The soldier nodded, relieved to hear the Yankee words. "We're looking for General Tomás Ortiz."

Carlos smiled and shook his head. "No, señor. Only me and my wife."

The soldier nodded and joined his comrades who had moved on to the next house. Up ahead another woman peeked through the door, staring at the rebozoed Ortiz. She opened the door wide and shouted at the soldiers in Spanish.

"You fools! That is Tomás Ortiz in a woman's dress!"

"Down that side street," Ortiz whispered. He was moving as quickly as possible without arousing suspicion.

"You fools!" the woman shouted again in Spanish. "Now you'll never catch him!"

A soldier waved a hand to dismiss her words, which they did not understand. As Ortiz and Carlos turned out of sight, they moved more quickly, heading toward the edge of the villa where, they knew, friends would help them. Here they had parted, Ortiz borrowing a water jug that he carried on his head as he walked away.

"Carlos!" The shout, nearer now, brought him back to the present.

That was the one to remember, Carlos thought. That treacherous woman who had tried to betray them to the Yankee soldiers. Luckily they had escaped in spite of her. And Archuleta, he had heard, had also escaped and gone south to Mexico. All of the others had been arrested.

"Carlos." The voice was at normal speaking level now and Carlos opened the door wide. "We need you in the rancho. There is to be a meeting. Something is up. In Taos."

"Taos? Let us make certain that there isn't another fiasco like Santa Fe."

Carlos joined his comrade and went out into the cold, crisp air that was clear now that the snow had stopped.

22

Tercero had seen the Vicar General from a distance as they
entered Santa Fe. It was that time of day when Vicario Ortiz
strolled around the central plaza. The faithful that he met would
drop to their knees, kiss his hand, and receive his blessing.

Tercero frowned, torn between his feeling for the pious who
paid their respects and his irritation at the pomp and ostentation
of the Vicar General. Not just his dress, but his entire manner.
His heavyset, overfed body. The shock of red hair under his hat.
The sausage fat fingers wiggling blessings in the air as if these blessings came from man and not from God. Worst of all, such a one
presided at the Church of Saint Francis—the humblest, sweetest,
poorest, most gentle saint in the true Church.

They rode past the plaza along the dirt street that led to the
church and the priest's house. Here they presented themselves to
the housekeeper who welcomed them with smiles and bows. The
new young priest from San Felipe Church. Yes. She had heard
about him. It was such a pleasure. Such a pleasure. The Vicario
would be back soon and would be delighted.

She trod around the room coltishly. Straightening here. Brush-
ing there. "The room is such a mess," she sighed over their pro-
tests. If it were any cleaner or neater, Tercero would be driven to
seek something more violable. Then she stopped in the middle of
her bustling and looked Tercero straight in the face. "Haven't we
met before, Father? Before you were a priest? I remember the face
but not the clothes. You wore a mustache then." Then she laughed
in embarrassment and red-faced, left them alone.

The two men exchanged looks as if to say: Now we are on to
something.

The dinner was over. A sumptuous meal in contrast to the
usual traveler's fare. The table had been cleared and they lingered
over a bottle of wine, enjoying its warmth along with that of the
fireplace.

"I have read the communiques," Vicario Ortiz said. "These
are troubled times. A conquered people are among the most lost
of humanity and have even greater than normal need of God."
The Vicario turned his face, flushed from wine and fire, toward

Tercero. The young priest could sense an unasked question behind the studied look. "It is good of you, young Father Rafa, to make such a personal delivery. The dispatches, routine business, might have been carried in the usual way. But then, I would not have had the opportunity to meet you. This is the first time, is it not?"

"Many years ago, Father, when I was a boy, my father, Don Francisco, brought me from Albuquerque to Santa Fe. You met us both then, my brother and me." Vicario Ortiz smiled. The question had gone from his face and he poured the remains of the wine into their glasses. "You probably do not remember. I was no doubt up to boyishness and had no inkling at the time that I would be called to serve God."

"Thanks be to Him that we meet again."

"Actually," Tercero continued, "it is through the good graces of Father Gallegos that I am here. My father is ill, and Father Gallegos has graciously let me be his messenger so that I might, at the same time, search for my brother. That is my father's wish."

Tercero sensed a pique of discomfort as Vicario Ortiz drained his glass and set it empty on the table with a sigh. Then a realization came over the young priest. One that shamed him with the indelicacy of the situation, if the rumors he had heard were true. And one that, at the same time, struck him with the irony and coincidence in human life.

Vicario Ortiz, too, had a brother. One who had been a soldier, a general in the Mexican army, and who opposed the new government. As if Carlos and Tercero had older models of what life might offer them—if life furnished any clues to God's will. How strange to see the contrast that a generation might make. Here the powerful churchman who would, no doubt, cap his career by being the first Bishop of New Mexico. An intimate of the Bishop of Durango. While he, a young priest, faced an uncertain future in a conquered country. And the Vicar's brother who had reached the highest ranks of the military, while Carlos had never decided whether to be soldier or a ranchero. Perhaps fate had decided that for him.

"Your brother, then, is he here in Santa Fe?"

"I don't know. He left his wife, his home near Albuquerque saying that he was coming here. He had been with Armijo's militia and was deeply upset by our failure to fight the Yankees."

Ortiz' eyes narrowed and he peered over his tapping fingertips that half obscured his face. "There are many who were upset."

191

"What advice, venerable Father, would you give to a young man in my situation?"

Ortiz' eyes narrowed even more. "In troubled times loyalties are pulled at from many directions. So be careful. Trust in God. Seek counsel only from the most trustworthy. Do not reveal more than is necessary or wise. Avoid dangerous entanglements. Go about your own business with respect for the most powerful. At one and the same time act as if no man is your enemy, yet deep down consider the possibility that every man is."

Tercero almost smiled. He knew the words came with all sincerity, although it was not the kind of answer he sought. After a few more words, he and Miguel excused themselves and went to their room.

"I could learn more in five minutes on the streets than in two such evenings with the Vicario," Miguel said in irritation.

He knows," Tercero said. "He knows something, but he will not tell. So we must seek elsewhere."

Señor Rivera blanched when Tercero walked into the little shop. Hurriedly, Rivera served the solitary customer, a woman, then ushered her out.

"What are you doing here?" Rivera asked fearfully. "In those clothes and with your mustache shaved. If they find you, it's the calabozo."

"You mistake me for someone else."

"Now, Carlos—"

Tercero sighed. "I am looking for Carlos. I'm his brother, José Antonio. Or don't you remember, Cousin?"

"Oh, my God. Two of you. I had forgotten. And you don't look exactly alike."

"Do you know where I can find Carlos?"

Señor Rivera brushed past him and poked his head out of the door to look in both directions. "Have you just come from Albuquerque?" Tercero nodded. "Have you heard the news yet? About the rebellion?"

"Only the briefest report."

"Hah. Rebellion. So-called. An act of fools. What a way to celebrate the birth of our Lord. They were all arrested. All but three and the authorities know two of them: General Tomás Ortiz and Colonel Diego Archuleta."

192

"And the third?"

"I know nothing, Father. No one in this town knows anything. Not just in fear of their lives, but also because of their loyalties. After all, fools though they were, Ortiz and Archuleta were our own countrymen."

"And Carlos—"

Rivera shook his head. "Six months ago, when the militia waited to battle the Yankees, I saw much of him. But the Yankees captured Santa Fe after that."

"Did he ever speak to you of a Señor Hammond?"

"Cómo no. The Yankee whose young partner was stabbed to death in an alley." Rivera lowered his voice as he glanced to the back of the shop. "It is only now that my niece, Dolores, has gotten over it. A new boyfriend. Another Yankee. A soldier this time. Yes. Señor Hammond I know—a trader. Carlos lost much money to him in cards. You are not the only one who has been looking for Carlos."

"Do you have any idea where Carlos might be?"

"I would not tell Señor Hammond. A Yankee. Nor anyone in authority. And I cannot say for sure. But if I were looking for a desperate man whose sympathies were violently anti-Yankee, I would go north. Toward Taos. Where there are many such men."

Tercero breathed a sigh of relief. "Then he is alive."

Rivera shrugged. "Ah, Padre. Who knows? Perhaps only God and a few fellow revolutionaries."

"Gracias, Cousin. I will listen quietly and speak carefully. It is one of those times."

"It is always one of those times for the poor, Father."

Taos lay north of Santa Fe about the same distance that Albuquerque lay south, some sixty miles. They tarried a few days in Santa Fe, hearing the news and rumors that fleshed out the story of the aborted revolt. Less than two weeks previously, Governor Bent had issued a proclamation regarding the plot and its defeat. Only two days ago the Governor had left Santa Fe for his home in Taos, satisfied that the rebellion was over.

While the streets were full of hearsay, people in private seemed to know nothing. At least the people Tercero and Miguel saw. The Vicario revealed nothing more than what he had said at dinner that first night. He asked politely about Father Gallegos. About

Albuquerque. Always in an ambiguous way as if other questions were veiled behind the apparent ones. Tercero began to wonder what was in the communiques he had delivered. Did they have to do with rebellion? The plot had extended as far south as El Paso del Norte and, if so, certainly Albuquerque was involved.

Even his cousin, Rudolfo Rivera, had no more to communicate. He did not acknowledge having seen Carlos in recent months. He knew nothing other than what he had already said.

With this contradiction of wild public rumors and private silence, it was with relief that the two young men headed to Taos one Sunday after early mass. The next day, cold and tired, they arrived at Padre Martínez' large house on the plaza. The Padre was attending to his school. A suspicious housekeeper made them welcome, such as it was, and Tercero brought in his belongings, then went across the plaza to church to pray.

Later that day the Padre returned and greeted them. His large, suspicious features studied them with intelligent interest—especially Miguel. Somehow there was no escaping the feeling that he had little love for Anglos.

After this brief but outwardly cordial welcome, Padre Martínez asked Tercero to his study. It was as if he did not want to speak in the presence of the blue-eyed foreigner. Miguel nodded his understanding to Tercero and joined other guests of the Padre.

Tercero quietly watched the man who was a living legend. Who had started schools, not just for boys but for girls. Who educated young men for the priesthood. A one-time member of the provincial legislature who dared suggest that it abolish itself since it had been delegated no power by the Republic of Mexico. Who alone of all the priests with power denounced the church for bleeding the poor with their fees for this and their tithes for that. Publisher of the only newspaper heretofore printed in New Mexico. A man now in his early fifties, at the height of his powers.

"What brings you to Taos, young Father Rafa? It is a long and cold ride from Albuquerque."

Tercero explained about his father's illness and the old man's wishes to find Carlos. He did not mention the gambling debt.

"It seems strange, Father Rafa, especially in these difficult times, for you to be riding with a Yankee."

"No more strange, Padre, than for New Mexico to have a Yankee governor from Taos. But Miguel is no Yankee. He is a

Gaélico, an Irishman, who has almost become a Mexican. He and my sister plan to be married."

"These are strange times."

The comment piqued Tercero. "Today, Padre, as we rode into Taos, there seemed to be many travelers on the road. Is there some special celebration? It was as if half the villages and pueblos from the surrounding country were riding to town."

Padre Martínez' face remained impassive although he hesitated as if collecting his thoughts. "No," he finally said, "there is nothing that I can speak of."

"I went to the church just after we arrived. As I crossed the plaza there was much activity. Men in the streets. Boisterous noises from the cantinas. Busier it seems to me than Santa Fe."

"Perhaps you would find your brother in the crowds."

"I thought you might be able to tell me."

A smile from the Padre. A quick shake of the head. Should I ask more? Tercero thought. Should I tell him that Carlos is no doubt with a band of revolutionaries? But why? he thought. Padre Martínez would certainly know what was happening in Taos. Nothing escaped his attention. Anything of importance that occurred was with Martínez' concurrence if not at his direction. No. The Padre did not want to talk. He viewed Miguel with suspicion and therefore viewed Tercero with less than full trust.

"What would you suggest?" Tercero finally asked.

Padre Martínez pierced him with a questioning look. How much should he tell this young man? Where were his sympathies? What did he already know?

"We have been conquered by infidels," Padre Martínez began. "I must speak plainly. I find that insufferable. There is only one true Church. One true God. Whom we must serve and defend with all our lives."

"But there are Yankee Catholics," Tercero protested.

Martínez froze him with an angry glare. "It is not a Catholic nation like Mexico. Or Spain."

"You feel there is so much danger?"

"It is our way of life—or theirs. There will be no compromise. First the military conquers. Then the civil government becomes gringo. Then the church and its priests fall in line. The people will follow. They will forget their past. Or if they do not forget it, they will despise it—and themselves. They will want to become gringos."

"But the United States is a republic, with freedom of religion and—"

"Young man, you tell me nothing new. Yes. The United States is a republic whose genius lies in its freedom of worship and its separation of church and state. But laws are one thing and how people live another. And attitudes are something else.

"There will be changes for us. Not all of them will be to our liking. As I told my boys in school, the United States is a burro that plods along better at the urging of a lawyer than of a priest. Did you know that my school no longer educates young men for the priesthood? I train lawyers now, for that is what the future needs."

Tercero did not know what to say. He sensed the bitter hostility in this powerful man of God. Yet he could not reconcile it with his vision of Jesus' message of love. And through the Padre's protest he thought he heard the refrain of personal power lost. Why not separation of church and state? Tercero thought. It was here, in this blurring borderline of authority, that both Spain and Mexico failed, leaving their frontiers impotent.

"So," the Padre continued. "You search for your brother."

"Do you know him?"

"I have met him. He strikes me as a true patriot. If I hear of his whereabouts, I will tell you. But now, I have other guests. I must not neglect them."

The Padre rose and led Tercero from the study. After dinner the two young men retired early. Tercero wondered what to do next. Perhaps tomorrow he could search the town for traces of Carlos. Surely the Padre could give him some suggestions—if he wanted to.

They dropped into a heavy sleep, tired from their journey. Once or twice during the night, Tercero heard strange noises: shouts, gunfire—but he dropped back into deeper sleep, convinced that he was dreaming.

Then he felt a hand on his shoulder and all of his senses leaped to attention. "Tercero." Miguel's whisper was damp on his ear. He could see the dark shape in the dim light of the fireplace and he sat up. "Something is happening," Miguel whispered. "I heard gunshots from outside. A terrible din."

Tercero threw back the covers and together they went to the door. They heard an angry voice from another part of the house. "I cannot condone these acts of murder!"

196

They crept out into the hall and peered into the sala at Padre Martínez, who was angrily berating a man who stood quietly in the center of the room, a handkerchief over his face like a bandit. The few others who were still awake sat spellbound, while huddled in alarm on one side of the room was a group of women and children who had not been at the supper table.

"There is no other way to describe what you've done, Montoya, except as murder. These women and children sit in terror, wondering what has happened to their husbands, brothers, fathers. God will punish you if no one else does. Despicable. No other word can describe—"

Montoya stood passively, not responding, his body in an attitude of resignation and shame. The refugees watched in horror, perhaps wondering if this revolutionist's mob would follow him into the priest's house to destroy them all.

Suddenly, while the Padre glared angrily around, breathing deeply to catch his breath, Montoya turned on his heel and left the house. He had not spoken a word.

Tercero and Miguel went quickly back to their room, slipped on their clothes, and joined the crowd in the sala. Padre Martínez was directing the housekeeper and others, who must have been his students, to make arrangements for their added guests. A young man came into the house from outside, slamming the door behind him.

"They've left Taos heading north," he shouted. "Governor Bent was shot to death. They killed Sheriff Lee, the prefect, the district judge, Bent's brother-in-law Pablo Jaramillo, and God knows who else."

"Has there been a general uprising?"

They all turned toward Padre Martínez. "Only that drunken mob." You could not tell what he was thinking from the solemn expression on his face. "Even now messengers must be racing to Santa Fe to spread the word. There will be no general revolt."

An older woman rushed toward the young man. Her hands were clasped tight and there were tears in her eyes. "Is there word of any others?" The young man shook his head.

Small groups began to drift from the sala, led by someone from the household, until only a few were left talking in whispers. As Tercero and Miguel rose to return to their room, Padre Martínez walked a few steps with them. His solemn face now seemed tinged with resignation.

"There's where you will find your brother," he said in a low voice. "Traveling with Montoya's mob. What started as a patriotic revolt against the overbearing Yankees turned into a drunken slaughter."

The Padre turned and went back to the business of the household, leaving Tercero and Miguel to find their way to their room and a restless sleep.

23

They stayed as guests of the padre while the battle flared briefly here and there in the surrounding countryside. There had been an attack on the American distillery at Arroyo Hondo where seven Yankees had been killed. Two more had been killed at Río Colorado. While at Mora, eight Yankee wagon traders had been captured and shot.

Word came that the Yankees had intercepted a rebel messenger and that troops and volunteers were on their way from Santa Fe. The two rebel leaders, Pablo Montoya and the Pueblo Indian, Tomasito Romero, marched south to do battle.

Meanwhile, it was quiet in Taos. Snow was falling; with rebels and Americanos on the road, it seemed best to await the outcome of the battle. Feelings in Taos were mixed. For the most part the populace did not take up arms to join the rebels—partly from loyalty, partly in outrage at the killing of friends and relatives by the rebels, and perhaps in aversion to killing and fighting. The consensus was that the rebellion was doomed. Its leaders had counted on a general uprising that had never occurred.

Two weeks after that fateful night at Taos the Yankees made their way into town, weary and cold, but grimly determined after having routed the rebels at Santa Cruz. The rebel survivors had retreated before the onslaught and had taken refuge in Taos Pueblo, just beyond the town. It did not take long for the battle to commence again. From Padre Martínez' house Tercero could hear the boom of Yankee artillery, knowing that it was just a matter of time. The pitiful rebellion was over.

"I must go help take care of the wounded and dead," Tercero told Miguel.

"I heard that the rebels barricaded themselves in the mission church at the pueblo. The Americans turned their cannon on the church and blasted it to ruins. Blasphemy!" Miguel spat. "I can't think of a more barbarous act."

Tercero sighed. "The Yankee colonel is a Catholic, too." He mounted his horse and trotted off to join Padre Martínez and the others. They were divided into groups, some to ride to the pueblo while others would help the wounded who had staggered back to town. Tercero joined the group headed for the pueblo.

"I am looking for Carlos Rafa," he said to the New Mexican wounded and captured that he met on the road. "Has anyone seen Carlos Rafa?"

Mute, expressionless faces looked past him, but still he asked until one startled man looked up and nodded his head. "At the pueblo with the Indians." He barely had strength to whisper the words.

"Carlos Rafa?" The prisoner blinked his eyes in assent. "Is he alive?" A shrug. Then the Yankee sergeant yelled at the man to keep moving.

Hope and alarm fought within Tercero. He watched for familiar faces among the troops headed toward the town. A wagon bumped along toward him and he peered into it searching among the wounded.

"Young Father Rafa." The hoarse words were in American.

There in the shadows, Tercero saw the Yankee officer from Albuquerque. "Captain Burgwin."

The alarm in the young priest's face must have been evident. "It's only a wound, Father."

"Vaya con Dios."

Then they were past the group plodding toward Taos with the road empty except for those riding to the pueblo.

The mission church was a pile of rubble. After bombarding the four-foot thick walls, troops had rushed forward with axes to chop their way through, then thrown hand grenades into the crowded building. The smell of blood and flesh was sickening. The Indians were removing their dead and carrying them back to the central pueblo while Tercero and the others scattered, looking for their own wounded and dead.

"Carlos Rafa?" Tercero asked each of the wounded that he went to comfort. "Carlos Rafa?" But no one answered. Only the cries and groans separated the living from the dead.

"East," one man finally said. "They rode east."

"Was Carlos Rafa with them?"

The man nodded. "East," he repeated. "To the mountains."

Impatiently Tercero continued his work, moving toward the east. He could see the signs of struggle, the direction that the battle flowed, in the abandoned equipment, dead horses, dead men. They had moved to the farthest perimeter of the battle toward the path along which the surviving New Mexicans had fled.

"Father! Over here." Tercero joined the man who called and helped clear away a dense pile of brush, alongside which a dark, clotted stain despoiled a patch of snow. "This one hid underneath. I can't tell if he's alive or dead."

Carefully they slid the body free. "My God," Tercero said, crossing himself. "It's my brother."

He bent over the still figure, feeling for a pulse and carefully opening the eyelids. Carlos' clothes were torn and stuck to his right side on a huge dark patch of blood. He was still and cold, and if he was not dead from the ugly wound, he might be frozen to death. Tercero's hands trembled and he started to cry. His companion clasped him on the shoulder.

"His lips are moving, Father."

Bending still lower, he put his ear to Carlos' mouth. "Before . . . I die . . . I . . . want . . . to kill . . . one . . . more . . . Yankee."

"There is barely a pulse, Father."

"Wagon!" Tercero shouted. "Over here! Another one."

Carefully they placed Carlos among the other wounded and dead.

He will not last, Tercero thought. It's a miracle that he is not dead already. With tears in his eyes he watched the wagon pull away.

Another shout. "Over here, Father! Oh, my God. This one's head is missing."

Tercero returned to work.

The wounded were cared for in Taos. The dead were buried. Some in Taos. Some, especially among the Yankee troops, in Santa Fe. Others in the little villages from which they had come. Families wept and prayed for victims, rebels and Yankees alike.

Carlos had been taken to Padre Martínez' house where Tercero watched over him with the help of the local doctor. But it was no use. After those first whispered words, he slipped into a state deeper than sleep but not yet death.

Tercero prayed at his bedside, relieved only by the concerned Miguel who brought him something to eat—he did not know what—it slid down as a lukewarm anonymous mass. Then Miguel brought him cups of hot atole to help keep him awake.

Carlos did not last the morning. In one last spasm of energy he opened his eyes wide and croaked out, "Mamá! The Yankees!" Then he slipped back. Tercero knew that it was the end. A terrible trembling came over him and he could not see for the tears in his eyes. He sat at the bedside, unable to pray, unable to think, feeling a deep heaviness that seemed a permanent part of him.

Finally, after an hour, thoughts began to come to him. Of how close he and Carlos had been as boys and how they had drifted apart. Of the family that he would have to tell. Of his mother and father. Ana María. The others. Of the fragility of human life—his own included. And the wonder that the race survived at all. That somehow that fragile thread went from each present-day survivor all the way back to Adam and Eve. Unbroken. Sustained by God's mercy.

"Tercero." It was Miguel's low whisper. "It is almost daybreak. I will sit while you rest."

He turned his tear-stained face toward this blue-eyed stranger who was already like a brother to him. He did not need to say a word. Miguel took his hands and there were tears in his eyes too.

"We will have to take him back to Los Rafas," Tercero said. "That is the only place for him."

"So young," Miguel said in a daze. "So young."

Together the two young men went toward the kitchen to get something hot to drink that might sustain them even briefly in their sorrow.

PART III

AMERICANOS

1847–1854

24

Together Tercero and Miguel brought Carlos' body home to Los Rafas for burial. "It is God's will," Don Francisco had said. "Carlos is happier where he is now than he was here on earth." Though there were tears in his eyes and his face was contorted with sorrow, Don Francisco grew steadily better from that day. The talk of spells and witches disappeared. He regained most of his old vigor when he was once again at work. He turned his thoughts from the son he had lost to the blue-eyed son he was about to gain.

Andrea's wedding was an event to remember. Like in the old days. For even in these uncertain times there were few Anglos in the county. So it was still as it had always been. As if they were Americanos in name only while life went on much as always.

Father Gallegos presided, with Father José Antonio assisting. Afterwards there was the fiesta with much food and music and dancing. Once again the house at Los Rafas echoed with the laughter of friends and family. Once again Father Gallegos outdanced them all.

But underneath the surface of the same old way of life, there were rumblings.

They had waited almost six months for the wedding in order to show proper respect for the departed Carlos. The ceremony had been one bright day early in June of 1847. Less than two weeks later Don Francisco received a visit.

"Patrón," the servant girl said timidly. "He is here. The man who came to see you just before Christmas. Señor García."

For a moment Don Francisco could not remember. García? What did he have to do with any García?

"This time, Patrón, he comes alone. The Yankee is not with him."

Now it came back with a sudden twinge of pain. "Have him wait in the sala. I will be there momentarily."

The reckoning, Don Francisco thought. Always there has to be a reckoning. He strode from the room out into the patio and surveyed the huge cottonwood tree that shaded the house. He felt an affection for that tree as if it were a human member of the family. Friend. Protector. Beacon when returning home from the fields, or town, or river.

That tree was like the land. An integral part of his life. A familiar part. Essential, it seemed, as a wife was to a husband or children were to parents.

There were three pieces of land left to him. Of all that had belonged to the Rafas when this place was first settled. Two of them were rich bottomland paralleling the Río Grande, while the third was pastureland far up in the hills.

The family house stood on the largest portion of the bottomland, perhaps two-thirds of the total. Just north of it and towards the river, separated by those small farms given to his married daughters and their husbands, was the other one-third that he still considered his own, though legally it was in Carlos' name.

No more, he thought. The day of reckoning. The slow erosion of what had once been an enormous tract had reached its final stage. What once two brothers had owned had, over the years, been subdivided and passed on to heirs. Then pieces had been sold to neighbors. Now, finally, one of these pieces was going to an outsider. An Anglo.

Don Francisco stepped up to the trunk of the cottonwood and patted it with his hand. There is still this, he thought, thanks be to God. It is not as if we have nothing.

Then he walked back into the house to meet his visitor.

"Don Francisco." The old gentleman bowed graciously to Señor García. "I am here, Don Francisco, as the legal representative of Señor William Hammond."

Don Francisco extended a hand toward one of the straight-back chairs and offered tobacco and corn husks for rolling a cigarillo.

"Señor Hammond," García continued, "is a man of business, a trader, and is somewhere between Santa Fe and Missouri in Indian country."

"So the lawyer comes."

Señor García's eyebrows raised as if asking: What do you mean by that? "Sí, señor. The lawyer comes." García handed over a sheet of paper. "This is the note, Don Francisco."

Again he stared at the signature. Unquestionably that of his son. The rest he still could not read since it was in American. He handed the paper back to García.

"My son is dead." Not saying what else he thought: Fighting the Yankees. Now that they've killed him, they want to take away his land.

Silence. The lawyer's mind considered the consequences. "I'm sorry to hear that, Don Francisco."

"His widow owns that piece of property now." More silence. More consequences to consider. "I cannot give to Señor Hammond what is not mine."

"This is unexpected."

"No one ever expects the young to die. Least of all the young." But this was not what García meant as Don Francisco well knew.

"What can you tell me about the widow and her circumstances?"

Don Francisco frowned. What was there that one could tell? "Her name is Ana María Gutiérrez Rafa. She has moved back with her parents. The Gutiérrezes have that little farm across the acequia madre, the main irrigation ditch, just east of the river. She is in mourning."

How little those few words told, Don Francisco thought. He could have been talking about someone's horse or pet goat. What it did not tell was how wild the deep-set eyes of his daughter-in-law were when Carlos' body had been brought home. Then the outburst in church during the funeral mass. A disgrace, some had said. Scandalous. Throwing herself on the rude wooden coffin, her screams piercing the hallowed silence of the church, until her brothers had to carry her hysterical from the building.

"Loca," the whispers buzzed. "She was absolutely crazy for her handsome husband and now that he is dead she has lost her mind."

"Guilt," others whispered. "Look. They had a barren marriage. No children. And you know Carlos. With his wine and his cards and his secret rendezvous. She hated him. She had even talked to Father Gallegos about him. She wished him dead. Then when he died— Guilt, I tell you. That is what drove her mad."

Ana María spent her days in church now, riding from her parents' farm on that stupid burro of hers. Praying. Cleaning. Consulting with Father Gallegos. Who knows? Perhaps she would become a nun. Somehow that was how Don Francisco had always seen her.

"The acequia madre," García asked, "where is that?"

"North of here, perhaps half a league."

"Does the Widow Rafa know about this debt?"

"I do not believe so, señor."

García sat quietly, pondering. This was a turn of events he had not expected.

"Don Francisco," he finally said. "Señor Hammond does not want that piece of land. He is a trader, a businessman, not a farmer. The land is not of primary concern to him. He would rather have the money that is owed him."

"You will have to talk to my daughter-in-law."

"Do you think she would understand that Señor Hammond would rather have the money than the land?"

"¿Quién sabe? It is not so much a matter of understanding as it is the ability to pay. This is a land-rich, money-poor country."

García looked at him sharply. "If he had to take possession of the property, Señor Hammond would just turn around and sell it. The money would go into his trading business. Better, Don Francisco, that you keep such property in the family. I know how it is. I come from a family such as yours."

"Señor, what can I say? You cannot make tortillas from adobe. I have even less money than when we spoke six months ago. As for Ana María—" Don Francisco shrugged. "My son had very little to leave her."

Señor García stood abruptly. "Don Francisco, I must thank you for your time. Obviously there is nothing that can be settled by us. I will see your son's widow. I'm sorry that it may turn out to be difficult. Muchas gracias, señor."

"De nada." Don Francisco walked him to the door and stood there as García mounted his horse and headed north.

206

Well, Don Francisco thought. That piece was already lost when I gave it to Carlos. Soon someone else will own it. So it goes.

Sighing, he closed the door and went to the patio to sit under his beloved cottonwood tree.

25

Some months after Ana María Rafa had signed over her property to William Hammond the Treaty of Guadalupe Hidalgo was signed, officially ending the Mexican War. It was February, 1848. However, for the new American citizens of New Mexico the war had been over long before. It had been eighteen months since Santa Fe had been occupied and twelve months since the last major effort at rebellion in Taos.

The year since Carlos' death had been a strange one for Tercero. It was as if the excitement of coming home for his first assignment as a priest, the American takeover, and Carlos' death had been a peak and now he was marking time.

True, there had been Andrea and Miguel's wedding, and Ana María's loss of the only thing of tangible value that Carlos had left her. His work with the church had settled into a routine, traveling for weeks at a time from one tiny village or pueblo to another to carry out God's work. But he knew something was happening inside of him. As if one year's crop had been harvested and the land had been plowed under to lie fallow for awhile. Now it was waiting for new seeds to be planted and this time the crop might not be corn. It might be beans. Or marigolds.

The visits to his family were infrequent. His work kept him away from Albuquerque most of the time. His companions were those few other priests that he encountered at the pueblo missions in the jurisdiction. These and the poor and simple faithful who gave him such joy with their warmth and openness.

But even here things had not changed with the coming of the Yankee. The poor were still poor. The conqueror was not really in evidence. It was as if a gigantic corral had been built around a herd of wild horses and though they still seemed free to live their old lives, there were now limits to it. With these limits also came the realization that some day a strange vaquero would climb over the fence to put a saddle on them. And still later some other stranger would mount and ride them to where he wanted to go.

Perhaps that was the seed that lay in the fallow ground of his soul. The conquering American military force had already built the corral around them. The strange vaquero on the fence looked like a lawyer—much as Padre Martínez had described. Soon, the mysterious rider would come to take them God knows where. Then, Tercero knew, things would change for him personally. He knew not how, but he knew they would.

Tercero sat quietly in meditation in his room. The priest's house was quiet since Father Gallegos was probably playing monte or faro in one of the gambling halls. He looked up distractedly at the knock on the door.

"Your brother-in-law," the housekeeper said.

Then Miguel Dalton peered in shyly. "I hope I'm not interrupting anything important, Tercero."

The young priest ushered him to the one chair and sat himself on the edge of the bed. Miguel closed the door and looked over his shoulder. "I'm ill at ease when I come to the plaza. It has changed. With American soldiers stationed just across from the church. It used to be quiet. Almost holy ground. Now you can hardly find the church for the soldiers and the traders and their customers."

"Yes," Tercero said. "It has changed."

"There is another reason that it upsets me to come to the plaza." Tercero looked away from the crucifix above his bed toward Miguel. "You know," Miguel continued, "that the American army fought their way into Mexico City in September. Right to the halls of Montezuma.

"When Mexico City surrendered, General Scott's men arrested some thirty deserters. Men who had fled the American army to join the Mexicans. A few were good Irish lads like myself. Many resenting the prejudices that Irish Catholics were subjected to by other Americans. Except for fate, I might have been one of those thirty men.

"I was told they were tried, convicted, and sentenced. They

built scaffolds on top of Army wagons in a plaza just two miles from Chapultepec. The prisoners, with ropes around their necks, were forced to watch the attack on Chapultepec. When it was overrun and the Stars and Stripes hoisted over the Mexican palace, there was a great cheer. The teamsters whipped their animals and the wagons jerked away, leaving the thirty deserters strung by the neck. A rather grim way to celebrate a victory."

"Where did you hear such a story?" Tercero asked.

"From some of the local soldiers. They thought it a proper comeuppance for traitors."

Yes, Tercero thought. And last year after Taos there had been another trial. This time of Mexicans and Indians. With once again a bitter accusation of treason. Yet, how in God's name could a civilized nation conquer a country and then accuse its revolting inhabitants of treason? Treason meant being disloyal to one's own country. How could one be treasonous to a conquering nation? So technically it could not have been treason. Was insurrection the more correct term? What did it matter to the accused men? Whatever the proper word, the outcome was a foregone conclusion. Guilty! The rope.

Tercero looked into Miguel's fearful eyes. "I have to leave," Miguel said. "Find some place that is not occupied by American soldiers. Some small, quiet place away from things."

"But how could anyone know? I am bound by the confessional. You have told no one else."

"I am afraid. What—what if someone recognizes me?"

"Do you think it likely that someone who fought in the interior of Mexico would find his way up here? The Yankee soldiers will have all gone back to the United States."

Miguel stared dully at the wall, eyes blinking, but reason was beyond him at the moment. "I fear being discovered."

"Where would you go?"

Again the dull stare. With his flesh tight over his face, Miguel looked even younger than his twenty-two years. A mere boy, Tercero thought. Confused and frightened.

"Andrea is pregnant!" His voice quavered. He turned toward Tercero as if his words had explained everything.

"That's wonderful. I will be an uncle again."

"So you see, I really have to go some place safe." Then he stood and paced across the small room. "There are American dragoons stationed here. A major contingent in Santa Fe. But there are little settlements, not even villages, back in the mountains. The country is beautiful up around Santa Fe. There would be places one could settle and not be disturbed."

Tercero sighed. "I have been to many such places. It is true one would not have to worry about Yankee troops. But it is still not always safe. There are the Apaches. The Navajos. Other tribes."

"I would rather face the Indians."

"Have you spoken to Andrea yet?"

"No. I don't know what to say to her. We have been happy here and she knows it."

"That will be difficult."

"I have to tell her. Don't you see? She will have to know the truth so she will understand. Then we can go to Don Francisco together. It will be difficult. Don Francisco has been like a father to me. He depends on me to help with the stock and the farm." Miguel shook his head. "He will be angry. Feel deserted. There is more work than he can handle alone."

"You must do what you have to do."

Miguel nodded. His confusion had dissolved and he acted like a man no longer torn. It seemed as if he had made a decision. He rose, ready to leave.

"I owe you so much, Tercero. My life. Do you realize that it has been almost two years since you found me in Los Bacas?" Tercero nodded sadly; Los Bacas no longer existed. "It was through your help that your father agreed that I could marry Andrea. You have been like a brother to me."

"I am your brother."

A firm clasp of each other's shoulders and Miguel was gone. His future is settled, Tercero thought. But mine is still unresolved. The mysterious rider has not yet come.

26

Time stood still on the ranchos. Miguel and Andrea moved north. The next year gold was discovered in California and though

210

there were but faint stirrings among the local people, there were many passing through the Territory of New Mexico from the eastern states.

"California!" they would shout. "There's gold in California!"

The brown-skinned paisanos would smile because they did not understand English and did not want to appear unfriendly. Then they would bend back over their hoes to work their fields.

Don Francisco managed his holdings with the help of his sons-in-law and servants. But Tercero could tell that he was getting older and things did not go as well as they had when Miguel lived on the rancho. Grandfather was still alive, if one could call it that. He slept most of the time and his memory had dimmed so that he did not always recognize the family, slipping back in time to another family with other names.

The wonder of all, though, was Ana María. She had lost her land, which William Hammond had promptly sold, but she had found a husband. It had shocked the Rafas, for many had seen her devoting the rest of her life to the church. Then, even more shocking, babies issued forth from her in profusion. Three in three years.

Perhaps it was this more than anything that agitated Tercero. All of those years the Rafas had talked in whispers about their infertile daughter-in-law. Well, it had not been so. Whatever had been sterile, unable to reproduce itself, had been in the Rafa strain. It had been a shock that had cracked the foundation of an intense belief and made them not only question the past but view the future with greater apprehension.

Then one day the word came to Tercero as he prepared to ride out once again from Albuquerque to the pueblos, missions, and ranchos in the outlying district. The New Mexican clergy was no longer under the jurisdiction of the Bishop of Durango. As Americans they were to have their own American bishop at Santa Fe. He had been nominated by a council in Baltimore. Pope Pius IX had appointed this American bishop; even now he was on his way from Kentucky. Where in God's name was Kentucky?

Worst of all, Tercero heard, he was not really an American. He was a Frenchman. The gross insensitivity of sending a foreigner to head the church of their newly conquered Mexican citizens was appalling. At least the Bishop of Durango was one of their own and understood them.

The news prompted other thoughts that had lain dormant

these past few years. Thoughts about the priesthood here in his homeland. A realization that perhaps here finally was the mysterious rider who would mount and spur the wild mustang in an unknown direction. Or was it a wild mustang? Perhaps, Tercero thought, that was vanity, and it was really a Mexican burro. Small, tough, and stubborn.

God and Caesar, Tercero thought as he went on his rounds in the hinterlands. Both God and Caesar had turned out to be Yankees and co-conspirators. And though the pueblos, the little villages, the ranchos that he visited were much the same as they had always been, it was an illusion. The stubborn burro was going to have to ride in a new direction determined by a new master. It was just a matter of time.

On those lonely miles on the desert and into the nearby mountains he thought about his church and his home. Already ambitions would be smashed. Vicario Ortiz would never be Bishop of New Mexico. Father Gallegos would never be Bishop of Albuquerque. Padre Martínez—who knows what secret desires lay hidden in his powerful breast? Whatever they were, they had met their match in the Americans.

Then, Tercero asked, what about my own ambitions? What had I wanted for myself? To be like other priests here in New Mexico?

There were many different kinds, he thought. Pious, hardworking ones who tended their congregations like gentle shepherds. Ones who brought the good word to the heathen Indians and who were revered and loved by their pueblo brothers. Somehow the missions seemed to draw spiritual leaders who epitomized the best in the clergy. Devout. Celibate. Giving.

Then there were others. In the little villages or towns where the Spanish-speaking lived. A motley group. Ranging from the devout to the indifferent. From the chaste to the worldly. Some of whom lived openly with their "wives" and children. No better—or worse—than some of the poor, ignorant peons. From the knowledgeable to the ignorant. Men who not only could not read but who barely knew their prayers, yet were supposedly spiritual leaders of their flocks.

Finally, there were the powerseekers. Men who, as in the medieval church, became men of the cloth because for those with ambition it was one of the three choices: church, army, or politics.

And there were old feudal kingdoms in New Mexico still ruled by priests. Like that of Padre Martínez in Taos.

Yes, Tercero thought, there was a wide choice of men of the church. As for himself, none of these choices seemed right. He was not cut out for the missionary life. Comforts were too enjoyable. Isolation among the Indians was no substitute for the company of more civilized men.

Celibacy did not seem like a healthy long-term condition for any man. Yet once vows were taken they must be kept. So the licentious living of some priests was intolerable from his point of view.

As for power? Tercero shook his head. That was something he could not understand. It was enough to rule your own life and live it well without the arrogant presumption of telling others how to live theirs.

So he fit no mold. In fact he had agonized over the question of whether or not he should be a priest at all. Why had he taken this route? He had thought about it much lately, following that thought back those few years to Carlos' death. Then moving slowly forward, curious to where that thought would take him, until he realized that it was *the* important question of his life and he must follow it quickly.

There had been no choice, he now realized. By tradition his older brother was the heir to Los Rafas. Carlos had been destined to be the don. The patrón. When necessary, the soldier. And by position, the one who would influence politics. It was all bound up in that one role.

So there had been but one choice for Tercero. Or rather, no choice. There was only the Church. Take it or leave it. A life of sacrifice. And the first sacrifice of all had been to take on holy orders.

Yes, Tercero thought. He was where he was because he had been an obedient son. Because tradition had defined his life's role and he had accepted it.

Now tradition had gone to hell. It was not just the death of the rebellious Carlos. It was in the circumstances of that death. A new master had taken charge and the old traditions were no longer valid. Life was at a standstill because new traditions had not yet filled the void left by the old.

As he slept under the stars, making his rounds from place to place, Tercero realized how right Padre Martínez had been that day in Taos. The United States, a republic, was like a burro that was better ridden by a lawyer than by a priest.

Yet, in those sleepless moments when he gazed up into the starlit blackness, another realization would overwhelm him. The infinity of God. A deep awe possessed him. Akin to terror. And he trembled as he watched the stars. Overpowered by the thought that God was everywhere.

After his trembling had finally stopped, a new, peaceful thought possessed him. Yes. God was everywhere. Out in the infinity of space. In the cold, distant pinpoints of stars. Yet He was right here. Now. Beside him. In the cool desert night. And even more. God was inside the lowest creatures on earth. The coyotes. The crow. Mesquite. A desert rock. An ant. God was inside *him*. He was, however, infinitesimally small, a part of God. One of God's children. He, as well as Jesus, could call Him Father.

The realization cooled his agitated heart like clear water cooled a thirsting man. His breathing slowed and a deep peace calmed him. It was easy to decide what to do, he thought. One must only follow God's will.

He closed his eyes and almost immediately he was asleep.

Father Gallegos stood watching him as he made ready to mount his horse. He had told only the priest of his intention. There was no point in telling anyone else until it was an actuality.

"I think a letter to the Bishop of Durango would have been enough," the older priest said.

"But he is no longer our bishop."

The angry red face looked up at him as he mounted. "We know nothing of this Frenchman. Suddenly he appears on horseback from the desert saying he is our new bishop. Any imposter could do the same."

"He has already been to Durango. It is all in order."

A stony silence. Then Tercero waved and headed north along the river toward Santa Fe.

Father Gallegos' reaction had surprised him. He thought that his superior would have been pleased to see him go. The five years they had worked together had not changed their relationship. The very popular, affable older priest was a different man with his subordinate. Irritable. Impatient. Shouldn't it have been a pleasure to get rid of such an assistant?

The weather was clear and warm and the ride up the Río Grande easy. Next day Tercero found himself once again in Santa Fe, waiting to be announced to Bishop Lamy. Wondering what kind of man this new Yankee bishop would be. Would they talk in Spanish? Did Lamy even know the language of the people he was to serve? Or would they speak in English, which Tercero knew only a little. Was he a warm, loving man? Nothing less would do for these brown-faced, child-like people of New Mexico.

A door opened and the housekeeper led him to a study where the slender, frontier-toughened man leaned over some papers on a desk. After a moment he looked up.

"Your Excellency," Tercero said in English.

"Please sit down, Father Rafa." He spoke in halting Spanish. "I have been rereading a message from your superior." The Spanish was interspersed with a word or two in English as he looked at Tercero with questioning eyes. "He writes that you want to abandon the ministry of God."

The words chilled Tercero: *Abandon the ministry of God.* They had a solemn, almost accusing ring to them. He studied the new bishop minutely while trying not to appear to do so. Surprisingly, he was younger than Tercero expected. Not much more than ten years older than himself. Perhaps forty years of age. His face was lined and tough like those faces exposed to the elements. Yet his eyes seemed warm, receptive. Perhaps the words had not been said in the spirit that Tercero had taken them.

"Yes," Tercero answered. "I am resigning from the ministry."

"Why?" When Tercero did not immediately answer, Lamy went on. "I have heard good things about you, Father Rafa. You are one of the priests that I had hoped would be a support and a source of strength for the work that must be done in New Mexico."

"It is time for me to return to secular life. To the life of my family. There have been many changes under the Yankees and I am needed there more than in the Church."

"There is no work greater than serving God. And change is inevitable. One cannot stop it by retreating to the familiar."

Tercero moved uneasily in his chair. "I have thought long and hard about that, Excellency. Out on the desert there is time to think. There is great truth in what you say.

"But I realized just recently that there are other truths just as important. That if God is infinite—which He is—and if God is everywhere—which the Church also teaches—then every place must be holy ground. Also—if God is first cause, then every deed must be a holy deed because God is the cause. So that being a priest is no more holy than being a farmer. Being in church is no more holy than being in the fields. And one must be what he must be.

"It was the arrogance of priesthood that disturbed me most. The notion that any one person knew how to talk to God better than any other person. That any person needed someone to intercede for him. One must speak directly, although one should listen to teachers. Learn from them. Then speak for himself."

"That is hardly an orthodox point of view, Father."

"True. We New Mexicans are not highly schooled in the philosophies of the Church. We are a simple people who have lived isolated from the world but not from God. If there is one thing I've learned being out among the peons, among the Indians, it is how little I know and how little it matters. The poor speak to God with their lives, not their prayers. They hardly need a priest to sanctify them."

"Then you condone ignorance, Father? You feel that a Catholic who does not know his prayers is just as much on the right path as the Catholic who does? The next thing you will tell me is that you believe priests should be married."

Tercero smiled ruefully. "There is something I have to ask before I answer that, Excellency. Is it true that women who live sinful lives here in New Mexico have been banned from the Church?"

The expression on Lamy's face hardened. For a moment he stayed silent as if struggling with whether or not to answer this unorthodox upstart.

"Yes," Lamy finally said. "The goings-on in Santa Fe are a disgrace to decent people. One of the town's leading ladies—if I may use the word—runs a gambling casino and a bordello. It seems to be the custom for riotous sin at night and church in the morning. So I have banned the women from church."

"Then you would have banned Mary Magdalene?" Bishop Lamy sat stonily. "What about the men, Excellency? Have they too been banned from church?"

"You don't agree with my decision, Father?"

Well, Tercero thought. The fat was in the fire anyway. What had made him speak out? The sternness he sensed in this bishop? The Yankee puritanism? Better to get on with it.

"It's not a question of disagreeing, Excellency. But if you look at it from another point of view—"

"There is no other point of view for sin."

"If you consider that fornication is an act requiring two, then to ban the women alone seems unfair. Even Jesus himself said—"

"I do not need a lecture about what Jesus said, Father."

Tercero flushed, but he persisted. "The women, Excellency, are few in number and they are Mexican by birth. They are poor and earn a living any way they can. The men for the most part are Yankee soldiers. They are rich by New Mexican standards and they seek their pleasures where soldiers usually do.

"Might it not make more sense to speak to the Yankee commander and tell him to order his soldiers to stop buying women or they too will be banned from church?"

It was as if the words had struck against a wall and bounced off. "Next you will be telling me that priests should be allowed to marry."

"The Protestants do, Excellency. Already there are Protestant churches here in Santa Fe with married ministers setting an example."

A reddening face. A stony, angry glare. Tercero had gone too far, but the bishop kept his temper in check the way he must have been capable of reining in a fractious horse.

"I'm sorry, Excellency. I came to speak to you about leaving the priesthood and instead I seem to be attacking you." A wave of the hand, dismissing the idea of attack. "Excellency, I do not believe that priests should be married or live in concubinage. When I took my vows, I took them in all sincerity."

"I'm glad to hear that, Father Rafa."

"I realize that not all of our priests feel the same. There are a few who live in open sin. I understand the problem you face, Excellency."

"I need help, Father. There are too few priests and so much work to be done. The Church is in sorry neglect. The faithful need their priests. They need to be taught. So there is need for schools. The sick need hospitals to care for them. Churches need to be rebuilt. The needs of the poor must be met by deeds, by organization, and by hard work. We need priests who care, and if I do not find them in New Mexico, I will bring them from elsewhere."

Tercero saw the quiet conviction in the bishop's eyes. Then Lamy stood and strode to the window to look out, his tall, gaunt frame silhouetted against the afternoon light.

"The soul is a garden," the bishop said. "We must plant seeds that grow into the love of God."

A pang wrenched Tercero's heart. He could sense a bit the vision that this man of God had. But the time to help had passed. His father was old. His grandfather finally bedridden and senile— only a matter of time. He felt the pull of duty and tradition. For him, serving God best meant going back to the rancho.

"If I could only help," Tercero said in all sincerity.

Lamy turned around with a beatific smile. "Then why don't you?"

Tercero looked away from the smiling bishop whose vision beckoned him. "I can't, Excellency. I have always agonized about rendering unto God and unto Caesar. Sometimes one needs to do both with the same act. That is where I am. I must go back and help my family."

The smile faded. "One must go where duty calls loudest."

"I hope you understand, Excellency."

"No one can be forced to be a priest."

Tercero stood and pulled a paper from his jacket. "Here, Excellency. My resignation."

The bishop took it and dropped it unread on the pile of papers on his desk. Then he extended a hand in a Yankee handshake. Somehow the gesture took Tercero by surprise. He had been so used to the more demonstrative Mexican way, where men would clasp each other's shoulders and pat one another warmly on the back. The handshake seemed cold to him, yet it was only the new custom.

"May God bless you, Father Rafa. If all our priests were as sincere and honest as you, there would be few problems in the Diocese of New Mexico."

"Adiós, Excellency."

As Tercero turned and left he heard Lamy's parting words, "Go with God."

218

27

Going back to work on the rancho made Tercero feel like a boy again. There was the same sleepy excitement in the early mornings when he would ride out to supervise the peons in the fields or ride farther into the higher grazing lands to see how it went with the few sheep that they had.

"Don José Antonio!" the men would shout, waving their hats as he approached.

Then in the hot afternoons, a rest in the shade with a drink of water would bring back memories of boyhood afternoons, resting in the cool shade of a tree after the hard work.

True, there were fewer servants to help them now. Almost none. What had once been thousands of fat sheep were now down to hundreds. Their land holdings had dwindled, with a small piece sold here to raise cash, another sold to pay for Grandfather's funeral, still another sold for a different reason. But there was enough left—the large acreage on which the ranch buildings sat in their cluster of cottonwood trees and adjoining it an equally large area which was exclusively farm.

Only on Sundays did Tercero ride into Albuquerque. Then he would escort his parents to church where they would meet his older sisters and their husbands surrounded by their various children.

"Well, Tercero," Josefa would tease. "Who is that young thing across the plaza making cow's eyes at you?" His face would redden and his eyes would stare straight ahead, not daring to turn and look. Josefa would laugh. "If you're nice to me I'll arrange an introduction."

Of course his other sister, Clara, would know other young ladies whom she would offer to introduce to him. While his brothers-in-law had sisters and nieces and cousins. There seemed no end to the eligible young ladies willing to meet an eligible bachelor.

There was always news of interest to exchange. A letter from Andrea and Miguel who had settled in a fertile little valley east of Santa Fe and were raising corn, beans, and children. The latest gossip of marriages, impending births—both in and out of wedlock—deaths, Indian atrocities. The new prosperity that rode in Anglo wagons across the plains and was displayed in stores just across the plaza from the church. The Yankees themselves. More numerous now but still a minuscule number whose dollars and energy had impact far out of proportion to their small numbers.

One Sunday morning one of Tercero's nieces ran excitedly to greet them as they crossed the plaza toward the church. "An Anglo lady here in Albuquerque is going to have a baby! Next week. And I'm going to watch."

Tercero looked at his parents. Señora Rafa had turned away in embarrassment, while Don Francisco, lost in thought, had not really heard and mumbled, "That's nice, hijita. Where's your mamá?"

"Atocha!" Josefa shouted. "You come right here and stop scandalizing your grandparents." Then to Tercero, who greeted her with raised eyebrows. "Our maid's sister works for the Anglo family. Half of the countryside plans to go into town to see this miracle."

"You know what?" Atocha said to her cousins hovering on the outskirts of the adults. "I heard that when an Anglo baby is born—" Then she began to whisper and the little girls began to giggle.

"Atocha!" Josefa boxed her ear and led her blubbering toward the church while the others followed in amusement, wearing their smiles into the building.

It was then that Tercero remembered. Father Gallegos had gone south on business to Old Mexico. He felt a pang of discomfort, for in the past under such circumstances it would have been he presiding at mass. As it was—

His curiosity did not last long. There was more than the usual stirring when the unknown priest entered, and quiet whispering passed along the crowd.

"Macheboeuf."

"The Frenchman."

"Lamy's hatchet man."

But the mass was still much the same mass as always until that pause in the ritual when announcements were made from the pulpit. The words rang out through the quiet. "By order of His Excellency, Jean Baptiste Lamy, Bishop of the Diocese of New Mexico, Father José Manuel Gallegos has been relieved of all priestly duties." Then the list of offenses—the causes for removal.

Few heard. Only the pronounced sentence seemed to echo in their ears. ". . . relieved of all priestly duties." An angry rumbling whispered through the crowd.

Tercero was torn by the pronouncement. If it had been in his power, he might have pronounced the same words years ago. Yet the words, when spoken by the Frenchman, left him uneasy and resentful. He knew how the New Mexicans would take it. "Another foreigner," they would say. "Our San Felipe Church for almost a hundred and fifty years is now in the hands of that foreigner."

Couldn't they have found a native priest who could have served this function? They had not heard the last of this. And as if in answer, the prayers of the congregation grew louder, like a swarm of angry bees buzzing at this intrusion in their hive.

Tercero could see the horses tethered in front of the rancho as he rode home from the fields. For some weeks now Father Macheboeuf had taken over the duties at San Felipe. There were some who had stopped attending mass, mostly those from the outlying ranchos, while those who lived in Albuquerque went as faithfully as ever. All waited apprehensively for Father Gallegos to return from Mexico, for until then nothing would be resolved.

The visitors were grouped about Don Francisco and Tercero heard their voices from the sala as he entered the house.

"No," his father was saying. "I am too old for such intrigues. The bishop has sent down his edict. It is our duty as good Catholics to obey."

"It is merely a show of friendship, Don Francisco. After all, Padre Gallegos has served our church for many years. He is not only our priest, he is our friend. How often have his heels turned a polka in this very room? I myself have tossed a card or two with José Manuel over the years. And which of us has not enjoyed his hospitality over a glass of wine?"

"Gentlemen!" Tercero strode in from the hall and greeted them. They were friends and neighbors. Men from the farms and ranchos outside of the villa proper.

Their spokesman's face brightened. "Don José Antonio."

"Don Pedro."

"Have you heard the news?"

Tercero looked around from face to face as if the answer might be there. "No, Don Pedro. I have not heard."

"Father Gallegos has returned from Mexico." The visitors' faces brightened for an instant, then lapsed into solemn intensity.

Don Pedro continued. "The Frenchman is off to the Indian parishes this week. There will be a surprise for him when he returns next Sunday."

"We come to ask you to join us," another said.

Don Francisco was glowering at no one in particular. Before Tercero could ask, Join in what? one of the visitors turned urgently toward him.

"Can't you see, Don José Antonio? That if, for some reason, Padre Gallegos must leave, then you should have been his logical successor. You assisted him for five years. You are one of us. Not like this foreigner—this Frenchman."

"But I am no longer a priest," Tercero said.

Don Pedro nodded in agreement and flashed a look of irritation at his companion. "We are not here to talk of what might have been."

"What is it that you want me to join?"

"This Sunday Padre Gallegos intends to reclaim his church. We plan a show of support from his friends. We come to ask your family to be there early when Padre Gallegos takes control of the presbytery."

"I go to mass every Sunday," Tercero said.

"What we want is your support!"

Tercero could see the look on his father's face. Support? What did they mean by support? Did they think that parishioners decided who was or was not to be their priest?

"I will be at mass as always," Tercero said. "I cannot speak for my father or mother."

Don Francisco nodded in agreement. "We will be at mass as always."

Don Pedro smiled and nodded to his companions. "We look forward to seeing you in church on Sunday." They left in a group, talking about the next rancho they were to visit.

Don Francisco sighed. "The bishop can do as he wants," he said. "They can no more overrule the bishop than they can stop the sun from rising tomorrow morning. It is inevitable."

Tercero nodded. Not only was Father Gallegos' ouster inevitable, it was the right thing in his opinion. Yet if he had stayed in the church, might not it have been he who would have taken over the parish? He looked at the tired face of his gray-haired father and thought about the field from which he had just come. No. His place was here. As for Father Machebeouf, he was an old and trusted friend of the bishop. His right-hand man. So things were not so simple. There were all these entanglements that pulled this way and that until things went their inevitable direction. Yes. His place was here on the rancho.

The church was crowded when Tercero and the family arrived. More crowded than he had ever remembered except perhaps for an occasional Easter or Christmas service.

Although they were almost an hour early, there was room only at the back. A few acquaintances nodded and one of them smilingly whispered, "Nothing like a good fight to get everybody to mass."

Tercero did not smile. He looked through the crowd. It was not the usual mix one saw at Sunday mass. There were very few from the villa of Albuquerque itself. Most were from the ranchos and little farms on the outskirts of the villa. Friends and supporters of Father Gallegos.

There was an air of excitement, of expectation emanating from the congregation. In a land where life was filled with the same day-to-day drudgery, this was drama of high order. Something to remember and tell one's children about. More exciting than the Yankee invasion, because that had been no fight at all.

Most listened to the words assaulting them from the pulpit, where Father Gallegos held forth against the Yankee encroachment by Bishop Lamy and Father Machebeouf.

"Excuse me. Please stand aside." The words, not quite a whisper yet not loud, parted the standing crowd and Tercero turned to see Father Machebeouf make his way into the church.

Ah, Tercero thought. That sly old fox, Gallegos. He must have locked the sacristy so Machebeouf could not enter by the side door.

But locked sacristy or no, the priest was making his way forward. Heads turned. Whispered words were passed. Father Gallegos continued as if he hadn't noticed, his words rising heatedly. Accusing the bigoted bishop and his priest of stealing God's church from its rightful owners. Accusing them of unspeakable sins.

Father Machebeouf walked boldly down the center aisle past the pulpit into the presbytery, climbed the few steps to the altar, turned, and stood quietly as Padre Gallegos continued.

Now there was absolute quiet in the church. Only Padre Gallegos' words knifed through the silence, though they were more hurried. As if he wanted to finish and look over his shoulder to see what Machebeouf was doing.

Then abruptly he was done and the silence seemed to focus on the other priest. All eyes turned toward Father Machebeouf. They waited expectantly, for there was no doubt that he had to answer.

"Dear friends in God. Fellow Catholics," he began. "There is no truth in these rash accusations made against Bishop Lamy and myself. As God is in heaven, the truth shall be known from the lie, the charitable from the grasping, the angels from the devils.

"As to the reasons for the removal of Father Gallegos from your church, we have already spoken. His scandalous behavior has made this more a church of Satan than of our good Lord. To remind you once again, here are the reasons."

He recited a list of particulars, much of which was well known, though many listened open-mouthed as if hearing for the first time. Not once did he glance at Father Gallegos, who stood impassively.

Father Machebeouf paused for a moment, his short, stocky body standing in the sacristy like an immovable rock. Slowly, dramatically, he removed a letter from his pocket and unfolded it, still staring powerfully at the congregation.

"I have here," he said, "a letter that I have received just this past week from His Excellency the bishop, who as you all know, was appointed to this diocese by our Holy Father, the Pope, the Vicar of Christ on earth. I will read it to you.

" 'To the parishioners of the Church of San Felipe de Neri, Albuquerque, Territory of New Mexico.

'Father José Manuel Gallegos has been suspended from the exercise of all priestly duties in the parish of Albuquerque. Effective immediately, Father Joseph P. Machebeouf is authorized to administer the affairs of the parish.

'By order of His Excellency, Jean Baptiste Lamy, Bishop of the Diocese of New Mexico.' "

Only when he finished reading the bishop's letter did Father Machebeouf turn toward Padre Gallegos, acknowledging his presence. Silently he folded the letter before he spoke.

"Father Gallegos. You have heard the reasons for your suspension and the bishop's order. Can you justify those actions which have led to your suspension?" No answer but a glowering, defeated look. "Would you care to answer, if you have any reply to make to me and to the congregation?"

Still no reply. Padre Gallegos seemed to physically contract, as if by making himself smaller he might disappear from this embarrassing defeat. Then he slunk from the church, leaving it in the possession of the Frenchman.

"Let us continue."

High mass was sung as if there had been no interruption.

The affair was not over. A few days later an emissary of Father Gallegos came to the rancho.

"We intend to confront the Frenchman!" the visitor said. "He will have to leave. We do not want him here. We want you to join us. Especially since you have worked with the padre."

Tercero looked at the man and wondered if he remembered. How many years had it been? Since the invasion. When a contingent of the padre's friends had met him as he rode out to the more distant villages of the parish. An ominous greeting when Tercero and Padre Gallegos had had their most open disagreements. He had feared for his life, he remembered. Had this man been one of the party that had met him? Or perhaps a brother or son? Had Gallegos forgotten? My God, how many years had they worked together in disagreement? It was inconceivable that the padre would expect him to be a staunch supporter.

"No," Tercero said. "I will not be a party to this. We cannot overrule the bishop."

The answer flared back angrily. "Ingrate! Traitor! You who have worked with the padre do not support him against this foreigner. A curse on you!"

Then the visitor turned and stomped from the house before Tercero could respond.

"What was that?" Don Francisco asked as he entered from the back of the house.

"Nothing."

The next Sunday at church the news was on everyone's lips. Just the day before a contingent of twenty-five or thirty had accosted the new priest. Ricos from the ranchos mostly. Friends of Padre Gallegos. With a few from the little villages on the ranchos. They had planned their timing well because the prefect was away and they could take matters into their own hands.

"We order you to leave!" was their insolent command. "We want none of your administration in this parish. And if you do not leave of your own accord, we will have recourse to other measures."

Tercero and the family leaned forward, waiting for the rest of the whispered story.

The priest was very polite. "I have come to take possession of this parish by order of the highest ecclesiastical authority, the Bishop of New Mexico. I take no orders except from that same authority. Take what measures you will, but I am a sentinel on guard. I will not quit my post. As the shepherd of this flock, I am ready to die for my sheep rather than abandon them."

They had nothing to say in reply. Flabbergasted and confused they rode away. Soon after the prefect returned to town. Violently angry, he threatened to arrest them all for their audacious threats. But Father Machebeouf calmed him. Asked him to do nothing.

A buzzing whisper rose from those gathered outside the church. "Here he comes," someone said.

"Good morning, Father," a voice rang out loud and clear.

"Good morning," came the response. Calm. Firm.

Slowly, respectfully, they started to enter the church while the priest stood outside greeting his parishioners.

As Tercero knelt he thought about the immense change that had come over this church. There would be more. Many of the changes would be improvements. No longer would their pastor be a dancing, drinking, card-playing roisterer. More austere leadership had taken over.

But with the change there would be a loss, too. It was as if many of the faithful would no longer be free to show their joyous, childlike sides in church. Guitar music was not appropriate to the mass, the new priest said. Joy was not part of the celebration. There would be an organ. Solemn. Deep. Appropriate. Whatever that meant.

In spite of Tercero's relief at Padre Gallegos' removal, there was a tinge of remorse too. It was almost as if God had, in the end, turned out to be a Yankee. And God's brown-faced stepchildren would have to learn new ways of loving their Father.

226

28

Tercero sat quietly in the family chapel, although it was almost as quiet in the house itself. There were only three of them now in this large place. His father, his mother, and himself. There were fewer servants, just as in the fields there were fewer workers and in the pastures fewer shepherds.

But it was not of the declining fortunes of the Rafas that he thought. And it was not, though the chapel was their holy place, of God. He was thinking about Gregoria Sánchez.

The "Old Maid," his sisters called her behind his back. She was already in her early twenties and still unmarried. Whether because she took care of her widower father or for some other less obvious reason, they did not know. It was said that she could ride a horse as well as any man. She worked her father's fields as well as the hardiest peon. She could shear a sheep. Make tortillas as tasty as cake. Her chile verde made one's mouth water just to think of it.

Sundays were the times he saw her. He remembered Gregoria from the time her mother died some years ago. He had officiated at the funeral. Been struck by the way she had taken charge while her father had drowned his sorrows in drink, wailing like a woman at the services. Exuding the smell of brandy. Having to be carried from the church blubbering incoherently.

She had been watching him, Tercero thought. The way he had been watching her. They saw each other only occasionally at first. As if they attended different services most Sundays. But their eyes acknowledged each other. Then, somehow, it seemed that both would be at San Felipe Church at the same time every Sunday. It had happened so gradually that only now did Tercero realize it.

Yes, he decided. This was the one. There was no question about it.

There was a rustling in the back of the chapel. Then the faint fragrance of food and powder approached. "Tercero!" The whispered voice was urgent, almost on the verge of tears.

"Yes, Mamá."

"It's your father."

When he turned he saw her, hands clasped over her mouth, eyes wide with fear. He followed her glance out toward the patio, walking quickly past the door. Don Francisco half sat, half lay across the wooden bench beneath the cottonwood tree. A maid was rubbing his hands and patting his face.

"He collapsed right here. I had brought him a message from the lawyer in town. He had barely opened it, barely looked at it, when he fell over."

There was a groan as Tercero bent over his father. Don Francisco's eyes fluttered. "Papá. Are you all right?" The answer was another groan. Tercero turned to the maid. "Go get one of the men." Then to Doña Estela. "We'll take him to his room."

They carried him and laid him on the bed, leaving Doña Estela to minister to Don Francisco. Carefully Tercero unfolded the crumpled message that he had taken from his father's hand and stood reading it outside the bedroom door.

"Dear Don José Antonio," it began in Spanish. *"I have done the preliminary work necessary to verify your land claims. As you know, claims will have to be filed with the Surveyor General of the United States as well as with authorities in Santa Fe. This will take time and money, both for the investigations necessary and for filing per the proper legal procedure. I know you will want to discuss it in person in more detail and it will also be necessary to discuss the fee. As of now your retainer has been exhausted so it is important that we meet soon so there will be no unnecessary delay in proceeding with your case.*

"Respectfully yours, Arnold S. Cole."

He refolded the letter and tapped it on his hand as he glanced at the closed door. So that was it, he thought. Don Francisco had read a message not intended for him.

That afternoon Doña Estela walked softly to the desk where Tercero was going over accounts. "I'm worried," she said. "Your father keeps saying: 'All is lost. All is lost.' He will not eat and he lies there as if he does not want to get well. It is almost like the time before—when he was bewitched."

"I'll speak to him."

"What was in the note?"

"Lawyer Cole asking for money."

"Ah—"

When his mother left the room, Tercero returned to the accounts. Finally he slammed his pen onto the desk. There was no sense doing this. He had been through it again and again. There

228

was no extra money. It was all they could do to stay out of debt.

Later that evening, just after supper, he crossed the patio to his parents' room. Don Francisco lay in bed breathing heavily. Tercero sat beside him to watch. After several quiet minutes, when it was apparent that his father was asleep, he began to silently recite a rosary.

Tercero was lost in the rote of prayer when a groan intruded. "Papá?"

The answer was weak—tired but pleased. "It's you, hijo."

"How are you feeling?"

"Not so good. I'm getting old." Tercero did not know what to answer. "Where's your mamá?"

"In the kitchen supervising the clean-up."

A long silence. "I envy you," Don Francisco finally said. His voice sounded more tired than ever. Drawn back in on itself. "You're a young man. In the full vigor of life with so much to look forward to." Then he lay silent again—the obvious words unspoken.

"You have years left, señor." Tercero thought of his grandfather, his namesake, who had lived a good many years—over ninety—until he had peacefully gone to sleep one night and not awakened in the morning. A blessed death after a long life.

"I'm old. I feel old." Then the awkward silence again before he continued. "Living has made me tired. Regrets. Nothing stays still. Everything changes. I feel old. Useless."

Tercero did not respond. What could he say? Did his father really want a conversation? He was an old man ruminating about his life. He was getting himself ready to die.

Don Francisco groaned, sighed, then spoke again in his tired voice. "There are only two things worth leaving behind on this cursed earth. Heirs and land."

"You have grandchildren enough. I think there were fifteen the last time I counted."

The groan came louder now. "Yes. But not a Rafa among them." Tercero looked away. He did not want to see the expression on the old man's face. "Hijo, how old are you now?"

"Thirty-one."

"Well. There's still hope." Tercero did not know what to say. "Anyway," Don Francisco continued, "your crazy brother—God rest his soul—he could not have helped there. Did you see? As soon as he was dead that wife of his started dropping children like a hen laying eggs. There was a curse on Carlos. God saw the life he lived and said, 'no more.' But you—"

"In due time, señor."

"And now. That—that letter." Don Francisco turned his guilty face toward the wall. "I did not realize until I opened it that it was for you."

"No matter. There was nothing you should not have seen. We've discussed these claims often. It is what happens when a new government with new laws takes over an old land."

"I thought—when we first talked to that lawyer—that we had paid him a great deal of money. That it was all we would have to pay. What do they do with all that money?"

Tercero shrugged. "Trips to Santa Fe. Trips to Washington. Filing papers."

"Trips? How much does it cost to go on trips? You just get on your horse and go. As for papers—nonsense. Anybody can scribble anything on papers."

Tercero nodded. The old man was right. Why should it cost so much? Even their whole attitude toward land was different. Anglos tended to see land in miniature, in quibbling detail. As if a foot or an inch more or less mattered. There was plenty of land—enough to be reckoned in miles, not inches. If one disagreed with a neighbor because an old boundary disappeared—that is, if lightning destroyed the tree that demarcated one person's land from another's—well, they could settle it like gentlemen. What did a few feet one way or another matter? There was enough for all.

"Tell me," Don Francisco continued. "How much more is this lawyer going to cost?"

"I don't know."

"Where will we get the money?"

Tercero started to answer, I don't know, but then he thought better of it. "We'll get it," he said instead.

Don Francisco sighed and seemed to relax now, to sink down into the bed instead of floating stiffly on top. "It all changes," he said. "In your grandfather's time—God rest his soul—we never worried about money. Or strange Yankee laws. There was more than we needed. Enough for all. It's as if the generations have seen a decline."

"The world changes, Papá, but God always remains the same."

230

For the first time a faint smile cracked the old man's face. He sighed again. "I'm always grateful that one of my sons was a priest. I have sinned my share in life. Regrets. Regrets. But to have a son who can intercede with God for you is a blessing few can claim." Don Francisco put a hand onto Tercero's hand and squeezed feebly. "Light a candle in the chapel for me, will you, hijo?"

"Yes, Papá."

Then Don Francisco closed his eyes while Tercero watched him drift slowly to sleep.

It was rare that Tercero came into Albuquerque on any day other than Sunday. He stopped at the sign that read: Arnold S. Cole, Attorney-at-Law. The client with Cole looked over his shoulder as Tercero walked in and lowered his voice, but the words were still audible. "—damned Mexicans. If the courts don't give me what's mine, I'll take it. No ignorant half-Indian is going to . . ."

The voice dropped even lower as Tercero sat to wait. The Anglo's face flushed, then his hard eyes glinted angrily as Tercero looked him directly in the face.

"Don José Antonio," Cole greeted. "I'll be with you in just a short while."

The conversation continued, in an inaudible whisper now. After a few more minutes, lawyer Cole's client rose. "I'll be back in touch with you," he said gruffly.

"Don't worry about a thing. The court will take care of this."

"It better."

They watched as the man glared at Tercero and left the office. Cole ushered him to the chair alongside his desk. "You got my note," he said. Tercero nodded. Cole smiled and waited, then flushed as Tercero did not go on to the obvious topic of discussion. The lawyer's smile faded. "Is there anything wrong?"

Again Tercero nodded. "The money we advanced you has gone very quickly," he said. A forced smile did not disguise the lawyer's anxious eyes. "I would like to see an accounting of the expenses if I may."

Cole blinked in surprise. Then again the forced smile. "Why of course. I don't have the papers with me, but I can certainly have them for you in a few days." But his eyes said more truly what he thought: You don't trust me!

231

"I hope you won't let a few dollars stand in the way of protecting your rights," Cole continued. "You've heard what's been happening in California?"

Yes, he had heard. How five thousand Californios had been inundated by gold-seekers, then by land-grabbers. But they were only five thousand, while here in New Mexico there were ten times that many.

"Without proper surveying, proper boundaries, the squatters moved in on some of the large ranchos," Cole said. "There was no legal way to remove them. No way at all short of bloodshed. We don't want that to happen here."

Tercero nodded. He had heard about the squatters. And he had heard more. About vast lands claimed for nonpayment of taxes. Either through lack of knowledge about Yankee ways or through out-and-out deceit.

"We have to do this legally," Cole said.

"Then we should do it together," Tercero said, meaning the New Mexicans, not the lawyer. "I have spoken to several on the ranchos in Los Rafas and Los Griegos. We want to be represented as a group. With one fee to be shared by all. There is no need for a dozen fees to pay for one trip to Santa Fe."

"Well now, Don José. You know that would never happen."

"Of course not, señor."

"There's nothing I'd like better than to represent all of the land grant claimants together."

"We plan to form a committee and elect our representative to work with our lawyer."

"Admirable. An excellent idea."

"And we share the expenses."

"Absolutely."

"Now that you have studied the problem, what is it that we have to do?"

Cole leaned back in his chair and stared at the ceiling thoughtfully. "The first thing, of course, is to form your committee and elect your chairman. Then you need to agree on a lawyer to represent you. This lawyer will prepare a petition for a hearing by the Surveyor General of the United States. At this hearing the petitioners will present their proof that they own the land.

"In the meantime, proof must be gathered. Each family must search through old papers—if they exist—for any documents to substantiate their claim. The original grants would be best. But, lacking these, proof must be sought elsewhere. In the old Mexican and Spanish archives for instance."

Tercero frowned. "We have lived on this land for a hundred and fifty years. How can anyone dispute that we do not own it, even if we cannot find old papers?"

"We must go by the law."

"How long will all this take?"

"It could take years."

In the meantime, Tercero thought, lawyer's fees and taxes continue unabated. "Years? But what do we do during those years?"

"The same as always, I suppose. Nothing will change much during that time."

No, Tercero thought. Only the ownership of our homeland. Only the laws that govern our lives and our future.

"Years," Tercero said, shaking his head. He rose abruptly. "Then we had better get started."

"Yes, Don José. It is time."

Instead of turning north toward the rancho, Tercero turned his mustang east toward the Sandía Mountains. It was early yet and he felt the need to be alone and out of his usual routine. The mountains beckoned, and he followed an old trail that he had ridden many times as a boy.

In his mind's eye he saw one of those times as a fusing together of all the good rides to the mountains. He was with his grandfather, old Don José Antonio II.

The trail began to rise and the boy, Tercero, turned to see how the near-blind old man was doing. He was doing fine, sitting ramrod-straight in the saddle, the sombrero tilted rakishly forward, shading his near-sightless eyes.

The boy smiled. Anyone who saw them from a distance would not know that the proud rider was an almost senile old man who could barely walk and could not quite see. There was still juice in the old dog. You could see it in the cruel spurs that gripped his boots. See it in the light touch of spur on horse flank as the old man sensed that he was falling behind.

"Grandfather!" Tercero shouted. "We'll be onto the mountain trail in a moment."

"Bah! Don't I know that? I can smell it."

Tercero slowed his horse and let the old man draw alongside. Grandfather sniffed the air, trying to filter out the smell of dust and other odors that masked the scent of piñon. Tercero looked at his grandfather's large Roman nose, the nostrils flared like those of an angry buffalo. That was a nose that in its prime could scent Indians before the Indians were aware of his presence.

"As a boy," Grandfather said, "I used to race from the Sandías all the way to the Río Bravo. Bareback. Like an Indian. Nobody could beat me." The old man patted the neck of his horse affectionately. "It must have been your great-great-great-great-grandfather, little mustang." Then to his grandson, "I'll race you to the summit."

"All right, Grandfather. But no cheating."

"On the count of three," Don José Antonio II said, ignoring the impertinence. "One. Two." He was gone. Laughing, Tercero followed him, restraining his horse so that he would not catch up too soon.

The trail was barely wide enough for two horses. Yet his grandfather's tough mustang raced along the familiar trail at breakneck speed, not needing a rider to tell him where to go.

In a moment their landmark, a large boulder with the name "Rafa" scratched on it, came into view. Tightly Tercero held the reins of his horse as he drew alongside his grandfather.

"Get back!" the old man shouted at Tercero. "¡Andale!" he shouted at his mustang. Then they reached the boulder, and his grandfather started to laugh. "I won!" he shouted. "I won! It will be a long time before you can beat the likes of me."

Remembering, Tercero smiled. He looked up the trail, half expecting his grandfather's ghost to shout out a challenge. Let's race!

But the race was over, he thought. Was ended that last time he had raced up this summit with his brother, Carlos, just a few years ago. That time, too, someone other than Tercero had shouted, "I won!" Won what? he thought.

Tercero saw the boulder just ahead. He drew his horse alongside and looked down the slope the way he and Carlos had those years past. The Río Grande Valley lay spread out before him. The villa. The farms. Off to the north he saw the thin line of the Comanche Trail threading through the property that his parents had sold to help him start his life as a priest.

Directly ahead to the west was the green line of growth that followed the river. North of the villa was Los Rafas. Although it was too distant to see in detail, he could picture every adobe house, every field, every line of irrigation ditch from memory.

The most northern section, that bordering Los Griegos, was the portion Carlos had left to his widow, who, in turn, had lost it to an outsider. The southeastern portion was where their rancho stood. The portions between were a crazy quilt of ownership. Uncles. Cousins. Others. With a few little pieces still belonging to Don Francisco and himself.

There! he thought, seeing one isolated field that still belonged to them. That is the piece I must sell to raise money for the lawyer.

Then, among the crazy-quilt patches of small farms, he pictured one in particular. Among the smallest. With well-tended fields stretching beyond a broken corral. The house tiny, its outside walls worn by weather and in need of plastering. In the house, the tall Gregoria Sánchez.

There are things one must do, Tercero thought. Carlos had to fight the Americanos. The acts that might have made him a hero in older days had left him a corpse. Padre Martínez had to fight for his people, his church, and his power—and he was still fighting. Padre Gallegos had become a politician, which was what he was all along. And now, he thought, the donkey that is democracy is being ridden by a lawyer. Padre Martínez' prophesy has come true.

Once again Tercero gazed toward Los Rafas. There is still home, he thought. Our land. One can still withdraw from the craziness of the world and survive in a manner almost the way it was in Grandfather's time. One can then pass on what one has left to his heirs.

Gently he patted his horse and headed him down the slope toward Los Rafas. Toward a small, weathered adobe house where Gregoria Sánchez would look up from her work and see him coming and say, "At last!"